4 Weddings AND a Feud

4 Weddings AND A Feud

MICHELLE McCRAW

CITY OWL
PRESS

4 WEDDINGS AND A FEUD
Forza Family, Book Two

CITY OWL PRESS
www.cityowlpress.com

Cover Design by MiblArt. All stock photos licensed appropriately.

Edited by Tee Tate.

For information on subsidiary rights, please contact the publisher at info@cityowlpress.com.

Print Edition ISBN: 978-1-64898-532-4

Digital Edition ISBN: 978-1-64898-533-1

Printed in the United States of America

CITY OWL PRESS
Escape Your World ◆ Get Lost in Ours

To the women, Italian-American or otherwise, who hold families together.

Chapter One

It's not a bachelorette party until the woo-ing starts.

"Woooooooo!"

Mary smiled when her passengers' yells penetrated the partition to the driver's compartment. But when the motor whirred to retract the convertible top and the sleek limousine started to sound like a human-powered ambulance, she knew the bachelorette party had taken a turn for the worse.

Not necessarily for the ladies partying in the back, but for the upholstery.

She glanced in the rearview mirror as she slowed to stop at a red light on the Las Vegas Strip.

Yep, the bridal party was standing on the leather seats, the petite blond maid of honor still wearing her stiletto heels.

Mary winced. Her brother was going to be *pissed* if she brought back Nick Cage with punctured leather.

The privacy screen was still up, so she couldn't simply holler back, "No shoes on the seats!" like her brother would've done. She put on the flashers. Ignoring the middle finger of the driver who zoomed around her, she got out of the driver's side, circled the front of the Escalade's hood, and stopped on the sidewalk next to the rear passenger door.

"Hey, ladies." She scanned each of the seven bridesmaids to identify the least-drunk one.

"Girl, I told you to keep the top on," a curvy Black woman said.

"I did! Look!" The blond bride, Bristol, glanced down at her shirt, which had "I'm the Bride" printed on it, not the most original slogan Mary had seen in many years of sending out bachelorette parties in the family's limousines. "No one's throwing beads anyway, not like Mardi Gras at home."

"Not *your* top," her friend said. "The limo's top."

"But I wanted to see the lights." Bristol pointed her champagne flute—Mary had stocked the limo with plastic, never glass for these types of parties—at the glowing Paris Las Vegas hotel. "I couldn't see the tippy top of the Eiffel Tower through the roof," she pouted.

"Ladies," Mary repeated, "it's not a good idea to stand while the limo is moving, but if you do, I need you to take off your shoes."

Finally noticing her, Bristol shouted, "Hey, Mar-eee!" She threw out her arms, knocking into her maid of honor, who toppled from the seat.

"Ooh, is she okay?" Mary leaned over the side of the limousine. The woman on the floor was the bride's sister, Mary recalled. Normally, she'd have memorized the names of all the party guests, but she'd had to step in for Rafe at the last minute, unprepared. All night she'd mentally called the maid of honor "Bristol's sister," which her exhausted brain had finally shortened into "Sistol." Sitting on the carpeted floor, Sistol swayed.

"Oh, hey, let's get you some fresh air." Vomit in the vehicles was the worst, and Mary couldn't spend hours cleaning and deodorizing the carpet tonight. She needed a good night's sleep for her big event tomorrow. She opened the side door, reached inside, and tugged Sistol onto the sidewalk. Her uncooperative pinky finger twinged, and she shook out her hand.

Perspiration glittered on the woman's pale forehead. "I don't feel so good."

"That's okay," Mary said. "I've got you." Gripping her upper arm, she shoved through the crowd of tourists and partiers on the sidewalk toward a trash can. When Sistol belched, Mary grasped her blond hair in one hand and pressed the other into her back, bending her over the opening just in time.

After emptying the contents of her stomach, too much booze and hardly any food, into the bin, Sistol straightened, still pale. "Sorry, I..."

"Don't worry about it, honey." Mary rubbed a circle on her back, the way her mother used to do when she was sick. "It happens all the time. Drink some water, and you'll be better in no time." It might even be true. She couldn't be older than twenty-five. Alcohol treated Mary better when she was in her twenties. Now thirty-six, she'd have a two-day headache if she drank as much as these ladies had.

But why come to Vegas for a bachelorette party if you weren't going to get drunk off your ass, dance in the limousine, and scream until your throat hurt? It was all part of the package Forza Elite Motors offered, with a fully stocked bar inside the limousine for cruising the Strip until two A.M.

Someday, Mary hoped to get a larger cut of the wedding action, beyond transportation. Then she'd be able to focus on the party planning she loved and leave the driving to someone else. Plus, with the extra money coming in, her brothers wouldn't have to work such long hours. None of them were as young as they used to be. Fatigue led to injuries like Rafe's.

She glanced at her watch. Ten minutes until two. Time to wrap it up so she could snag a few hours of sleep before she had to set up her brand-new booth at the wedding expo.

Snugging an arm around Sistol's waist, Mary led her back to the group of women, who'd attracted a crowd of equally drunk men. Bristol leaned over the side of the limo and huffed at the short veil clipped to her rhinestone tiara.

Gently, Mary pushed herself between the men and the car and opened the door to let the still-pale Sistol inside. "Sorry, guys, can't you see she's taken?" She shut the door.

"Not yet, she ain't." The cowboy hat–wearing guy closest to the limo sucked on the straw of his glowing yard-long cocktail.

The drunken douche would've never talked back to either of her brothers. It was one benefit of their tank-like builds. "Afraid so," Mary said. "And her fiancé's a lot bigger than you. Think Jason Momoa."

"Whoa." The guy stumbled back.

The bride protested, "No, he's—"

"In fact," Mary interrupted, "it's time to get you back to him. Night, guys. Ladies, shoes off if you're going to stand on the seats." She checked that the women followed her instructions, then circled around to the driver's seat and punched the ignition. The engine purred to life like her brother Michael's cars always did.

Michael had offered to drive the party tonight. But he'd spent the day repainting his pet project, a '71 Mustang Mach 1, and the paint fumes always gave him a headache. Her other brother Rafe, who was scheduled to drive tonight, had broken his finger in the shop when a car hood had unexpectedly crashed down.

Rafe had argued that he could still drive with his splint, but years later, she remembered the agony of a broken finger. She'd been only eleven and all too aware of her family's precarious finances when she'd hidden her hand in the pocket of her school uniform skirt. It was only later, when the side of her hand swelled and she couldn't hold a pencil, that she finally told her dad what had happened and he took her to the ER. By then it was too late, and her pinky was permanently crooked.

She'd taken better care of her baby brother than that, driving him to the ER herself and putting the enormous deductible on her credit card. He couldn't drive tonight's bachelorette party with the pain meds, and none of their part-time employees were available that night. That left her, the co-owner of Forza Elite Motors, to do it.

Someday, if her plans worked out, they'd have full-time employees who weren't named Forza to pick up the slack. But until she'd achieved her dream of branching out into event planning, she was stuck as the backup chauffeur.

Signaling, she pulled the limo into the porte-cochère of La Villa. The hotel's location toward the end of the Strip meant it wasn't quite as crowded as the larger ones in the prime locations, but Mary was glad to see people entering the revolving door. She hoped it would be even busier when she came back in a few hours for the wedding expo.

She heaved her tired body from the driver's side, circled the hood, and opened the rear passenger door. The fresh air had done its job, putting color back in Sistol's cheeks. She leaned on a friend as she shuffled toward the door.

Bristol waved exuberantly. "Greg!"

The groom, a slender man no taller than Mary and certainly no Jason Momoa, scurried toward the limo.

Bristol bounded to him and all but fell into his arms. "Why aren't you at your bachelor party?"

"They're still in the suite watching...uh, a movie. But I missed you." He pushed his glasses up his nose. "Did you have fun?"

"The best time. Thanks to Mary."

Mary realized only then that she'd been watching the couple like a creeper. She busied herself by scanning the interior for forgotten shoes and handbags. She picked up a tiara, which had "MOH" spelled out in rhinestones.

"Can you give this to Sis—to your sister?" She held it out to Bristol, but Bristol was lip-locked with her groom.

Mary sighed. She'd seen some couples too caught up in strippers and porn to remember what they were celebrating during their weekend in Vegas. But Bristol and Greg were adorable. He'd left his bachelor party to check on his bride, and now they'd spend the night together.

Would she ever find a love like that?

She shook it off. She didn't have time for romantic love. Besides, she had all the love she needed from her brothers. Her family. And tomorrow at the wedding expo, she'd find customers for her new side hustle, enough to pay off Rafe's medical bill and maybe even enough to find the security they all craved.

Chapter Two

Alessandro Villa hardly noticed how his Italian oxfords sank into the thick pile of the silk Persian rug as he paced across it. The unfamiliar bubble of hope made him soar like a tourist on the zipline over Las Vegas Boulevard.

"Alex?"

"Say that again." Gripping his phone, he planted his feet and stared at the polished mahogany surface of his desk.

"The rumor is that the Paradise is for sale," Lev said.

His heart thudded in his chest. He'd never thought this day would come, the day when he could show everyone how far he'd risen above the rubble his father had made of their lives.

"You want it, right?" his real estate operations manager prodded. Alex had been silent too long.

"Yes." He didn't have to think about it. "You know I do."

"The gaming board will have to approve it."

Alex heard what Lev didn't say. He'd had a prickly relationship with the board since he'd opened the doors of his casino, La Villa. In Vegas, he didn't think there was such a thing as too over the top, but the gaming board disagreed.

"They'll approve it." He'd use all the levers at his disposal to ensure they did. He'd even grovel to his chief critic, Ray Richardson. He had a feeling Ray would demand it.

"Listen." A note of worry softened Lev's tone. "Remember, it's not personal. It's business. Stay focused."

Alone in his office, Alex grinned. "I'm always focused. I'll keep it professional." Just like the Rissos had kept it professional when they'd bought the hotel at a fire-sale price after the feds seized the Villa family's assets. He'd never thought the Rissos would sell, so he'd never dared think about what he'd do if he had the opportunity to buy his father's old hotel and casino. Turning the Paradise into La Villa II—no, La Villa *Prime*—a world-class resort, would prove to everyone he'd risen like a phoenix.

No, he'd go a step further. He'd demolish the Paradise. Wipe that dump from everyone's memory, and maybe they'd forget the humiliation his father had brought on their family, too. He'd build something truly ostentatious in its place. A neon-encrusted skyscraper would be an appropriate middle finger to everyone who'd doubted him.

"Anything else, boss?" Lev asked after they'd worked out their bidding strategy.

Alex's euphoria waned as he remembered why he'd called Lev in the first place. "Yeah. I need you to find a job for Dante Campo."

"Again?"

"He's a good worker from a good family."

"One of those statements is true," Lev said dryly.

The Campos were a good family, but they'd fallen for his father's swindle and lost more than money. Mr. Campo died from an aneurysm a few days after Alex's father had been arrested, leaving Mrs. Campo to care for her two young sons. Alex would be making up for it until the day they carried him feet first out of his casino.

Though the older son wasn't making it easy. "We just haven't found the right job for Dante yet," he said.

"What went wrong with the restaurant?"

"He set the kitchen on fire. A small fire, but my executive chef threatened to quit if I didn't get him out of there. Maybe he'd be good at clerical work at your office. Less risk of fire."

"That kid will find a way," Lev grumbled.

"He's promised to be on his best behavior. You'll find him something?"

"Yeah, yeah. Send him over."

"Thanks." Alex breathed out a sigh. He'd kept Donna Campo's boys employed since they were sixteen. Joey, who worked in his event planning department, was a good worker. Dante had always proved more of a challenge. Still, helping him was the least he could do for the family that had lost everything because of his father.

He disconnected the call and set down his phone. Propping his hands on his hips, he surveyed his desk. It was clear of clutter and papers as usual, though work always waited on his laptop. He should review the operations report, but he had too much adrenaline coursing through him to sit still. He needed to move.

Mentally flipping through the day's activities at the hotel, he found a target for his energy: the wedding expo downstairs. Evie, his head event planner, should have it under control. But at the winter expo, she'd pulled in only eighty percent of the new business he'd been expecting. Six months later, he'd ensure that she was implementing the new tactics they'd discussed.

Going to the door, he pulled his suit jacket from its hanger and shrugged into it. He buttoned it then, glancing in the mirror, smoothed it over his flat stomach and straightened his shirt collar. When all was in place, he opened the door, told his assistant where he was going, and rode down the elevator to the mezzanine.

Only Alex and Lev, who'd seen it in its shabbier days, would have recognized the mezzanine as the top two floors of the budget motel he'd bought ten years ago. He'd hardly slept for a year, worrying over the amount he'd borrowed against his bar to turn the rundown place into a luxury casino and resort. Now, instead of cramped rooms and dim hallways, the mezzanine's high frescoed ceilings soared over plush carpet, which was currently awash with frothy white tulle, the overpowering scent of roses, and the nervous titters of people about to drop thirty Gs on four hours of cheap champagne and a band that arrived in their mom's Kia Carnival.

He pasted a smile on his face and strode in. But he didn't go straight to his booth in the center of the room. He forced his feet to slow as he took a meandering circuit of the expo.

Brides stopped to flutter their false eyelashes at him. Most of them didn't know who he was, but they liked his bespoke suit and wolfish grin. Vendors waved at him. La Villa hosted at least one wedding reception every weekend, and he'd worked with every major florist, caterer, and wedding chapel in Las Vegas.

"Alex!" The owner of the city's premier Elvis impersonator agency clapped him on the shoulder. His name was Orville, but he didn't let anyone call him that.

"Elvis! Looking good. I see you're enjoying the peanut butter, banana, and bacon sandwiches." Alex gestured at the stretched middle of his sequined jumpsuit.

Elvis leaned in closer. "You wouldn't believe it, but I've had more requests for, let's say, a more full-figured Elvis lately. People like a wedding officiant who seems more like your cool uncle than a sex object."

"Cool, huh? More like eccentric."

"Don't forget flamboyant. Why get married in Vegas if you're not all-in on the razzle-dazzle?"

"True." Over-the-top glamor was what La Villa promised with its gilded statues and frescoed ceilings. Not to mention the casino dealers with their faux-leather corset tops, short shorts, and fishnets. And every weekend, glitzy events brought in a steady stream of cash.

He glanced at the hotel's gold-and-white booth in the center of the room. Wait. Why weren't there any potential customers in it? Brides should have been poring through the galleries of photos or at least taking the ribbon and organza-wrapped candies. Distractedly, he excused himself and hurried to the large, carpeted square in the center of the room where his event planner leaned against the gilded copy of Michaelangelo's *David*—his little golden pecker had to be poking her in the back—staring at her phone.

"What are you doing?" he barked.

Evie bobbled her phone. "Don't scare me like that! I'm checking on the Murray-Achebe cake."

"You're supposed to be drawing in clients for next year's weddings."

Fire sparked in her usually placid gaze. "My immediate concern is tonight's reception. If that goes poorly, no one will hire us for a wedding next year."

"You should have everything in hand for tonight. You've got to be more strategic."

She squared her jaw. "Strategy is your job. Mine is ensuring every event goes flawlessly and reflects well on La Villa."

"Strategy is everyone's job." How could she not see it? The only way he'd gotten himself and his mother out of the poverty his father had landed them in was to look years into the future, to set seemingly impossible goals, and to work his ass off to achieve them. Now thousands of people depended on his success. Strategic thinking was why he was standing in a hotel he owned in a ten thousand–dollar suit.

She pursed her lips and crossed her arms.

"I'll show you how simple it is." He turned to face the bustling aisle and cracked the knuckles on his right hand. There. A meandering mother-daughter pair. When he grinned, the mother's steps faltered. It was almost too easy.

"Good morning." He reached out his hand, and the white woman took it, just like he knew she would. She stepped onto the carpet, tugging her daughter along. "Who's getting married?" He glanced between them like he couldn't tell. It was a rare day when someone surprised him.

"My daughter, June. I'm Valerie." She didn't release his hand. That was fine. Alex continued to pump it slowly.

"Your daughter? I was sure you were sisters." Evie shifted, and he could sense her eye-roll.

Valerie tittered. "I've been married for twenty-five years. Everything is so different these days, and I'm a little overwhelmed. The last wedding we went to, there wasn't even a formal invitation. We got invited on Facebook."

"Ah, no." Alex clicked his tongue sympathetically. "Here at La Villa, we value tradition." Actually, he valued whatever would make him a sale, and today, that would be embossed, hand-addressed invitations. "Our in-house wedding planner, Evie, will help make June's special day truly unforgettable." When he turned the full force of his smile on the bride-to-be, her gaze went glassy. He had them.

"Why don't you start by telling Evie what you have in mind? Then she can tell you how La Villa can make your wedding dreams come true." He shot his wedding planner a meaningful stare, and she nodded almost imperceptibly. If she couldn't close the sale he'd served up to her on a platter, he'd cut her loose. He couldn't afford dead weight in his organization.

With a dip of his chin, he stepped away from the women and almost bumped into the muscled form of someone he knew. Rafe Forza, towed by a suited man and woman he didn't know. Rafe was almost unrecognizable with his hair gelled into place and wearing khakis and a logo golf shirt instead of his usual mechanic's coveralls. His eyes were wild like he didn't like where this situation was headed. But Alex still remembered the sickening snap of his nose when Rafe's fist connected with it almost twenty years ago. He smirked and let them pass unmolested.

If Rafe was here, that meant... Alex scanned the room. Yes, there it was. The Forzas' elegant black booth with the red script *Forza Elite Motors* on the sign above it. But it was missing the person who held the family business together. Mary.

Alex widened his search and found her in the next booth over, her voluminous dark curls and expressive brown eyes calling to him like a beacon. Or maybe it was her olive skin, which seemed to glow like she'd swallowed the early-summer sun.

The sign over her head read, *Forza Events*. Events? That was new. Putting on his most careless swagger, he sauntered toward the corner booth and paused a dozen feet away to observe.

Mary stood before a pair of men, her hands doing at least half of the talking. In the air before her, her fingers shaped an imaginary layer cake, possibly with flowers on it. Gears would've more fitting for a motor-head like Mary. Back in high school, she'd scoffed when he'd told her he was taking his car—his first one, a BMW, before it was repoed—for an oil change. She had him drive it to their shop and showed him how to do it. They'd put on matching coveralls from the rack, and she'd swiped grease off his cheek with a rag.

He'd laughed, wondering why anyone would worry about the hundred dollars the service would've cost at the dealership. What an arrogant prick he'd been. Little did he know how useful the skill would be in the lean years ahead, when he'd changed the oil in his next car, an ancient Ford Escort, more times than he could count.

What was she doing with that second booth? He stepped closer.

Chapter Three

As she talked to the engaged men, a tall figure loomed in her peripheral vision. Mary's heart thudded in her chest. Not because of Alex's glossy dark hair and sharp brown eyes or the way he moved like a desert wolf, silent and powerful. It was because she was on his turf.

Back in high school, they were friends. Then they were enemies. Worse than enemies, they were strangers for the four years she was away at college. Then she discovered what her brothers had done. She tried to make up for it with kindness, but he was so closed-off now they'd never regained their old closeness. Now they met occasionally as acquaintances. As colleagues in the Vegas tourism industry. When La Villa needed to arrange transportation for their guests, Forza Elite Motors was the first company they called. Mary tried to return the favor by recommending La Villa when a party asked for a casino recommendation, but she knew her brothers often drove the guests to one of Alex's competitors.

There was nothing like an Italian-American grudge.

And there was nothing like Alex's dark gaze that seemed to see right into her soul. Their history, combined with his keen intuition, meant he knew all her hopes and dreams. Why she had a booth in the wedding expo he hosted.

She wished she understood him half as well. Maybe then she'd have known he'd break her trust.

She rubbed the twinge at her breastbone, just under the buttons of her black golf shirt. Why was he even down here? He should be up in his office in the tower, making deals with Japanese billionaires or whatever hotel magnates did. She'd hoped to keep her side hustle on the down-low a little longer, until Cierra's wedding was over and she could upload the photos to her website portfolio. She prayed every night for one successful event that would give her the credentials she needed to grow a successful business. One that would ease the financial pressures on her family.

Mary had always been the one who had it all together, who helped others. Not the one coated in nervous sweat, offering steep discounts in exchange for a review on The Knot. Never the one who needed help. Especially not in front of Alex Villa.

The shorter fiancé cleared his throat, and that's when Mary realized she'd been deep in her own head and hadn't heard what her potential client had asked.

"I'm sorry, it's so loud in here." The event was packed, and the brides-to-be filled the room with boisterous chatter. "Could you say that again?"

"I asked about your experience." His downturned lip told Mary he questioned her intelligence, too.

Alex raised an eyebrow and curled up one side of his mouth into that smirk that said, *Yeah, I'd like to hear this, too.*

Screw him. She stood up straighter. "I have twenty years' experience in the wedding industry. Since I was fifteen, I've worked at my family's limousine business, where I've handled transportation for all kinds of events, from bachelor parties to formal weddings. Going beyond transportation, I've consulted with brides and grooms, arranging reservations for restaurants and activities. We have a four-point-eight rating on Yelp. People love us because we treat everyone like family."

"But you haven't actually planned any weddings," the taller fiancé finally spoke up.

Mary tried to keep the wince off her face. "I'm working on one right now. But because my business is new, I can offer—"

"You won't find a more detail-oriented planner." Alex stepped forward. "Mary knows every vendor and every venue in Las Vegas. And she drives a hard bargain. She'll get you more than you expect for your budget."

Mary forced her smile wider. Who was he to swoop in here and try to rescue her? She could take care of herself. Her family, too. She'd been doing it since she was tall enough to reach the stovetop controls. She needed to do a better job of marketing her business. Like Alex. Even though La Villa was far from the action at the heart of the Strip, it was busy all the time. His dad, also a casino owner, must have taught him all his tricks.

"We'll think about it," the first man said.

"Take my card." Mary handed it to him. Instead of the white tiger they used in the car business, the logo on the dove-gray cards was a blue-eyed panther wearing a flower crown.

"Don't think too long." Alex rested his arm across her shoulders. "Mary's schedule books up fast."

As the couple walked away, Mary allowed herself a single sniff of Alex's expensive cologne before she ducked out from under his arm. "I didn't need that. I can take care of myself."

"I know you can." His brows scrunched together the same way they used to in math class. The grooves between them were deeper now. "But I thought you could use the assist. I'd have done it for any other friend."

Would he? Since graduation, he'd cultivated a reputation as a businessman with a relentless focus on success. She nodded at his much fancier booth in the middle of the room, staffed by Evie McAlister, his very capable wedding planner. She had screens and screens of photos in the gallery on La Villa's website. "I'm the competition now, you know."

He flashed that secret smile they used to share. "I'm proud of you for striking out on your own. Following your dream."

"But what about—"

"Vegas is a big town," he said. "There's plenty of business for both of us. Besides, everything I said was true. You'll be amazing at whatever you set your mind to do. As long as you don't undervalue yourself."

"Undervalue myself?"

"I heard you, about to offer those guys a steep discount. People don't want a cut-rate wedding. They want value. Which you can deliver at full price."

She gritted her teeth. Had she been that obvious? "It's a catch-22. Customers want experience, which I don't have."

"Yet." He flashed her that confident smile, the one he'd always used on her before they had to give a presentation in school. "Customers will come, don't worry."

She wished she felt that certain. She'd stepped into the family business after it was established. Starting new was unfamiliar territory. Alex had done it with his piano bar. Then, instead of taking the safe route by taking over his father's casino, he'd bought that old motel he turned into La Villa. She supposed she could take his advice. They could be friendly competitors. But she'd stop there. Older and wiser now than she was when she'd given him her heart, she knew better than to trust him.

She took a step toward her other booth, where a thirtysomething Southeast Asian woman lingered in front of the poster that showed their limousines. Where was Rafe? He'd said he'd be right back.

"Sorry, I have to..." She tipped her head at the potential customer.

"Of course." He nodded but stayed where he was, surrounded by the dove gray, petal pink, and hydrangea blue of her booth.

As she talked to the woman about limousine options for a girls' weekend, she wondered again where Rafe had gone. He was supposed to be handling the car booth. With his adorable cleft chin, he could charm women without even trying. In fact, before he'd wandered off, his splinted finger had seemed like a draw for them. Everyone wanted to talk to the cute guy with a visible injury, especially when they found out how shy he was. It seemed the fewer words Rafe said, the more business he brought in.

Mary never had a problem talking to people. Fifteen minutes later, the woman walked away, having booked Nick Cage. (The stretch convertible was every woman's favorite.) Mary knew the names of everyone in the group and which ones were most likely to get out of control. She noted them in the file so Rafe, whose finger should be fully recovered in time to chauffeur them, could keep his eye on party-girl Samira.

She glanced at her party planning booth and was shocked to find Alex still there. He was using that damned grin on a beautiful Black woman. Mary huffed. Really, the man had no shame, flirting with someone in *her* booth. He was probably keeping actual customers away. Mary strode over to shoo him off.

"...can offer you a full service, from invitations to honeymoon planning. Mary is committed to quality. Plus, you'd be hard-pressed to find a better negotiator in the city. You won't be disappointed."

She stopped so suddenly her shoe caught on the carpet, and she had to windmill her arms to stay upright. Alex was selling her unproven business? What was his angle? Once she regained her balance, she hurried over.

"Hi." She stuck out her hand. "Mary Forza, president of Forza Events."

"Hello. I'm Rochelle Richardson."

"Nice to meet you, Rochelle."

"Rochelle is Ray Richardson's daughter," Alex said. The words were heavy with meaning.

Mary blinked. Ray Richardson owned several high-end restaurants in town and was the president of the gaming commission. He was one of the most well-connected people in town. His daughter's wedding would be a who's who of Las Vegas VIPs. Whoever secured that wedding would be at the tip of everyone's tongue for wedding planner recommendations.

No pressure. "T-tell me more about your vision for your wedding."

"At this point, I'm just hoping not to have to get married at the drive-through chapel. Though I guess"—she tittered nervously—"that's one benefit to coming home to Vegas to get married. I, um, thought I had more time, but, well..." She put a hand on her flat belly. "The universe gave us a sign to move things along. I want to get married before I start showing so I don't look like the Luxor in my wedding photos."

"Congratulations!" Mary clapped her hands. "Believe me, you won't be the first bride in this town who needs a little give in her gown. I know a boutique with beautiful designs for every body shape. How much time do we have?"

"We want to get married by the end of July."

Less than two months? That was going to be tighter than Rochelle's wedding gown.

"How many guests are you inviting?" Mary asked.

"Not too many. About five hundred?"

"Five...hundred?" While summer's heat made it the least popular time to get married in Vegas, pulling off something that size, even in sizzling July, would be daunting.

Rochelle's smile faded. "You don't think you can do it?"

"Of course I can do it," Mary said. "*We* can do it. But you're sure you don't want to wait until after the baby's born?"

"My fiancé's family is pretty conservative. We think they can overlook the math if we're married before the baby comes. And after, I imagine I'll be too tired to want a big party."

"I understand. And what did you have in mind as far as the ceremony and reception?" Mary pulled a notepad from the pocket of her khakis and jotted down the notes.

"My fiancé and I are lawyers in LA. We don't have time for a lot of fussy planning, so I want it all done for us. I was thinking something all-inclusive, you know? A big block of hotel rooms for out-of-town guests and anyone who doesn't want to drive home after. His family might not be big drinkers, but my family? We party hard." She chuckled.

"And a wedding might be a celebration of love," Mary said, "but it's also about merging two families. Establishing relationships for the years ahead. Does your mother have opinions we should consider?"

Rochelle's lips thinned. "My mother died when I was little. Breast cancer. It's just Daddy and me."

"I'm so sorry. I lost my mother when I was a girl, too." Mary blinked to keep her tears in check. This conversation wasn't about how much she wished her mother were still around to see what she'd made of her life and to stand beside her at her wedding someday.

"What about your dad?" she asked. "Does he have opinions?"

"Always." Rochelle smirked. "But in the end, he wants me to be happy. So we're doing it my way."

Mary heard the subtext: Rochelle was just as much of a force as her father.

"If money isn't a consideration and you're looking for something all-inclusive and easy, I think you'd be better off going with one of the major hotels. Like La Villa." Reluctantly, she gestured at Alex. "They'll provide rooms for your guests, plus they can host both the ceremony and the reception in one of the large ballrooms, assuming there's availability. Their food is to die for. Alex lured the chef away from a Michelin-starred restaurant in New York. Plus, they have an onsite wedding planner to make everything go flawlessly. And if you're looking for Las Vegas bling, this is the place to be." As if to prove her point, one of La Villa's buff waiters meandered by in his short leather centurion costume and offered them bottled water.

Busy admiring his thickly muscled thighs, Rochelle fumbled her bottle of water. "I see what you mean."

Alex picked up smoothly, "We'd be happy to host your wedding, Rochelle. I can arrange availability on the day of your choice."

If Mary knew Alex, he'd boot a President to make space for the Richardson wedding. He relied on the favor of the gaming commission for his business. Especially after the shenanigans he'd pulled when he opened the casino.

"I couldn't work with you both?" Rochelle glanced between them. "I just assumed you worked together, since..."

"We're old friends," Mary interjected. "We help each other out. But I can assure you, La Villa is a fantastic choice for your wedding."

"The hotel isn't what I was expecting, not after all the griping Daddy did when you opened it." Rochelle glanced at the tray ceilings, frescoed in the style of the Sistine Chapel. "It's beautiful. But I'd love to work with you too, Mary. I feel like you get me."

Mary shot her a rueful smile. "I do. That's why I can tell you La Villa is the best choice. Alex's planner, Evie, will take care of you. She's been doing it longer than I have, and they can offer the full service you're looking for."

"Of course," Alex said. "I'll personally see to it that every one of your needs is met. That your wedding is unforgettable."

"Unforgettable, huh?" She pursed her lips. "Okay. I'll talk to your planner." She flashed Mary a regretful smile. "It was nice meeting you, Mary."

"If you need transportation"—Mary waved at her other booth, where Rafe still hadn't returned—"Evie knows where to find me."

"I'll give you a call." Rochelle tipped her head toward La Villa's booth. "Shall we?"

"I'll be right there," Alex said.

Rochelle nodded and headed to the center booth.

"Don't you want to be sure she doesn't get pulled off course before she gets to Evie?" Mary propped her hands on her hips.

"Don't be that way. We could've partnered on this wedding. Why did you insist on giving it to me?"

"Partnered?" Mary dipped her chin. "You have a wedding planner. You don't need me. Besides, we both know we aren't the best of partners."

He laid his hand over his heart. "Someday you'll forgive me for my youthful indiscretions."

"Nope. Especially if you try that fake flirting bullshit on me. Save it for someone who doesn't know you like I do."

His full lips twitched downward. After all these years, Mary still didn't know how to interpret that expression. It looked like pain or regret, but she knew better than to think Alex Villa ever experienced either of those emotions. He only inspired them in others.

He lifted her hand to his lips and kissed it. "You break my heart, Mary Theresa Forza."

You broke mine first.

Chapter Four

Forza Elite Motors' first customer of the day was a finance bro from New York City who wanted to explore the desert. After she sent him off with a Land Rover and a kiss of her fingers to the framed print of Saint Christopher, Mary stepped through the door into the shop. She'd expected to find Michael, but there were two coverall-clad rear-ends poking out of Nick Cage's engine compartment. Prince's "Cream" blared from the sound system.

Mary switched it off. "Rafe! What are you doing here?"

Twin thuds on the hood told her she'd startled them both. Her brothers turned, rubbing their dark hair.

"How many times have I told you to ring the bell when you come in here?" Michael growled.

"The bell would've startled you, too. Rafe, you're not supposed to be working with your hand. Let me see it."

Rafe hid his right hand behind his back and waved his filthy left hand. "All good here."

She propped her fists on her hips.

Huffing out an exasperated breath, Rafe showed her his other hand. He'd put a plastic baggie over the splinted finger. "See? I'm being such a good boy."

"Don't sass me, or I'll make you drive on the night of Garth Brooks' show."

"You wouldn't," he grumbled.

"I would. You'd sit in traffic for hours, and you know how handsy his fans get."

Rafe shuddered. "Sorry."

"That's better. Now, where did you wander off to yesterday? I had to break down both booths by myself. It was lucky I ran into the Pollinzi boys. They helped me carry it to the truck."

Michael ducked back under the hood.

"Just some pictures," Rafe mumbled.

"Pictures? Wait, you didn't fall for one of those card slappers, did you? You know the girls on the cards aren't actually looking for dates."

"No! Dammit, I'm thirty-two, not twelve."

"Then what do you mean by pictures?"

"They wanted to take some of me, okay?"

"Clothes on or off?" Michael kept his head in the engine compartment, but his shoulders shook with laughter.

"Clothes on! Clothes on, Ma." Rafe raised his eyes to the high ceiling and crossed himself.

"But what about your hand? You left your splint on, right?" Mary eyed it. The purple bruising was visible through the plastic bag.

"It wasn't my hand they wanted pictures of."

"Wait, what?" Mary gasped.

"My face! My face!" He waved his splinted hand at his stubbled chin and red cheeks.

"Mugshots?" Michael's voice echoed from under the hood.

Rafe didn't dignify that with a response.

"Look, their model didn't show," he said, "and they asked me to step in 'cause I'm about the same size as him. They gave me a tux to wear, and I stuck my hand in the pocket. No big deal."

"Pictures for what?" Mary surveyed her brother. He was cute, but she'd never thought of him as model-handsome, especially with his cheap haircut and beat-up mechanic's hands. He wasn't even as good-looking as their other brother, Gabe, who might share their genes but had soft hands from working in an office. Alex, she heard, got his nails manicured and his hair trimmed every other week at his hotel's spa. *He* was a man who belonged in a photo shoot. Not Rafe.

"Dunno." He ducked his head. "Some promotional thing."

"Did they pay you?"

"Not yet. They said they'd mail me a check."

Mary shook her head. That was her brother Rafe, always stepping in to help someone and never looking out for himself. He'd never see that check. How many more sales could they have made at the expo if he'd been doing his real job at the booth so she could've sold some wedding planning services? Enough to pay for his visit to the emergency room?

Like he'd read her mind, he said, "Sorry I abandoned you. How'd you do at the expo?"

"I booked eleven parties, three wedding transports, and one conference VIP shuttle service."

"Not bad." Michael backed out from under the hood and straightened his back with a grimace. "How about the other booth?"

She hated that his back was hurting. At almost forty, her oldest brother's body had taken a beating from working on cars since he was thirteen. He'd supported their family for so long. If Mary could get her planning business off the ground, they could hire help and he wouldn't end up perpetually stooped, working himself into the ground the way their father had done.

She shook her head. "Not great. A bit of interest, but no sales. I had to give a big one to Alex because the bride wanted more than I could offer."

"Alex Villa?" Michael narrowed his eyes as he wiped grease from his hands with a rag. "You talked to that dirtbag?"

"We're cordial acquaintances. You should try it sometime."

"But why?" Rafe asked. "After what he did..."

"We were friends before. It was my mistake to think we could be anything else."

"It was his mistake to stand you up," Michael growled.

"And you made him pay for it. Even though I asked you not to." She'd been glad when Alex got his nose fixed a few years after she'd come back from college. Every time she'd seen the crooked ridge in it, it reminded her of the pain she'd experienced that night.

"Little shit," Michael muttered.

Rafe gave her that searching stare he always did when someone mentioned Alex. Like he was looking for the tiny piece of her heart that had broken off and still belonged to her former best friend.

"He helped me at the expo yesterday. He talked up the planning business to potential customers even though he didn't know about it until he saw the booth."

Michael muttered something that ended with, "in your pants."

Mary ignored it. Alex had no interest in what was in her pants, not when they were in high school, and not now. She was grateful he'd crushed her hopes when he did. She'd never have gotten over it if she'd been the first of those poor women who paraded around on his arm for a month before he dumped her for the next pretty woman.

She checked her watch. "Go home and rest, Rafe. Tonight's party is in Grace Kelly, and you pick them up at seven."

Rafe glanced at the classic black stretch Cadillac in the next bay. "She's ready to go?"

"Just needs a final polish," Michael said.

"I'll do it before I leave," Rafe said.

"I got it," Michael insisted.

Leaving them to work it out, Mary stepped back through the door into the small lobby. Maybe she'd send their mailing list a coupon code for her planning services. Alex didn't know what he was talking about. If offering a discount was the only way to make a sale, it wasn't selling herself short.

He'd been the first one to show her she wasn't worth as much as she'd thought.

Chapter Five

Alex never sweated. But today, standing in front of the gaming commission, a drop skidded down his back under his dress shirt and caught at the waistband of his trousers.

He resisted the urge to tug at his collar. He'd thought wearing a tie would help his case. All it had done was constrict his air supply and capture the heat around his torso.

He sucked in a breath through his nose as Lev, behind him and in charge of the laptop, desperately flashed up another chart. It showed the solid growth of La Villa after its first lean year, when Alex had done anything he could to lure customers in from the more popular center of the strip.

One of the commission members shuffled through his papers. Another looked at her phone. The other three scowled at Alex. He shot them his most affable smile, hoping it masked his nervousness.

The gaming commission had never been fans of his. Alex hadn't tried to hide who his father was or what he'd done. Instead, he'd done everything he could to show them he'd never follow in his father's criminal footsteps. He'd double- and triple-checked every required form, he'd poached the most reputable casino manager from one of the big casinos, and he'd partnered with Jack Sweetly, the most upstanding investor in Vegas.

When no one else had offered for the falling-down piece of shit, they'd grudgingly approved his purchase of the budget motel with its unrestricted gaming license. They'd probably thought with the money he'd sunk into the operation and the nonexistent foot traffic at that end of the Strip, La Villa would fizzle out within a year of opening, and after someone razed it to build a strip mall, they could give the gaming license to one of the bigger outfits in the heart of the Strip.

But they didn't understand how desperately Alex wanted to succeed.

They'd been shocked at the scantily clad women he'd hired to lead crowds of people from the center of the strip to the ass-end of it where he'd renovated the dilapidated old motel into a grand casino and resort. They'd been appalled at the tiny shorts and revealing tops his dealers and waitstaff of all genders wore. But those gimmicks kept people in the casino at La Villa, and soon people wanted to stay in the hotel, too. Gamblers and nongamblers wanted to eat in the authentic Italian restaurant with the exquisite wine cellar Alex cultivated on his trips to Tuscany.

And he'd do the same with the Paradise, if they'd let him.

From the head of the conference table, Ray Richardson sliced a hand through the air. "Hold on, please."

Lev froze, mid-gesture at the graph that showed the sharp rise in La Villa's gaming taxes, which only proved how profitable the operation was.

"Do I understand correctly that you plan to demolish the Paradise?"

Alex's left eye twitched. He'd worked hard with his lawyers to bury that detail in the paperwork they'd submitted. But Ray Richardson hadn't risen to become the president of the commission by missing details.

"That's correct," Alex said. "My team doesn't believe the building is worth salvaging."

Richardson glanced at his colleagues with a grim smile. "The newer members of this commission might not recall that Mr. Villa's father formerly owned the Paradise. I wonder if the demolition of the casino has something to do with erasing that history?"

Alex put up his palms in a pretense of openness and honesty. "It's a business decision. Renovations would cost far more than a rebuild."

Richardson tipped his head to the side. "Is it really your intention to rebuild, or will you leave the empty lot as a screw-you to everyone who doubted you, including this commission?"

It was like Richardson had a window directly into Alex's brain. How did he know that thought had tempted him? Years of construction fences, billowing dirt, and noisy machinery would be the perfect fuck-you to the commission and to the other properties on the Strip. It might even drive more traffic to La Villa's quieter end of it.

But in the end, Alex was a pragmatist. The risk was too great, and he wouldn't put his and his mother's security on the line. Revenge wasn't worth the expense.

He forced his grin even broader. "I'm a simple businessman, interested only in what my partner, Jack Sweetly, and I see as a solid investment." Tossing in Jack's name always shored up his legitimacy. "We fully intend to build a grand resort, bigger and better than the Paradise ever was. The plans are in your packets."

Not one commission member glanced at the glossy folders in front of them. Their stares were hard and cold.

"We'll discuss your proposal in a private session, Mr. Villa," Richardson said. "The vote will occur in our next public session on August first. In the meantime, we'll contact you if we have questions."

Alex opened his mouth to argue but stopped at Lev's slight shake of his head. Instead, he flashed the commission members a tight smile. "Thank you."

He forced his trembling fingers to gather the papers in front of him.

"It'll be fine," Lev muttered as the commission members and

their support staff filed out. "Our offer is the best they're going to get."

But was it? As much work as he'd done to redeem the Villa name, memories in Vegas were long. Especially where a swindle was involved. Would he ever erase the stain his father had left on it?

"Villa." Richardson stood next to him, his brown eyes narrowed.

Alex swallowed. "Yes, Mr. Richardson?"

"I understand my daughter has decided to host her wedding at your hotel."

Alex kept the surprise off his face. He'd sent over the contract on Monday, but today was only Wednesday, and he hadn't received the signed copy yet. "I'm gratified she's chosen La Villa to host her celebration."

"I tried to talk her out of it," Richardson said unapologetically. "But she's stubborn. Like her father."

Alex squared himself up. "She wants the best, and that's La Villa." None of the big hotels would bend over backward like he was offering to do, not even for a wedding as big as Miss Richardson's.

"Don't fuck this up, Villa." Richardson's jaw was granite, and Alex heard what he hadn't said. *If my daughter's wedding isn't perfect, you'll purchase the Paradise over my dead body.*

"I wouldn't dream of it, sir."

Chapter Six

I t was a nightmare of his own making.

Alex's temper was always smoldering, like the embers at the end of the bonfire parties they used to have out in the desert back in high school. Usually, he kept a bucket of water nearby to douse any flame-ups and covered it all up with a smile and a fuck-all-this attitude.

The smile had failed, and the bucket must have been filled with gasoline instead of water because the fire had raged out of control today. And now he was paying for it.

"So...who's going to run the Sweetlys' party?" His assistant, Yasmin, leaned on the doorframe of his office as the elevator doors shushed closed behind Evie, whose anger lingered like smoke in the hall. "Joey Campo's a good kid, but I don't think he can manage this."

His pulse still roared in his ears. He cracked the knuckle of his middle finger, then he set his palms on the smooth surface of his desk to cool them. No, the rest of the staff would run right over Evie's doe-eyed assistant. "I'll do it."

Yasmin raised an eyebrow. "You don't know the first thing about managing parties."

"How hard can it be? I'm sure Evie left a file somewhere."

"Harder than you think. Besides, Jack expects you to be at the party shaking hands and looking good, not sweating over how to get another case of champagne at the last minute. Next time, maybe don't fire your event planner hours before an event begins."

"You can do it, then." Yasmin had worked for him almost since the beginning. She knew everything about his operation.

"Oh, no." She shook her head. "I have plans tonight."

"Cancel them. I'll pay you double overtime. *Triple*," he amended when she shook her head again.

"No can do, boss. It's my nephew's graduation."

Alex groaned and buried his head in his hands. Who could he coerce to manage the party at the last minute?

A brilliant idea struck him, and he raised his face. "Mary!"

"You want me to pray with you?" Yasmin pursed her lips. "You know I'm not Catholic."

"Not Hail Mary," he said, though this was a desperate act. "Mary Forza. Get her on the phone, please."

"On it." Yasmin went to her desk outside his office, and a minute later, his phone buzzed.

Taking a deep breath, he forced a smile onto his face and picked up the handset. "Mary."

"Hello, Alex. What's up?" A keyboard clacked in the background.

"You busy?" he purred like they both had all the time in the world.

"Always," she said. "It's Saturday, and we've got two bachelor parties tonight, plus some airport transportation. What can I do for you?"

He remembered how she used to gripe about driving people to and from the airport. The drivers earned a pittance for the hours they sometimes waited, especially during times of extreme weather. The Forzas' cut had to be even smaller. She must not be able to turn down customers. He hoped once she got the planning business off the ground, she could kill off the airport shuttle.

"I have an opportunity for you," he said. "An event planning gig."

The keyboard clicks stopped. "You want me to plan an event?"

"Here's the best part: the event is already planned. All you have to do is execute it."

"Execute? When?"

He winced. Leave it to Mary to cut right to it. "Tonight."

"Tonight? What happened? Is Evie sick?"

"Not exactly."

"Then what *exactly?*"

He'd known Mary too long to bullshit her. Alex rubbed the spot over his eyebrow that twinged. "She booked the Richardson wedding into the small ballroom. The small ballroom for a five-hundred-person event! I already freed up a hundred rooms by making a deal with the Bellagio. The goddamn Bellagio! If she'd asked me, I would have shuffled things to free up the grand ballroom, but she didn't. We argued, and I...I let her go."

"You fired your event planner over a ballroom mixup. That you could have easily resolved. And you've got an event tonight?"

Put that way, it seemed ridiculous. But in the heat of the moment, he'd only seen how Evie never did things his way. Which was the only correct way. "I can't afford for anything to go wrong with the Richardson wedding." He had to wrestle back control of this conversation. "Tonight's event is an anniversary party." A high-stakes one, but he wouldn't reveal that. "Look, I'll pay you five thousand dollars if you can be here within the hour."

"I don't know, Alex." She paused. "My brothers would be on their own tonight."

Ah. She'd given him the lever he needed. "But I need your help, too."

She was silent a moment, so he added one more incentive. "I'll give you credit for the entire event. You can add it to your event planning portfolio."

"I couldn't. It would be dishonest to claim that I'd done the whole thing."

Of course. Mary had always been honest. Incorruptible. That was why he didn't regret standing her up all those years ago. He'd only have dragged her down into the dirt with him. So he appealed once more to her benevolence. He let his voice go soft, like it pained him to beg. It truly did. "Will you help me? Please?"

"Dammit, Alex." But he could hear the laughter in her voice. "Toss in a day of spa treatments, and you've got yourself a deal."

That evening, between the soup course and the entrée, Alex found Mary in the hotel's kitchen, her dark hair piled on top of her head with a clip and sweat glistening at her temples. Wearing a knee-length black dress with chiffon sleeves that revealed her muscular arms, she stood at the stainless-steel prep counter, loading dinner plates onto a server's tray. Her shoes were black, too. Sturdy, service-able, unsexy heels like she'd wear to church. But when she raised up on her toes to lean over the counter to grab a plate, her calf muscles rounded in a way that made him wonder what they might feel like wrapped around his waist.

No, he reminded himself, she was a good girl. Not the kind of woman he dated these days. She was doing him a favor tonight. He'd thrown away his chance for anything else long ago.

He crossed his arms, not budging when a server brushed against his suit as he hurried past. "You're an event planner, not a sous chef."

She blew her bangs off her forehead. "Tonight, I'm whatever it takes to make this party run smoothly. And your kitchen doesn't have an expeditor, so I'm it."

"Thank you. The party has been flawless."

"I'm only executing on Evie's plan. It's not hard." She set down a plate a little too forcefully, and the tray wobbled. Alex grabbed it and steadied it.

"Looks like hard work to me." He nodded his thanks to the

server as she lifted the tray of meals and carried it out to the dining room floor.

Mary shook out her hand. Did her broken finger still bother her after all these years? Something he hadn't felt in a long time panged in his chest.

She started filling the next tray. "I like hard work."

"I know." Back in high school, not only had she earned all A's on her report card and served as the secretary of the young entrepreneurs' club, but she'd worked after school at the family business.

"You do, too." She pierced him with her clear-eyed gaze for just a moment before she glanced down at the plate in her hand and handed it back to the saucier. "This one's missing the balsamic glaze."

"I do like to work hard. But I play hard, too." He winked.

Mary's lips tightened for a second. "You make no secret of that. Now get out of my kitchen and back to your guests."

He chuckled. "Come join the party when you can. I'd like to introduce you to the hosts."

"Really?" She fanned her face before reaching for the next plate. "I'm a mess."

"You're beautiful." It was true. Her face was flushed, and concentration made her deep brown eyes sparkle. Even the sweat-dampened curls framed her face attractively. He wanted to reach out and coil the one at her nape around his finger, but he'd ceded the right to touch her long ago. It was a good thing she didn't bother to look up at him, or she'd have caught the weakness on his face.

He turned to leave. "I expect you to join me for dessert. I'm saving a seat next to me."

"Ha!" she barked. "That'll be the day, when there's an empty chair next to Alessandro Villa."

But Alex kept his promise. As soon as the first tray of chocolate mousse emerged from the kitchen, he excused himself from the seat he'd borrowed at the councilwoman's table, next to her flirtatious daughter. He returned to his seat just below the head table and pulled up a spare chair himself, then waved to a server to bring a fresh place setting.

The anniversary couple had finished their desserts and descended from the head table to chat by the time Mary finally joined him. She'd let down her hair, and the curls cascading down her back were frizzled.

He rose and kissed Mary's warm cheek. Her hair smelled sweetly of balsamic vinegar and chocolate. "Jack and Janet, I'd like to introduce you to the woman who's responsible for tonight's successful party. Mary Forza, of Forza Events. Mary, meet Jack and Janet Sweetly."

"Hello, Mary." Janet shook Mary's hand. Janet's petite frame and short gray hair couldn't have contrasted more with Mary's solid build and voluminous dark locks. "Do you work with Evie? She was so helpful with all the decisions about the party."

"Well, I..." Mary turned wide eyes to Alex.

"Mary stepped in when Evie was unexpectedly...unavailable."

"Unav—"

He spoke over Mary. "Hasn't she done a beautiful job?"

"Exquisite. We've been so well cared for. Haven't we?" Janet nudged her husband.

"Yes, yes." He tugged at his tie.

"Stop pulling your tie, dear," Janet said. "You've gone positively feral since you retired."

"Semi-retired," Jack said.

"What do you do, Jack?" Mary asked.

He smoothed down his tie. "I own an investment firm here in Las Vegas."

"Jack helped me buy this place." Alex gestured to the frescoed ceiling. He'd paid some local art students ten thousand dollars to paint it, but it looked like a million bucks.

"It was a solid investment. I wish all my projects were as successful." Jack raised his champagne flute.

Smiling, Alex tapped his glass to Jack's. "May our next partnership be just as lucrative." The list of people Alex trusted with a deal like the Paradise was so short Jack's name was the only one on it. He'd asked his friend for a lot of money to buy the hotel, and he was leveraging Jack's reputation, too. Yet he'd almost ruined Jack's party. He owed Mary for rescuing it. She'd turned the snake eyes he'd rolled into a win-win.

"The return on my investment in this place keeps my wife in baubles." Jack tilted his head at Janet. She wore diamond drops in her ears and a diamond eternity necklace. Plus, there was her whopper of an engagement ring, snuggled up next to her sparkly wedding band.

Janet patted Jack's shoulder. "You know I don't care about that, darling." She touched her necklace. "Well, maybe I do care about it. A girl likes a little bling, you know?" She winked at Mary.

Did Mary like bling? He'd never seen her with anything but her mother's gold cross at her neck. From his observations, Mary dated nice men from church. Accountants. Hotel managers. Teachers. Alex barely kept from curling his lip. Not the kind of guys who could cover her in diamonds the way Jack did for Janet. The way she deserved.

Alex had lost count of the jewels he'd given to girlfriends. But Mary wasn't like the women he dated. She'd demand more than a few gemstones. She'd want all of him, even the dark parts he kept hidden. More than he could ever give.

"You two are so sweet together," Mary said. "I don't think it's the diamonds that have kept your love alive for forty years."

"No," Janet said, "it's the little things. He always asks me about my day. And after dinner, he mixes me a little cocktail before he washes the dishes. And puts them away." She hummed out a little sigh.

Mary echoed it. "You found yourself a winner."

Alex kept in a snort. It couldn't be that easy to win Mary's heart. Mary's man would have to get along with her lunkhead brothers, go to Mass every Sunday, and be exactly the upstanding, honorable member of the community Alex wasn't.

He'd done her a favor by not showing up for prom.

Jack curled his hand around Janet's. "Let's make a last round of the party so we can go home."

Janet's eyes widened. "We can't leave our own anniversary party early."

"Not even for..." Jack whispered something in her ear.

His wife blushed. "Maybe everyone is almost ready to go. Lovely meeting you, Mary. Thanks for all you've done tonight."

Mary said, "It was my pleasure. Happy anniversary."

"Thank you, dear. And thanks, Alex." Janet kissed his cheek. "The hotel is spectacular, as always."

When the couple walked away, Alex indicated the chair next to his, and Mary sank into it.

"Tired?" he murmured as he scooted her chair closer to the table.

"Only my feet. I'm not used to wearing heels for this long."

He sat and leaned toward her. "Get used to it. You're my new event planner."

She'd already picked up her dessert spoon, but she set it down with a snort. "What the hell are you talking about?"

"You've done an impeccable job tonight. You need experience for your portfolio to build your business, and I need an event planner, at least temporarily. Someone has to plan the Richardson wedding."

She narrowed her eyes, then dug her spoon into the chocolate mousse. "You can thank Evie for the impeccable party when you beg her to come back." She popped the spoon into her mouth, and her shoulders lowered as her long eyelashes fluttered closed.

He cleared his throat and looked anywhere but at her plush lips as she eased the spoon out from between them. "I'm not asking Evie to come back. Our relationship was always...contentious. You and I work well together. I need the Richardson event to go perfectly. I'm seeking the gaming commission's approval for a new business venture."

Tilting her head, she stared into his eyes. He held steady under her gaze, letting her peek at the vulnerability under that word, *need*.

He tried never to need anything, but he could trust his old friend Mary not to take advantage.

"You'll let me run the wedding my way," she said. "No interference."

"Under two conditions. First, I've got an assistant planner, Joey Campo. He's part of the deal."

Mary tilted her head. "If you have an assistant..."

"Kid's only twenty-two. He's not capable of running a wedding of this significance. But he's got a good work ethic, and he can help you."

"That's not a terrible condition. What's the second?"

"Being La Villa's wedding planner has to be your sole focus. Let your brothers handle the shop."

"Primary focus," she amended. "I can run this event and support my brothers, too."

"As long as I'm your priority."

"You mean the wedding."

"Of course. The wedding is your priority."

"Then I'll do it. For my full fee plus a second spa day."

"Be sure you try the white truffle facial."

"I'm looking forward to the four-handed massage. With your two buffest masseuses."

"Deal."

She extended her hand to shake his. As he cradled her work-roughened hand in his, he knew he'd gotten a bargain.

Chapter Seven

In her insufficiently air-conditioned office, Mary's palms were sweaty. She resisted the urge to wipe them on the skirt of the black dress she normally wore to funerals but now had become her wedding planning uniform. Instead, she clasped them primly in her lap.

No, don't hide your hands. The remembered advice from who-knew-where hit her like a cattle prod, and she moved her hands to the surface of her desk with a sticky thwap. She cleared her throat.

"What do you think of the proposal?" she prompted Teagan. "Do you have any questions?"

Mary had transformed her windowless office off the lobby of Forza Elite Motors, where she usually did the books, into her wedding planning headquarters. She'd removed all the car posters and photos of her brothers in their chauffeur suits and tricked it out with stock photos of brides, grooms, and cakes. Someday, she'd have her own photos to put up. Whole albums. But for now, she was in the fake-it-till-you-make-it phase.

The giant bouquet of magenta roses Alex had sent after she'd helped at last week's anniversary party perfumed her office. She inhaled their scent and hoped it covered the smell of her sweat as she waited for Teagan to look up from the blush-pink proposal.

The bell tinkled in the lobby. Rafe was covering the counter during her meeting with Teagan, but working at the desk bored him, and he usually wandered back into the shop where he blasted Aerosmith too loud to hear the door. She held her breath until she heard his voice. If she could keep up her professional pretense a few minutes longer, she might make this sale.

Finally, Teagan looked up. "I'm still trying to figure out what's missing. Why your services cost so much less than every other planner I've talked to."

She liked that about Teagan. She said what she was thinking. It had been easy to put together some concepts since Teagan already knew what she wanted. A good thing, with only a month to plan it.

She owed the bride straight talk. "I'm just getting my business off the ground. Honestly, I need customers for my portfolio, so I'm discounting my rates temporarily. I promise you'll get excellent service."

"I love your proposal. And I know Twyla said all the plans were up to me, but I think she'll love them too. I'd like to move forward."

Mary held herself back from leaping across the desk to hug her newest client, who didn't seem to be the hugging type. "That's fantastic. All you have to do is sign the last page and give me a t-ten percent deposit."

She kept her wince on the inside. Alex never would've stuttered over asking for a deposit. She smiled brightly at the bride-to-be.

"Of course. Can I pay you with Moo-Lah?"

"That's fine. My username is at the bottom of the proposal."

Raised voices, one of them Rafe's, filtered through the closed door. "Could you excuse me for just a minute?" Mary asked.

Teagan hadn't fully finished her *yes* when Mary closed the door behind her and stepped into the lobby. A red-faced white woman glared up at Rafe, who scowled back at her.

"Mary, tell this lady we don't have a pink Cadillac, so she couldn't have reserved one."

Mary had lost track of how many times she'd reminded her

brothers the customer was always right. Though in this case, Rafe was right. They didn't own a pink Cadillac.

"What seems to be the trouble?" Mary asked the customer.

"I called last Saturday afternoon and talked to this guy to reserve a Cadillac. Pink! I know I said pink. And today I show up, and it's boring black."

"She didn't talk to me," Rafe grumbled.

"It doesn't matter, sweetie," Mary said through gritted teeth. "Why don't you go back to the shop while I take care of this?"

Rafe grunted and shuffled through the door. Mary turned her brightest smile on the customer. "I'm so sorry about the inconvenience. We do have a vintage white Cadillac, or if you want something a little flashier, I've got a red Ferrari."

"A Ferrari, huh?"

"At the same price we quoted you for the Cadillac." They'd rent it at a loss, but she hoped this way, the woman wouldn't squawk about Forza's bad service all over town.

"No discount for my trouble?"

Mary forced a grin. "Ten percent off."

"Done. Where do I sign?"

"One moment." Mary stuck her head through the shop door. "Michael, could you please do the paperwork on Christie Brinkley?"

He poked his head around the hood of his freshly painted blue Mustang. "Rafe's supposed to be handling the desk."

She hated pulling him off his passion project. But the rental business was the priority for all of them. She used her firmest voice. "I need you, Michael."

"Fine." Wiping his hands on a rag, he sauntered toward the door.

She smiled at the customer. "Michael will take care of you. Thank you so much for your understanding." She scrawled *10% off Presidential rate* onto a sticky note, slapped it onto the computer monitor, and scurried back to her office.

"Sorry about that," she said, closing the door.

Teagan looked up from her phone. "My wedding will be your

first priority, right? No splitting your attention with"—she waved at the closed door—"that? I know I've left it pretty late, and we don't have a lot of time."

What was it with everyone wanting to be her first priority? Last weekend, it was Alex, now Teagan. Too bad, her family was always first. But until she could get her business revved up, weddings would be a close second. She could handle it.

She flattened her trembling palms on the desk. It would be a race to get it all done this summer. Teagan and Twyla's wedding was only a month away, the weekend before the Richardson reception. But Teagan was planning an intimate ceremony for their closest family and friends, and she loved the outdoor venue Mary had proposed. A good thing since all the air-conditioned options were booked. It was a small party she could organize in her sleep, a blip compared to the Richardson event the following weekend.

"Of course. Nothing will distract me from your big day." Mary smiled as the lobby door tinkled again. Ms. Grumpy Pink Cadillac must have left at last.

After she made copies of the contract and scheduled their next meeting, Mary escorted Teagan out of the office. But the lobby was full of men. And tension thick as incense at a bishop's Mass.

She sucked in a cooling breath through her nose and rushed to open the door for Teagan. "See you Monday!" She hoped her expression looked like a smile and not a grimace.

"Bye." The tiny line between Teagan's eyebrows told her it was a grimace.

Mary tugged the lobby door closed. Alex, whom she hadn't seen at Forza Elite Motors since they were in high school, gripped a box protectively. Both of her brothers stood in front of the counter, clenching their fists. She could smell the testosterone. Or maybe that was the scent of motor oil on her brothers' coveralls battling Alex's cologne.

"What's going on?"

Not breaking eye contact with her brothers, Alex said, "I came to give you this."

"She doesn't want anything from you," Michael growled. "Not your stinking roses, and not whatever's in that box."

"Your sister and I are working together," Alex said. "This is business." His white knuckles contrasted with the lightness of his tone.

"Don't you have people to run your errands?" Rafe's voice rumbled like the V8 engine on his pickup.

Alex's gaze swept from Michael to Rafe. "I couldn't trust anyone else with this."

Rafe sniffed the air. "I smell a liar. Don't you, Michael?"

"Stinking liar," his brother agreed.

"Boys, go back to the shop." Gently, Mary pried the box from Alex's hands. He cracked his knuckles.

"What's in the box?" Rafe stepped forward.

The box was less than a foot long on each side and surprisingly light. Mary pushed past her brothers to set it on the counter and lifted the flap. Inside a nest of shredded paper was a bubble-wrapped item about the size of a small teapot. She pulled it out and carefully unwrapped it.

It was a delicate ceramic statuette of a Black couple, the man wearing a suit and the woman in a puffy white gown. The woman's hair was a 1980s-style mass of coils that reminded her of the cover of Janet Jackson's *Control* album.

"A cake topper?" she asked.

"Rochelle's parents'," Alex said. "She wants to use it, and I thought it might inspire your plans."

"How sweet." She turned the statuette in her hands. Wanting to use the topper meant tradition was important to Rochelle. That she remembered her mother and wanted her to have a place in her wedding even if she couldn't be there in person. Mary got it. She wished she had a memento like this from her parents' wedding, but they'd done a city-hall quickie, perhaps to hide the fact that Michael was already on the way. Their stern-faced Catholic grandma knew how to count months and, unlike Rochelle's family, wouldn't have celebrated an early-arriving grandchild.

If her family had been more supportive, would Mom have worked herself into illness and an early death? Would she still be around to give Mary a hug and tell her she was doing a good job? And someday, in the far-distant future, if Mary finally met a nice man and decided to marry, would she have sat in the front row, tears sparkling in her eyes?

Mary wiped a tear from her own cheek and glanced up to thank Alex. But Rafe was standing practically on top of him.

"I don't know what's going on here, but no one makes Mary cry," he growled.

"He didn't—"

Michael spoke over her. "You've delivered it. Now get out." He pulled a socket wrench from his pocket and tapped it against his palm.

Mary stepped between them. "Stop. This is ridiculous. Thanks, Alex, for bringing me this. It's going to give me a ton of ideas." An inspiration board started to come together in her head. A white layer cake with frosting flowers, the topper nestled into the top layer. Or a more modern cake, architectural and austere, possibly something textured, with the topper as a throwback element. Eighties and nineties hits sprinkled into the dance mix. And if Rochelle wanted one of those retro ballroom skirts, it would go a long way to hiding her baby bump.

"I'm glad you appreciate it," Alex said smoothly. "I expect I'll see a lot more of you all, now that we're working together."

"Won't that be nice, boys?" Mary said. "Like back in high school." Alex used to come to their house for Sunday dinner after Mass. Then, while Rafe and Michael washed the dishes, Alex, Mary, and her dad would go into the garage and tinker with whatever project Dad had going on in there. Alex's help was usually limited to handing over the right size socket wrench because he didn't know a fuel injector from a spark plug, but he seemed to enjoy chatting with Dad. Alex had never come out and said it, but she suspected his father wasn't nearly as generous with his time.

"This guy was an asshole back in high school," Rafe said,

squaring his jaw. "Still is, only now he's got fancier suits and manicures."

"Rafe, be nice." Where was a bucket of water when she needed it? She'd dump it over her brothers like a pair of angry cats.

Alex pulled his phone from his pocket. "Looks like you aren't so averse to the idea of a fancy suit yourself, Rafael." Carelessly, he flicked a thumb over the screen, then turned it toward Rafe.

Rafe's face went as red as Mary's Corvette.

She set the cake topper on the desk, then grabbed Alex's hand to see what he'd shown Rafe. It was a photo of Rafe in a tux, gazing into the middle distance, his hand—the one that still had a splint on it—shoved into the pants pocket. "Holy crap, Rafe," she gasped. "How'd they make you look so hot?"

Alex cleared his throat and pressed his phone into her hand. "Scroll. There's more."

"No!" Rafe's expression was pure horror. But of course, she had to look.

She flicked through a few more poses. Damn, was his jaw really that sharp? In the suit, he looked almost as good as Alex. As she scrolled, she noticed he lost the tie, then the shirt was unbuttoned at the base of his neck, then at the middle of his chest. Then the jacket was gone. Her fingers froze on the next photo, where Rafe lay on a bed against white sheets, shirtless, bathed in a light that called to mind early mornings, waking up next to someone who'd rocked your night.

"Rafe." She looked up, eyes wide. "You said you kept your clothes on."

"What?" He snatched the phone from Mary.

Michael peered over his shoulder. "Holy shit. That looks like porn."

Rafe put his hand over the screen. "They said they wouldn't use that one. How did you get these?"

Alex shrugged. "I know everything that goes on in my hotel."

"I kept my pants on." Rafe shot a pleading gaze at Mary. "I promise."

"Too bad you can't tell in that shot," Alex said. He was enjoying her brother's discomfort far too much.

"Fuck you." Rafe looked like he wanted to hurl the phone at Alex, but he only shoved it roughly into the front of his dress shirt. "Delete those, like I told the modeling agency people to do."

Alex looked down at the phone, a devilish smile curling his lips. "I don't think so. These photos bring me far too much enjoyment."

Usually, Rafe was the steady one, but this time, Michael held him back. The tendons in Rafe's neck stood out, and his face had gone almost purple. "Fuck you and your bullshit! Delete those, or so help me, I'll take a mallet to your phone!"

Mary planted her hands on the lapels of Alex's sport coat and pushed him back a couple of steps. "That's enough, Alex," she hissed.

Alex blinked down at her like he'd just remembered she was there. "I, um, I guess I got carried away."

"I guess you did." Why had he whipped out those photos? Though in a way, she was glad he had. It reminded her that Rafe was still her younger brother and, apparently, still needed protecting. Why had he posed shirtless for the modeling agency? Why had he agreed to pose for them at all? And why hadn't he let her review whatever release he'd signed? She was the only one of them who'd taken college-level business classes. Unlike Rafe, she dealt with contracts every day.

Which was why she had to narrow her focus to where it was needed: her family. No more partnerships or big weddings. She could plan Teagan's and Cierra's weddings while she got the boys and the shop in order, but that was all.

Alex began, "Look, I'm sorry..."

Mary plucked the cake topper off the desk and folded it into its bubble wrap, then carefully nestled it back into its box. She handed it to him. "I can't do this. I need to look after my brothers. And my own business here."

"But you—"

"No. I can't," she repeated. She'd been distracted at the wedding expo, and that had caused all this trouble.

"What am I going to do without you?" His brown eyes deepened, threatening to suck her in.

"Not her problem." Michael stepped forward. "Now get out of our fucking shop."

"Mary?" Alex held the box between them as if hoping she'd take it back.

"I'm sorry, Alex. You'd better go. Find someone else to plan the wedding."

His jaw hardened, and it was like he'd drawn a shade over his pleading brown eyes. They went cold and glittery. "Fine. I will." He turned on the heel of his shiny loafers and walked out, the bell dinging merrily as the door swung shut behind him.

Deliberately, Mary turned her back and didn't watch Alex's fine ass walk toward his Ferrari. "You okay, Rafe?"

"Yeah. I'm really sorry."

"Don't worry about it. Find me that release you signed, and I'll call the modeling agency."

"Thanks."

Mary reached for him and pulled him close. "I'm always here for you. Don't forget it."

He rested his chin on the top of her head. "Thank you. Michael, you want in on this? Mary gives the best hugs."

"Nah, I'm good. Try to stay out of fucking trouble, okay?" He opened the shop door.

Rafe's arms tightened around her. "Yeah. Okay. Sorry."

Mary held Rafe a little longer. "It'll be okay. We're family, and we've got each other's backs."

"Family," Rafe repeated. "I can always count on you."

"Always."

Chapter Eight

Alex stomped into his office, carefully set down the box with Rochelle Richardson's cake topper, then flung himself into his chair. His chest felt tight, and his neck was still sweaty from the effort of holding in his anger as he fought Friday afternoon traffic on the drive from the Forzas' shop to his hotel.

One by one, he cracked the knuckles on his left hand. Then he repeated it on his right hand. The practice usually soothed him, but today it gave him no relief. Holding in this much anger couldn't be healthy. He was too young for a heart attack.

Though he canceled most of his appointments with his therapist, he remembered a helpful exercise she'd taught him. He blew out his frustrated breath, then drew in a long, cool one through his nose, visualizing it as a light blue gas that he held in his lungs for a count of four as it slowly turned from blue to pink. Then he exhaled it from his pursed lips, slowly, for another count of four.

By the time he'd repeated the exercise four times, his head felt cooler, and his pulse no longer hammered at his neck.

"Goddamn therapy," he muttered as he glanced down at his desk and the neat stack of printed emails and letters Yasmin had prepared for him. He usually went through the mail right after lunch. He'd opened the package from Ray Richardson, holding his breath like it was a bomb. He'd thought the gaming board president might have sent a snarky representation of his chances of buying the Paradise, like a plastic bag full of water to represent his snowball's chance in hell. But it contained only the cake topper and a terse note: *Rochelle asked me to send you this.* He'd rushed to Mary's office like a giddy fool.

Why had he gone to her place of business and poked the bear? Showing Rafe those humiliating photos had filled him with the glee of retribution, especially when he remembered the last time he'd seen her brothers together, when Michael's fist to his stomach knocked the breath out of him right before Rafe's left hook smashed his nose. Twenty years later, he still remembered the sickening crunch.

He might have started the drama to put that meathead, Rafe, in his place, but he couldn't deny that it was Mary who pushed him past the safety barrier. He'd been aroused at the sight of her bathed in the shop's cheap track lighting, her brown eyes ablaze with righteous fury.

He was like one of the gamblers on the casino floor who'd lost every dollar in his pocket and begged for a few hundred in credit to get back on Lady Luck's good side. He'd let dopamine and adrenaline, not reason, take the driver's seat.

And now she'd not only kicked him out, she'd quit. He was well and truly fucked.

Doubly so, he realized as he scanned the first printed email. Yasmin had scrawled the word *Important!* across the top, which was saying something since she only printed the ones he couldn't afford to let trickle to the bottom of his inbox under the weight of all the urgent ones. It was a brief note from one of the gaming board members Alex had spent time cultivating into a friendly, who often shared insights from the board's discussions. The email noted that Richardson doubted Alex's commitment to collaboration with the big players on the Strip, citing the feud he'd started when he'd pulled that Pied Piper stunt to attract customers to La Villa.

Collaboration might be fine for someone like Mary Forza, but

Alex had never played well with others. He'd doubled down on self-reliance after his father destroyed the Villas' reputation and Alex had to rebuild it from zero.

When he'd opened La Villa, he'd done what he must to draw gamblers from the flashy center of the Strip to the ass-end of it he'd been able to afford. He wasn't trying to hurt anyone but to survive. Once people had discovered La Villa, he'd cultivated it into a haven for gamblers and tourists looking for all the Vegas amenities on the more peaceful end of the Strip. La Villa was a sexy and elegant respite from the hawkers and showgirls and drunken revelry closer to the main action.

Not that there was anything wrong with the Strip. The Paradise presented the perfect opportunity for him to put his stamp on it. To bring the Villa elegance to it while embracing the glitter and glamor.

La Villa Prime would symbolize the end of his ten-year feud with the big players on the Strip. Once he'd secured the Paradise, he'd play nice.

Alex scanned the email again and caught something he'd missed the first time. *Mr. Richardson also noted your antagonism with Michael and Rafe Forza, upstanding members of the Las Vegas tourism community.*

God dammit! It was like Richardson had a spy camera into Alex's brain. His hotheadedness had put not only Richardson's daughter's wedding in danger but also his bid to buy the Paradise and the redemption he'd worked so hard for eighteen years to earn.

He had to convince the board that their interests were aligned. An email wasn't enough. He'd have to prove it to them. And what better way than to make Rochelle Richardson's wedding the event of the season? No, he'd make it the event of the *year*. He'd show her father what he was capable of. Then Ray Richardson would finally believe Alex's purchase of the Paradise was good for Vegas.

He slid the email aside, revealing a large, cream-colored envelope. Yasmin had already slit it open but left the contents undisturbed. He pulled out a heavy card, a traditional wedding invitation.

Cierra Louise Dallencourt &
Sawyer Charles Leverton
invite you to share in their joy at their wedding
Saturday, August 9
at 3:30 in the afternoon
Semi-formal attire

So Cierra was getting married. Did women usually invite their exes to their weddings? It was a first for him.

He flipped through the inserts and paused at the reception card. It was deep red with a white swoosh across it that highlighted the black script.

Reception begins at 6:30, Desert Flower Country Club
Come at 5:30 to be entertained by an aerialist

Aerialists? Only in Vegas.

Alex wished he'd thought of entertainment like that for the Richardson wedding.

Cierra was one of his more dramatic exes, so it was fitting she'd bring pulse-pounding excitement to her wedding. He'd been savvy enough to end their relationship in public, at a very expensive restaurant overlooking the city, after he'd bought her a delicious dinner and the best bottle of cabernet in Vegas. It didn't stop her from tossing her wine in his face, ruining his suit, and screaming to everyone in the restaurant that Alex was a dog.

Maybe she'd invited him to her wedding to supply additional entertainment.

No way would he let her humiliate him in public. Not with the Paradise deal on the line.

He checked the "will not attend" box on the response card and tossed the whole packet of invitation garbage into his outbox. Then he pressed the intercom button on his desk phone. "Yasmin," he barked. Silence. Shit, it was after six. He switched to her voicemail. "Send Cierra something nice for her wedding. A case of that pink Prosecco she drinks and a dozen champagne flutes."

A tentative tap made him look up. A slender, dark-haired man stood in the doorway, his posture ramrod straight, his wide brown eyes slingshotting Alex back to the day he'd looked into the big, brown eyes of a toddler perched on his mother's hip when she'd come like an avenging fury to their door. But the boy was grown... ish now.

"Joey." Alex stood and circled his desk to shake his hand.

"Mr. Villa, hi. You wanted to see me?" A drop of sweat trickled from his temple.

"Come sit." Alex waved his hand at his guest chair.

When they were both seated, Alex leaned back. "How's your mother?"

Joey blinked. "Sh-she's fine."

"You still live with her, yes?" Alex waited for the boy's nod. "And she's getting by? Your father's pension is enough for her to live on?"

"Yes, sir."

Joey and his mother didn't know it, but the pension was fiction. Although Alex and his mother had sold everything they had to pay back the principal people had invested in his father's scheme, he knew that wasn't enough to sustain Mrs. Campo and her three children long-term. As soon as he'd been able to afford it, Alex had set up the "pension" with enough trusts and shell corporations in between that Mrs. Campo would never know it had come from one of the people she blamed for her husband's death.

"Excuse me, Mr. Villa," Joey said, his voice trembling, "are you firing me?"

"Firing you? Why would you think that?"

Joey shrank back at Alex's outburst. "Be-because you fired my boss?"

"No, no." Alex tried to chuckle, but tension tightened his

throat. "Now that Miss McAlister is gone, I'm promoting you. To chief wedding planner. It even comes with a raise."

If anything, Joey's olive skin turned paler. "Ch-chief?"

Shit. Rochelle was going to eat the boy alive. Alex pinched the smooth bridge of his nose. He had no choice. His temper had gotten him into this mess, and with Joey's help, he was going to blast his way out of it.

"Sure," he said. "First order of business is the Richardson wedding at the end of July. I'll need you to take charge of that."

Joey's eyes grew impossibly wider. They were going to roll out of his head and onto the silk rug, and then who would coordinate the Richardson wedding?

"It's going to be fine," Alex said. Though what was he going to do if it wasn't? "Evie left a file, plus a playbook of how she plans weddings. Everything is in here." He passed the boy a tablet.

Joey glanced at it, but Alex could tell he saw nothing but his own fear.

"Spend the weekend familiarizing yourself with it. Ask me questions. In fact, set up a weekly meeting with me, and we'll work through any issues together." Ray Richardson would never let him buy the Paradise if his daughter's wedding was anything less than dazzling. He'd never get his redemption. "In fact, better make it twice a week."

Joey's Adam's apple bobbed, then he let out a small cough. "Yes, sir."

He scrambled out of his chair and was halfway to the door when Alex called, "Joey?"

Joey froze like a rabbit about to be flattened by a semi.

"You forgot this." Alex waved the tablet.

Joey scurried back to snatch it from his hand and then disappeared faster than you could say, "You're screwed, Alex."

He sank his head into his hands. This had to work. Sure, Rochelle had seemed to connect with Mary. But she was a lawyer who understood how business worked. She'd accept the personnel change as the business decision it was.

Regardless, bad news, unlike wine, didn't improve with age. He'd leave her a voice mail about the change in wedding planners, assure her that her needs would be met and her expectations exceeded, etcetera, and deal with any fallout on Monday. He pulled up his copy of Evie's file on the Richardson wedding and dialed the bride's number.

To his surprise—and disappointment—she picked up.

"Hello, Rochelle. This is Alex Villa. How are you today?"

"Hi, Alex." Her voice was slightly muffled with wind noise. "I'm leaving work early for a change. I guess you're still in the office?"

"I am." He took a deep breath. "I'm calling to let you know we had a change in personnel. Our newly promoted chief wedding planner, Joey Campo, will be taking lead on your wedding. You can expect—"

"Hold on. What happened to Mary?" The wind noise disappeared, like she'd rolled up the windows in her car.

"Mary's fine. She's just no longer working on your wedding."

"Why not?" The two words hit his breastbone like rubber bullets.

"We had a...difference of opinion. However—"

"Are you serious right now? No. We are five weeks out from my big day. We can't afford to play around with this."

"No one's playing. It's a simple change in personnel." Alex took a deep breath. "Joey is a qualified—"

"No. This is my one and only wedding. Mary gets me. I don't care about your difference of opinion. Get her back, or I will go full-on bridezilla on you. Understand?"

He rubbed his tired, scratchy eyes. "I don't know that she'll be willing to come back."

"Nuh-uh. Listen to me. Tell her I asked for her. Tell her I need her. Remind her I am hormonal and pregnant." Her shaky voice had risen an octave.

"Maybe you should pull over."

"Don't fucking tell me what to do, Alex Villa. You need to work through your shit and get Mary back. Daddy didn't want me to work with you, but I insisted that you—that *Mary*—would give me a lovely wedding. Don't prove me wrong."

"I underst—" The line went silent.

Shit. It shouldn't have surprised him that Rochelle could be just as hard-assed as her father, but she'd seemed so sweet when he met her at the expo. When Mary had been there to smooth everything over.

If he fucked up this wedding, he'd never get the Paradise. Someone else would buy it, and he'd die a little inside every time he looked at the shabby old high-rise, thinking of how he could've finally destroyed the loathsome reminder of his miserable past.

He needed Mary back.

He scrubbed his hands down his face. The only option left was to grovel.

Chapter Nine

The Forzas' house had hardly changed in the twenty years since he'd last been welcome here. Like the other homes in the neighborhood, it was small, with stucco walls and a red tile roof. The Joshua tree in front had grown taller than the roof. He wondered if it had bloomed in the spring. Although the yard was landscaped with stones, cacti, and yuccas, a pot of cheerful yellow lantana flourishing on the porch showed off Mary's green thumb.

He reached for the enormous bouquet of blue hyacinths. The woman at the flower shop said they were best for apologies, and he'd bought every stem they had. After locking his car, he strode up the front walk.

He paused for only a second at the bottom of the steps up to the house. The last time he'd been here, only a week before prom, Mary had made a giant tray of lasagna. God, her lasagna was delicious. He never ordered it at a restaurant anymore because it was always a lifeless imitation of hers.

After dinner, they'd ended up in the garage, where her dad was tinkering with a '64 Mustang. It looked like shit on the outside, but the engine was so clean they could've eaten their dessert off it. Her dad had let him help replace the belt on it and had clapped him on the shoulder after. They'd laughed over the greasy streak on his preppy button-down shirt.

He could imagine how much Mr. Forza hated him when he didn't show the night of prom.

In the weeks leading up to prom, he'd planned it all out. He'd bring her flowers. Not like today's armful of hyacinths but a corsage in a clear plastic box. A single red rose, surrounded by a spray of tiny yellow roses and delicate baby's breath he'd bought to symbolize his hope to turn their friendship into something more. His pulse had pounded when he'd imagined sliding it onto her wrist. Kissing her soft cheek and inhaling her coconut shampoo. Weeks later, he found the corsage desiccated in the refrigerator, the roses brown and lifeless, and chucked it into the trash.

How many times had he imagined what could've happened if the investigators hadn't showed? He'd have marched up these steps, his head held high, and shaken Mr. Forza's hand. He'd have promised to drive safely, not have a drop to drink, and have her home by whatever time her dad had said. And then Mary would have walked in, wearing...

He sighed and trudged up the stairs. He didn't deserve to imagine her dressed up for him. He'd asked her to prom under false pretenses. He'd known his father dealt with some shady people in the past—he'd never forget the night a pair of thugs broke the fingers on his father's left hand and threatened to do the same to thirteen-year-old Alex—but he'd promised he'd gone straight.

He hadn't.

Alex's black BMW, his tux, and even Mary's corsage had all been bought with stolen money. Honest, upstanding Mary would've been sickened to know about the college funds, the retirement accounts, the rainy-day savings that had disappeared into his father's pocket. Or rather, into that money pit, the Paradise.

He'd done her a favor by not showing up that night. He wouldn't allow himself to think about what could have happened if he'd taken her to prom. Even if his dream of leveling up their friendship had come true, it would've all gone to shit when she learned his life was a lie.

He rang the bell. Seconds later, a shadow passed behind the window shade, followed by the soft shuffle of footsteps on hardwood. When they paused, he imagined her leaning forward to peer through the peephole, deciding whether to let him in or order him to go away.

Ten long seconds later, the deadbolt clicked, and the door swung inward. Mary stood in the doorway, her curls piled on top of her head with a clip, her black work polo untucked over—he gulped—pink leggings that had looked like bare legs for a moment, and old-fashioned scuff slippers on her feet.

"What are you doing here, Alex? We said everything we needed to at the shop today."

"I—" He licked his lips. "These are for you." He extended the hyacinths to her and held his breath.

Her eyes softened as she took in the bouquet. Of course she knew what they meant. It was her business to understand the language of flowers. She took them from him. "Thank you."

He cleared his throat. "I'm sorry I was an ass today." If he had more time, he'd take it slowly. Leave it there. Send her more flowers at work on Monday. Something that meant friendship. But he had to turn around Rochelle's wedding ASAP. "Can we talk?"

She tilted her head, and one curl floated across her forehead. He wished he could brush it aside, twist it around his finger and let it spring free. But he didn't have that right. He never had.

"Okay." She turned and led him toward the kitchen. He closed and locked the door, then followed.

The kitchen used to be yellow with light wood cabinets, but it had been repainted in a vibrant orange-red, and the cabinets had been painted white. The round white table in the corner was the same one where he and Mary used to do homework together, guzzling those disgusting Pepsi Blues her brothers liked. The chairs looked more rickety than he remembered.

When Mary reached into an upper cabinet for a clear vase, her golf shirt rode up, showing the generous curve of her ass. Quickly, Alex looked away. That peek at her delectable shape was not for him. Not today. Not ever.

The Forzas' refrigerator had always been covered in photos, stuck to it with kitschy Las Vegas souvenir magnets. Now that it belonged to Mary, it was no different.

He walked over, drawn to the photo of Mr. Forza, seated in what appeared to be the church's fellowship hall, surrounded by Mary, Michael, and Rafe. He looked frail, as he had at the end. "I miss your dad."

Mary ran water into the vase. "So do I."

The prayer card from his funeral Mass peeked out from under a Viva Las Vegas magnet. Alex's own copy was stuck in the family Bible at his mother's place. They'd gone together to pay their respects, but Alex had sat in the back pew.

Nearby was a photo that surprised him. "What's this? Are your brothers wearing...lederhosen?"

She chuckled and peered around his shoulder. "We went to my brother Gabe's amusement park in Ohio. I don't think you've met him. That's him in the green shirt. He was adopted and only came back into our lives last year. His fiancée, whom you met last year, is the entertainment director, and she let us all dress up in the costumes from the show."

"Let you?" He eyed the mulish expressions on Michael's and Rafe's faces.

"Okay, more like let me. And made Michael and Rafe. I suspect Gabe was into it, though."

Gabe did look happy, with his arm slung around his pretty fiancée. She wore a white gown, the stiff skirt encrusted with sparkly crystals. Alex remembered how she'd sung like an angel at his piano bar. On the other side of Gabe, Mary absolutely glowed in a red satin gown that did amazing things to her bustline.

"You looked incredible."

"Thanks. It was a little tight, and I kept thinking I was going to pop a seam."

Alex grunted and turned away. If he looked too much longer, he was going to pop a seam in his trousers.

"Wine?" Mary asked.

The tightness in his chest loosened. She must have liked the flowers. "Please."

She pulled a bottle of Chianti out of the refrigerator. "Sorry, it's nothing fancy."

"It's fine." He kept himself from wincing. Since the wine was cold, he wouldn't be able to taste it anyway.

She poured him a glass and handed it to him. Then she tucked the vase of hyacinths against her chest and carried it to the tiny living room. She set her glass of wine on the glass-topped coffee table, then centered the flowers next to it. Tucking one foot under her, she sank into the corner of the sofa.

Like everything else in the house, the sofa was small, with only two cushions. Alex wedged himself into the other corner, giving her as much space as he could. He sipped his wine and found it not terrible, despite the wrong temperature. "Is this a Chianti Classico?"

"It's my favorite." A pleased smile curled her lips.

"Have you ever been?"

"To Italy?" She snorted. "Not exactly in my travel budget. I suppose you have?"

"I try to go every couple of years. Most of the hotel's wine cellar is Italian, and I go for research."

"Research, huh? Must be nice." She sipped her wine and regarded him over the rim of her glass.

Right. Groveling time.

"I apologize again for showing Rafe those photos. I...I got carried away."

"You sure as hell did," she said. "There were a dozen better ways you could've let me know he'd done a shirtless one."

Any one of the dozen could have brought them closer together instead of pushing them apart. "I'm sorry. Truly."

"Alex, I'm always going to side with my brothers. They're the only family I have."

"I know." They'd stood together even before their father died. "I shouldn't have laughed at him."

"No, you shouldn't. But it reminded me of my priorities. I need to support my brothers. I can't be away working some big wedding when they need me. If I'd been there for him at that photo shoot..."

"What would you have done, Mary? He's an adult. Would you have held him back from that opportunity?"

"Opportunity?" She snorted. "More like exploitation."

"Is it exploitation if they promised not to use the shirtless one and if they paid him five Gs for the rest?"

"Five *thousand?* Are you serious?"

"Check's in the mail. I told you I know everything that goes on in my hotel."

She sipped her wine and stared at a spot on the coffee table. Five thousand was probably a lot to a family like theirs. Was she thinking of all the things they could do with it? But a windfall wasn't in his best interest. Not if he wanted to get her back on the Richardson wedding.

He knew kind-hearted Mary would eventually forgive him. She'd forgiven him for standing her up at prom. But this time, he didn't have years to wait. It was time to grovel.

"I feel terrible about what I did. How can I make it right?" He splayed his open palms.

"The flowers were a nice touch. And coming here. I can never stay mad at you for long."

He gusted out a sigh. "Ah, Mary. I don't deserve you."

"Deserve me?" She arched her brow. "Of course you don't."

His stomach clenched. "I didn't mean—"

She laid her hand on his knee for less than a second, but it was enough to send a wave of warmth straight to his belly. "I'm kidding. When did you get so serious?"

That night the investigators came. But he couldn't say that. "I honestly am sorry. And I'll personally ensure the modeling agency destroys all copies of that photo. If that's what Rafe wants."

"Ask them to give the original to Rafe and let him decide. And destroy all the copies. Including that one on your phone."

He pulled his phone from his pocket, scrolled to the photo, and showed Mary each step as he deleted it from the device and the cloud backup. "Better?"

"Better." She drained her wineglass. "Now that's settled—"

"There's something else." He reached for her hand and held it. "I need you, Mary."

She blinked her eyes wide. God, he could get lost in their brown depths.

"Rochelle needs you, too. We can't do this wedding without you."

She slipped her hand from his and rubbed the back of her neck. "Of course you can. You have an entire staff—"

"None of them are as good as you. Rochelle doesn't want to work with anyone else. She asked me to remind you that she's hormonal and pregnant."

Her eyes softened. "She only thinks she needs me."

"You know as well as I do that the customer is always right. Please, Mary. Come back. If not for me, then do it for Rochelle."

"What about the boys? They can't run the shop without me."

"I'll double your fee. You can use it to hire help at the shop."

"Double?" Her eyebrows rose.

"Triple." He hated the desperate tone of his voice. But there was nothing for it. The Paradise was on the line.

She smirked. "How did you become a casino magnate with those terrible negotiation skills?"

He shrugged. "Just lucky, I guess. Does that mean you'll do it?"

She paused for a moment, and he could see her weighing her family against the money. Which she'd undoubtedly use to help her brothers. Finally, she said, "I'll get started tomorrow." When she lifted her chin, the warmth again filled his stomach.

Like her namesake, she was the queen of angels, and he was nothing but a sinner. But he'd keep that hidden. He couldn't afford to lose control again. Not if he wanted the Paradise.

Chapter Ten

The next day, Mary sat at the counter at the shop as the mail carrier handed her the usual handful of bills and junk mail. Mary talked with her for a minute about the weather—hot—and the car business—slowing for the summer—when a thin envelope slid out from the pile and landed on the three-ring binder Mary used to organize her thoughts for Rochelle and Rohaan's wedding.

She turned it over in her hands. It was addressed to her brother Rafe, and it came from Starring Role Talent Agency. She frowned at it. Was this the check Alex had told her about?

As soon as the mail carrier got into her truck, Mary carried the envelope to the back, where Rafe polished Grace Kelly for her night out. A plastic bag covered his splinted finger.

"A letter came for you," she said.

Rafe didn't pause his polishing. "Hold on to it for me? I'll look at it later."

"No, I think you should open it now."

He straightened. "I'm not being audited, am I?"

"Just open it." She held it out.

He walked the few steps toward her and took the envelope just as the bay door opened and Michael drove the Presidential through, bringing in a blast of hot air.

Mary planted her hands on her hips as Rafe fumbled the envelope with his broken finger and finally managed to break the seal. He pulled out two sheets of paper folded into thirds. He scanned the first one, breathed a sigh of relief, and flipped to the second sheet. When his gaze caught on the bottom third, he froze.

"What is it?" Mary asked.

Michael ambled over and peered over Rafe's shoulder. "Looks like a check."

"It's the payment from that photo shoot I did during the wedding expo. It's...it's five thousand dollars."

"Should've asked for more for the nudes," Michael grumbled.

"There weren't any fucking nudes!" Rafe elbowed his brother in the belly. "This letter says they've emailed me the photos to use in my modeling portfolio and they've destroyed their copy of the shirtless one."

"Why the fuck do you need a modeling portfolio?" Michael asked.

Rafe ducked his head. "I don't."

Mary cleared her throat. "What are you going to do with the money?"

He held out the page with the check. "Take it. You paid my medical bill."

Mary took it from him. "Five thousand dollars is more than the insurance copay for your finger. There'll be some left over."

"I think we should use it to hire someone to help you, Mary," Michael said. "You can't work full time here and plan weddings, too."

"Sure, I can," she said automatically.

"But you shouldn't have to," Rafe said. "Look, I know this money won't go very far, but you should have this chance to follow your dream."

Mary glanced between her two brothers. "I've got the deposits from my three weddings. I was planning to use the money to hire help for you guys."

"Three weddings?" Michael said. "I thought you only had Cierra and the two women with the funny names."

"I, um, agreed to take back the one at La Villa. Last night."

"Last night?" Rafe raised his eyebrows.

Mary straightened a corner of the paper in her hands. "Alex came over and asked me to reconsider. And I did."

Rafe shook his head. "I hope he begged."

"He apologized. And tripled my fee."

"Triple?" Michael's eyes goggled. "You sure there isn't something more he wants?"

She drew herself up. "Can't I be good at what I do and get a bonus for doing it on a compressed schedule?"

"Of course you can," Rafe said. "And that only goes to prove that you're the one doing the extra work. You should get the help."

She looked down at the check. "Until the wedding planning takes off. Then it's your turn for a break. You guys work so hard."

Michael crossed his thick arms over his broad chest. "We like hard work."

Rafe hesitated for only a moment before nodding. "We do. Besides, this isn't you taking a break. You're doing more work. Hire an assistant."

"I'll get someone to work the counter part-time. I've only got three weddings so far. I shouldn't need an assistant for that."

Michael shrugged. "Up to you. Did you have someone in mind?"

"Actually, I think I do. Evie McAlister. She's the wedding planner Alex fired. She could probably use a part-time job until she can find a full-time wedding planning gig."

He snorted. "You and your soft heart. Are you sure she's right for the job? Why'd Alex fire her?"

"Does it matter?" Rafe said. "Dickhead doesn't know his ass from his elbow. Hiring someone he fired sounds like justice to me."

Mary's chest tightened. She hated that her brothers still held a grudge against Alex. Especially when she'd be working with him on

Rochelle's wedding. But seeing more of each other could be the chance for them all to smooth over that history. Her brothers would see that Mary had forgiven him, so they could, too. And Alex would see how important her family was to her. He'd dial down his animosity.

They'd all be friends. Just like back in high school. But this time, she wouldn't fall for Alex, no matter how kind he was. Or how good he looked in a suit.

Chapter Eleven

W hoever created La Villa's elevator music should have their ASCAP card revoked. How could someone turn the Pussycat Dolls' "I Don't Need a Man" into a lullaby?

It didn't take much to make her sleepy these days. She loved planning weddings, but the highs and lows were getting to her. Evie had accepted her offer. Burned out on bridezillas, she'd welcomed the opportunity to help Mary with the car business. So Mary had spent all day Monday training her on the inventory and rental systems. It was only last night that she'd had time to narrow a selection of invitations for Teagan and Twyla's wedding.

She'd devoted this morning to Cierra's wedding and cake tasting. Although she'd laughed until her stomach ached at watching Cierra's and Sawyer's overblown reactions to each bite of cake, the sugar crash and headache that followed made it difficult for her to focus on the walkthrough of the reception venue with the aerialist. When she'd stumbled over nothing in the grassy area where her friend Saanvi planned to set up her aerial rig, Saanvi had asked Mary if she was okay. Of course, she'd nodded and said she was fine.

She had to be fine. She had a third wedding to wrangle. And it was only a month away.

She'd worked on her binder for the Richardson wedding

between customers on the weekend and during her lunch break Monday, but it wasn't as complete as she wanted it to be. And she didn't have time to get organized tonight since she had to drive. Thank goodness it was a sixtieth birthday and not a bachelor party like the ones Michael and Rafe were handling. She hoped they'd end the night before 2 A.M., but the last time she'd driven a group of mature ladies, they'd stayed out until sunrise.

Five minutes' rest would help.

She leaned against the mirrored wall of the elevator as it ascended toward Alex's office and let her eyes close for a second.

She opened them again when someone bumped her hand, sending shooting pain from her crooked finger up her arm. The jolt of adrenaline popped her eyes open. Dammit, she'd missed her stop, and the elevator had returned to the ground floor. "Thirty-three, please," she said to the man in full-body gold makeup standing next to the panel. He looked like the copy of Michaelangelo's *David* downstairs except for his teeny tiny gold Speedo. He nodded and pressed the button.

She gripped her tote bag with the heavy binder as the elevator rose. She couldn't be off her game on the call with Rochelle and Rohaan. To ensure their wedding went perfectly—and earn her new, tripled fee—she couldn't afford to make any mistakes.

This time, she got off on the correct floor. The receptionist pointed her to the corner of the building, and she hurried to the impressive-looking pair of dark wood doors. A woman with gorgeous brown skin and white hair smiled at her from a desk just outside the doors.

She rose. "You must be Miss Forza. I'm Yasmin."

"Please, call me Mary. And I'm sorry I cut it so close."

"It's fine. Go right in, and I'll connect the call."

Mary pushed open the heavy door. It closed silently behind her, and she stepped onto the thick rug. Alex's office was almost as large as her entire house, ten times bigger than her tiny office at Forza Elite Motors. What would she do with all this space? She wouldn't have to keep her growing collection of ribbons, tulle, and favor bags in her guest room closet, that's what.

Unlike the public areas downstairs with their Renaissance-style paintings, Alex's office was decorated in a simple, contemporary style. A giant wall-mounted video screen overlooked a long conference table on one side. On the other side was an expensive-looking seating area under a watercolor of red roses. Fresh peonies spilled from a vase on the coffee table. She inhaled their fragrance.

Alex leaned a hip against his desk and stared out the enormous window with a view of the Strip and its cluster of hotels. In the daylight, they looked sun-bleached and ordinary, letting the hazy purple mountains behind them steal the show.

Mary couldn't see his face, but his back was more relaxed than she remembered seeing it since high school. Well before graduation. What did he see out his window that soothed him?

Although she could have watched him and speculated forever, the call with Rochelle was set to start in just a couple of minutes. When she cleared her throat, he turned and smiled.

"Mary. Thank you for coming." He stepped around the desk, buttoning his blue sport coat. He looked handsome and well-rested, like always. There were no dark shadows under his eyes.

Mary stopped herself from patting at the concealer caked under hers. "Of course. I'm looking forward to earning my tripled fee."

He chuckled, but she could tell he didn't believe her. They both knew she'd caved because of the way he'd reached for her hand and said, "I need you, Mary." She'd been powerless to resist the plea in his bottomless brown eyes.

She was a sucker, and she hated herself for it. Someday, she'd be able to say no to him.

Today wasn't that day.

As he approached, his cologne wafted into her nostrils. Vanilla, with something spicy. And a flowery note, too, but that could've been the peonies. Despite the afternoon sunlight streaming through the window, standing beside him was like walking through a garden at night, brushing against soft leaves and silky petals.

His hand landed lightly on her back, and he gestured at the conference table with the other. "We can take the call there."

His hand felt...nice. Warm. Solid. Like the friend she used to rely on. She let him guide her to the conference table. He pulled out one of the cushy leather chairs, and she sank into its cloudlike softness.

"Can I get you anything? A drink?" he asked.

The phone on the conference table trilled.

"No, thank you. Sorry I was almost late."

"It's no problem," he said. "You're right on time." He pressed a button on the phone. "Hello, Rochelle. And is Rohaan there, too?"

"We're both here," a low voice rumbled through the speakerphone.

"Hi, Alex," Rochelle said. "Is Mary with you?"

"I'm here," Mary said. "Hi, Rochelle. And it's nice to meet you, Rohaan." She pulled the binder from her satchel, wincing when her pinky finger twinged. "Let's get started. First, we'll confirm your date. It's the last Saturday in July, right? July 26th?"

"Wow, that seems really close," Rochelle said. "We're a little over a month away. Are you sure you can pull it off in time?"

Mary circled the date on the fact sheet, then smiled at Alex. "Of course. We've got the hotel owner right here. There's nothing he won't do to ensure everything is in place for your special day."

"Absolutely," Alex said. "And Mary will handle anything La Villa doesn't already have."

"Okay, next up is the number of guests. Rochelle, you said about five hundred?" Mary held her pen above the figure on the sheet.

"That's what I was thinking, with all of Daddy's business contacts," Rochelle said, "plus our families. How many of your family do you think will travel, babe?"

"It's not far from LA to Vegas," Rohaan rumbled.

"You could charter a bus," Mary said.

They were silent. Had they never ridden a bus?

She added, "Or reserve a car on the train?"

"You could charter a plane," Alex said.

"Yes," Rochelle said. "Don't you know someone who runs a charter service, babe?"

While Rochelle and Rohaan discussed the merits and drawbacks of offering their guests air transportation, Mary let her eyelids close for a moment. She couldn't imagine the cost of flying over a hundred people from LA to Vegas. Or having five hundred people to invite to her wedding.

The Forza family was scattered. Her grandparents were long gone, though she had some cousins somewhere near Chicago and some others up in San Francisco. They'd never been close. She had friends at church and plenty of business acquaintances, but she didn't need them to be part of her wedding. She'd need only her brothers, Gabe's fiancée, and her groom to make the day perfect. There was a perfectly serviceable room at the courthouse where she'd have a brief, fuss-free ceremony, then they'd go to her favorite Italian restaurant and stuff themselves with pasta and braciole. Tiramisu was even more delicious than wedding cake.

The honeymoon, though? That's where she'd spend her money. If they couldn't afford to get away, they'd get a room at the Bellagio and pretend they'd gone to Italy. They'd lounge by the pool, then wander through the gardens, and have a romantic dinner on the terrace. At night, they'd make love while they watched the fountain show from their hotel room window. She and her groom would fondly remember the romantic getaway years later as they rocked on her front porch, hand in hand.

Something hot and smooth nudged her hand, and she flicked her eyes open. Alex nodded at the cup of coffee he'd set in front of her.

Crap, had she fallen asleep, dreaming of her own wedding, and missed what Rochelle and Rohaan said about theirs? She opened her mouth to apologize, but Alex laid a finger across his lips. Rochelle and Rohaan were still debating whether their guests would appreciate the convenience of a chartered flight or prefer to make their own ways to Vegas.

She sighed and mouthed, "Thank you," as she lifted the porcelain cup printed with La Villa's crest to her lips. It was just how she liked it, the coffee strong and lightened with a touch of cream, no sugar. An almond biscotti perched on the saucer. She dunked it into her coffee, then bit into the crunchy cookie as she half-listened to the bride and groom.

"What if we work with a travel agent instead?" Mary asked. Alex looked up from his phone. "That way, your guests could make their own schedules, but your travel agent could track when everyone is coming in. I know someone great who's local."

"That could work," Rohaan said.

Before Mary could make a note of the decision, Rochelle said, "But wouldn't it be easier if everyone came on the same flight? Then we could charter some party buses from the airport to La Villa." They were off again. Though Rochelle and Rohaan seemed to really listen to each other and want to reach an agreement they could both live with.

Alex sighed and cracked a knuckle. It rocketed her back to their high-school days, when he had to run through the knuckles on both hands before every test. He said it helped when he was stressed. What did he have to be stressed about? All the planning was on Mary.

When he glanced at his phone, it clicked. This meeting was taking him away from his regular work, which was probably frustrating. *Too freaking bad, Alex.* He'd dragged her into this. She should be back at her office helping Evie and her brothers and working on her two other weddings. He could suck it up and be here with her.

Huh. Which was exactly what he was doing. Why did he care so much about this wedding? Sure, it was big, and it would make La Villa a lot of money. But couldn't he have sent what's-his-name, Evie's assistant? Joey. That's who should be here, not Alex.

While the couple continued to debate charter flights, she rolled back her chair and stood. The caffeine and sugar were helping, but moving would keep her awake. She wandered to the seating area and sniffed the flower arrangement. Heavenly. Peonies always made her think of weddings. She wondered if Alex knew they were said to bring financial success and happiness to newlyweds.

She meandered to his desk. It was solid, with a thick slab of wood on the top and a front that went all the way to the floor. Mahogany, if she wasn't mistaken. She trailed a finger across its smooth, clutter-free surface. Alex must keep his keyboard and papers in the drawers on the other side. A flat-screen monitor stood in one corner and a pair of paper trays occupied the other side, currently empty.

There was exactly one framed photo on the desk. She picked it up. She remembered Alex's mother from high school and church events long ago. Mary hadn't seen her in years, not since her father's funeral. From the photo, she guessed why. Mrs. Villa looked wafer thin, her skin practically translucent. Her hair and clothes were gorgeous, like always. But her smile was crooked, only one side turning up.

Mary knew Alex's father had died while she was still in college, and she looked around for a photo of him, but there was none. Ditto for photos of Alex himself or any of the women he'd dated over the years. Gently, she set the photo back in its place. It must mean a lot to him.

"So, a chartered flight, then," Rochelle said.

Mary returned to the conference table. "Okay. Rohaan, I'll note that you'll set that up with your contact. Next on the list is invitations. Did you like the samples I sent?"

"I liked the simple ones," Rochelle said, "but Rohaan liked the more traditional ones, so we'll go with those."

"Are you sure?" Mary asked. "I can look for something you're both happy with."

"No, I'm good," Rochelle said. "There are other things I care more about."

"Perfect. I'll order the invitations. Once you send me the guest list, I'll get them hand-addressed and in the mail. Next on the list is the reception music. Yesterday, I sent you demos from three bands that are available that night. Did you get a chance to listen to them?"

As they worked through her list, Alex sat with his elbows on his knees, tapping on his phone. Good thing this wasn't a video call.

While the couple debated salmon versus shellfish, Mary heard a soft pop. Alex was at it again, staring at the carpet, cracking his knuckles. Laying a hand over his, she mouthed the word, "Stop."

But what did she want to stop? The tingles that raced up her arm and lodged in her heart to reignite the ones still left over from his touch on her back? Or the unexpected fire in his eyes when he looked up at her?

He covered her hand with his and murmured her name, his mouth kicking up into a devilish smile on the last syllable. Had he rolled his chair closer? Suddenly, he was in her space. The scent of vanilla enveloped her. His smile showed off his lips, pink and smooth with a slight luster to them. His top lip had a sharp bow in the center. If she leaned forward just a tiny bit, she could kiss it.

"Mary?"

She blinked and slipped her hand out from between Alex's. "Sorry, Rochelle. Could you repeat that?"

"I asked if you thought potatoes or pasta would go better with the salmon."

Mary stared at the speakerphone, a much safer place to look than the light brown rings around Alex's pupils. "Potatoes, definitely. With five hundred people, keeping them warm during the service will be much easier. And there are so many variations. Maybe fingerlings with garlic and dill?"

After they'd scheduled a tasting for the following weekend when the couple would be back in Vegas, Mary summarized the decisions they'd made and outlined the next steps.

As Alex disconnected the call, she stood. "I guess I'll see you—"

"Just a minute," he said. "I have an idea."

"An idea?" Her heart thudded in her chest. Must be the caffeine. She rubbed her blouse over her breastbone. "Let's hear it."

"I think this wedding could use a little more pizazz."

"Pizazz." She crossed her arms. "I think with a month to plan it and a semi-secret baby on the way, we've got enough drama."

His lips quirked up on one side. "Someone I know always says, 'Why get married in Vegas if you're not all-in on the razzle-dazzle?'"

She squared her stance. "Because this is where Rochelle's family lives. She's looking for a simple, elegant wedding. Not one of your three-ring circuses with gold-painted *David*s in G-strings serving signature cocktails. Remember, I'm the wedding planner. You're just the venue. You promised me no interference."

"It was only an idea." He tilted his head. "Are you okay?"

From the scratch in her throat, she could tell she'd gone shrill in shooting down his razzle-dazzle. "Sorry, yes. I'm a little run-down. And I should go." She lifted the heavy binder and shoved it into her bag. "I'm driving tonight."

"Mary."

She couldn't help but meet his gaze, dark and dangerous. His smile was gone, replaced by a tight press of his lips.

Stop looking at his lips!

"Yes?" Looking into his eyes was also a mistake. They tugged her in like a whirlpool.

"You're not driving tonight."

"Of course I am." She sucked in cool air through her nose. She was back on solid ground. He wasn't intentionally smoldering at her. He was bossing her around. Again. "I run a business, same as you. Sometimes you must power through."

"Believe me, I understand powering through. But you're not safe to drive now, much less at 4 A.M. Can't Rafe or Michael do it?"

"They're also driving. And none of our part-timers can do it on a Tuesday night. So it's down to me."

"I'll do it," he said, his jaw like granite.

"You?" she scoffed. "You don't have a taxi license."

"I used to. It was one of my jobs after high school."

Wait, what? A job? Hadn't he inherited his father's white-collar business like the prince he was?

Before she could ask, he continued, "If you're worried, you can ride with me. But you're not driving in that condition. In fact, I'll drive you home."

She lifted her chin. "My car's here. I'll drive myself home. But..." Even if he no longer held a taxi license, he had to be more alert than she was. "I will let you drive tonight. Meet me at the shop at six."

"I'll pick you up from your house at 5:45."

She huffed, "Fine," and heaved her bag to her shoulder.

"If you brought a laptop or tablet to meetings, you wouldn't have to lug this binder around." He straightened the strap on her shoulder.

"Noted for when I can afford a laptop or tablet. And quit nagging me, or I'll change my mind about tonight." She zipped the bag closed.

His hand landed on her lower back, not a press but a gentle support as she moved toward the door. Wait, how was she supposed to storm out of here, her pride intact, while he was melting her with the soft touch of his palm?

She stole a glance at him. His gaze was directed at the door, and despite the soothing weight of his hand on her back, it was intense, like he could burn through it with sheer force of will.

She never wanted to be what he glared at like that.

Or did she?

Chapter Twelve

"Admit it." Mary leaned against the outside wall of the jazz club, a mischievous twinkle in her brown eyes. "They're adorable."

"Adorable monsters," Alex grumbled. He'd assumed she was driving a bachelor party. He'd not only drive but provide protection for the tempting chauffeur. With this party, the only protection Mary needed was from being overly coddled by the grandmotherly ladies.

Who also happened to be party animals and, as he could see through the window, were dancing cheek-to-cheek with men they'd just met. *Younger* men.

He wished he were dancing instead of standing outside this club, hands in his pockets like a chump. Specifically, dancing with the raven-haired beauty who also had her hands in the pockets of her black trousers, her black jacket thrown open to catch the night breeze.

"Is chauffeuring always this boring?" he asked.

She fluffed up like an angry cat. "No one asked you to come."

"I'm sorry." He winced. "I didn't mean it like that. I meant...the waiting. Driving a taxi, I was mostly moving, not killing time. I know you like to keep active, same as me. How do you pass the time?"

She shrugged. "I listen to audiobooks. Mostly about business. In fact, I've got one on my phone..." She patted her pocket.

No! Why had he said something so thoughtless? He was usually better at conversation than this. Having Mary near him again after all these years was messing with his head. He glanced through the window. The birthday girl was twirling with one of her friends.

"Mary." He stepped closer. "Dance with me?"

"Here?" She shifted her gaze along the busy street.

"It's only tourists. They won't care." He held out his hands, palms up.

She hesitated for a long moment. Then another. Finally, she placed her rough palm on his.

He didn't let her second-guess it. He tugged her toward him, into the circle of his arms, anchoring her with a hand on her waistband. He couldn't hear the melody of the music in the club, but he felt the bassline in the soles of his feet, in the thudding of his heart, and he shuffled his feet to it.

She gazed up at him, her eyelids drooping and her blinks slow enough to tangle her thick eyelashes together.

Ever since she'd touched him earlier during their conference call, he'd been unable to think of anything but touching her again. And now they weren't limited to a simple press of hands. His palm spanned the curve of her waist. Her fingertips rested on his shoulder, inches from his thundering heart. He clasped her other hand, wishing his palm weren't sticky with nervous sweat.

This was what their senior prom should have been like. Well, not like *this,* with drunk people catcalling as they stumbled past on the sidewalk. And the club's jazz was much better than their class's song, "Can You Feel the Love Tonight." But the neon lights of the Strip glowed in her hair, and he could imagine they were stage lights scattered by a disco ball. Her scratchy polyester pants were nothing like a satin ball gown, but her curves were soft under his hand, and for a second, he let himself imagine tasting her plush lips as he skimmed his fingertips under her starchy white shirt.

He leaned in closer to chase the scent that teased his nose. Lemons. No, it was sweeter than that. Oranges. Like the polish he'd smelled on the limo's upholstery. On Mary, it made him remember a citrus orchard he'd visited in Tuscany a few years ago, the delicate white petals falling around him like snow. He wished...

"What do you wish?"

He grimaced. He hadn't meant to say anything out loud. He was not about to reveal that he'd been wishing he could whisk her away to Tuscany to see how her eyes would sparkle in the moonlight, away from the neon of the Strip. So, he said another thing he wished as he looked into her sleepy face. "I wish you didn't have to work two jobs."

It was the wrong thing to say.

She reared back. "I don't *have* to work two jobs. I *want* to build up my wedding planning business. And, as I recall, you're the one who begged me to help with Rochelle's wedding."

"I know." He tightened his grip on her waist so she wouldn't spin out of his arms. "I only meant I wish you could spend more time doing what you love and less time doing that." He tipped his head toward where the limo was parked.

Her chin jutted out. "I love working with my brothers too. They need me."

If he still believed in any of the religious nonsense he'd been raised on, he'd have turned his eyes toward heaven in a prayer to the Archangel Gabriel to help him communicate better. He was skilled at getting his point across. Not tonight.

"You can't keep burning the candle at both ends," he said.

"Can't I?" Her dark eyebrows lifted. "I bet you hustle all the time. Why is it okay for you to work hard but not for me?"

He closed his eyes. Took a long breath. "I was only trying to care for you the way you care for everyone else."

"Well, stop. You suck at it." But her lips twitched.

"Do I? Suck?" He curled the corner of his mouth into what he'd been told was a devastating smile. "Or do you secretly enjoy being cared for too?"

Was that the neon, or did her cheeks turn pink?

"I think you do," he crowed. "I'm going to—"

"Alex?"

A tall woman in a sparkly dress stood beside them. Caught up in the bubble he'd created with Mary, he hadn't noticed anyone else on the sidewalk. This wasn't a tourist. She was...Fi...no, Vi... She danced in one of the shows. And they'd fucked a couple of times, more out of convenience and boredom than from any genuine connection.

The woman flipped her blond hair over her shoulder. Her white teeth sparkled. "What a surprise to bump into you here. Are you going inside?" She stepped closer, almost between him and Mary, forcing his hand off her waist. Though he kept hold of her hand.

"Hi, V," he said smoothly. "Let me introduce you to my date, Mary Forza." This was nothing like a date, but it was easier to explain than that he was driving a limo and relieving their boredom by dancing on the sidewalk.

Mary's eyebrows had all but disappeared into her hair. She stuck out her hand. "Sorry, I didn't catch your name?"

"Violette." She scanned Mary up and down, her gaze lingering on her frumpy chauffeur's suit. "Call me sometime, Alex. We'll...dance."

He gave a noncommittal head bob and turned his back to Violette. But Mary's stare followed her into the club.

Her lips thinned. "Why do I not think Violette was complimenting your actual dancing skills?"

He stepped closer. "Why? Am I not a good dancer?"

"Oh, you are. As I recall, your mother made you take lessons. But I think she was referring to something more...horizontal."

"I have no idea what you're talking about." Mary's smile told him he could get away with the playful lie. "But it doesn't matter. I'm positive I don't have her number anymore."

"Oh." She tugged her hand from his.

"What's wrong?"

She fiddled with her shirt cuff. "I was having such a good time I forgot what you're like."

He put a hand over hers to still her fingers. "What am I like?"

She fixed her gaze on her hands. "You, um, back in high school, you dated. A lot."

For one dizzying, heart-stopping moment, he thought she was finally going to ask him why he'd stood her up at prom. Heat washed over him and prickled in his cheeks. What would she think of him if she knew his secret? She'd walk out of his life and never return. He couldn't risk it. Especially not now, with the Richardson wedding and the Paradise on the line. As much as he hated it, he summoned up the old lie he'd prepared but never had to tell her.

Miraculously, Mary didn't go there. She kept at his dating history like it was relevant. "You do the same thing now. But now it's flashier. More dramatic. Like you're trying to prove something. You're not trying to prove anything to me, are you? I know you called me your date, but we're friends, right?" She finally looked him in the eye, the type of vulnerability Alex could never show shining right there on her face for anyone to see.

"Of course we are, sweetheart." *Sweetheart?* Where had that come from?

Mary stomped her foot. "You don't have to turn on all that bullshit for me, you know. I'm your friend. Not one of the women you *dance* with."

"But you did dance with me." Alex stepped closer until the front of his suit jacket brushed hers. He let his gaze fall on her red lips. They beckoned to him, soft and plump. He didn't know if it was the neon or the music or the way his hands had mapped the shape of her while they danced, but suddenly, he wanted to have her lipstick smudged across his lips for Violette, the birthday party, and all the tourists to see. "Friends can dance."

She blinked her eyes wide for a moment. Then she planted her hand on his chest and shoved him back a step. Her lips twitched with a smile that didn't make it to her brown eyes. "Right. Friends. Call me up the next time you need a platonic dance partner."

Platonic was the farthest thing from his mind right now, and he opened his mouth to say it, but the club's door opened, and the birthday partiers spilled onto the sidewalk, their voices still loud from talking over the music.

"Mary! Alex!" one of them shouted. "We're ready to sit while someone else dances. Take us to the strip club." The women all hooted.

With a wicked grin, Mary handed the key fob to Alex and said, "Yes, ma'am."

A couple of hours later, Alex pulled the limousine into the porte-cochère of the birthday ladies' hotel and stepped out to open the door. Mary beat him to it, and by the time he'd rounded the long hood, she was already helping the ladies heave themselves from the low vehicle.

"Have a good night," she said. "Thanks for using Forza Elite Motors."

"Thanks, Mary. Thanks, Alex," the birthday woman said.

His smile froze as his phone buzzed in his breast pocket in the specific rhythm he'd assigned to his mother's care facility. Ice careened through his veins.

Turning his back and stepping to the other side of the car, he reached for his phone. "Hello?"

"Mr. Villa, I'm sorry to call so late, but she's gotten pretty wound up. She's asking for you."

He tried to suck in one of those calming, blue breaths, but it was no use. His lungs could only take in fast sips of air. He'd seen her two days ago, on Sunday. What could have happened?

"It's no problem," he said. "I want you to call me when she needs me, no matter the hour. I'm on my way."

"Thank you. We'll see you soon."

Mary was all alone, leaning against the limo, when he turned back toward her. He hated to end the evening like this, but he had to get to his mother.

"I'm sorry. I have to go. There's a situation I have to deal with."

"Oh." Her lips turned down. "I guess a hotel runs twenty-four-seven."

"It does, but—" He stopped. Telling her about his mother would open parts of himself he'd rather conceal. Then his gaze fell on the limo. His car was parked in the Forzas' lot. "I'll call a rideshare."

"That's silly. I'll drop you at the hotel. It's just down the street. If you'll give me your keys, Rafe and I'll drop your car at La Villa in the morning."

"No, I...I'm not going there."

"Oh? *Ohh.*" Her eyes widened. "You're meeting Violette?" She grimaced. "Or someone else?"

"No. No!" As easy as it would've been, everything in him rebelled at the thought of Mary thinking he was leaving her for another woman. His shoulders slumped. "It's my mother."

Chapter Thirteen

"Whoa. Fancy," Mary said after Alex flashed his key card at the sensor and beckoned her through the door into the nicest lobby she'd ever seen—and she'd visited a lot of high-end hotels in her hometown.

Alex said nothing. Fair. He didn't want her here. He'd made that clear through his silence as he'd gripped the limo's steering wheel. But after he'd told her why he needed to get to the nursing facility in the suburbs, she'd needed to come. Why? That was complicated. He probably thought it was curiosity. That she wanted to witness how far his snooty mom had fallen. But she didn't think it was that, or at least, it wasn't all that.

She'd come here for Alex. For the terrified look in his eyes after he'd gotten that call. He looked like he needed a friend. And that's what she was. Even though she'd felt like a whole lot more when he'd held her in his arms outside the jazz club. Around women, he had one setting—smolder—and he couldn't turn it off.

Friends, she reminded herself. She cared about him, and she couldn't let him go alone to check on his mom late at night.

Though, from the tension in his shoulders, he probably would've preferred it.

She sympathized with the person whose job it was to keep all this white marble tile clean as they passed a couple of seating areas. Vases of cheery flowers brightened the dimly lit space, which must get fantastic light during the day from the large windows. Soothing landscapes and still-life paintings adorned the wood-paneled walls.

"Evening, Kim." Alex stopped at the desk, which looked nothing like a hospital counter. It looked like the one in his office, a regular wood office desk with a bouquet of daisies in a vase. "I have a guest tonight."

"Good evening." The white woman smiled at her. "Could I see your ID, please?"

Mary handed it over, and the receptionist used a tablet to scan it before handing it back. "Go right ahead, Mr. Villa."

He stepped around the desk to the elevator doors. When he scanned his keycard at the pad, the door slid open. Inside, he scanned his card again and pressed the top button. The silence stretched long between them on the ride up to the sixth floor. A million questions tickled the tip of Mary's tongue, but she held them back. Alex would speak when he was ready.

The elevator doors opened, and she stepped through into a hallway that could've belonged in any hotel in the city except for the faint scent of disinfectant. The marble, wood paneling, and artwork continued here, and there was another vase of flowers on a table at the end of the hallway. God, the florist bill in this place!

Doors lined the hallway. She jogged to keep up as Alex strode down the hall to the last one on the right. He paused before it, his head bowed.

"She's changed a lot since you knew her. Some of it's because of my dad. A lot of it's because of the stroke she had a few years ago."

A stroke. Of course. She remembered the crooked smile in the photo on Alex's desk. When he paused for several seconds, she asked, "Will she remember me?"

Shoving his hands into his pants pockets, he kept his face averted. "There's nothing wrong with her memory. Though she gets confused sometimes. In addition to the physical effects, her emotions are heightened. And when she gets emotional, they call me. I can usually calm her down."

Remembering how frail his mother looked in the photo on Alex's desk, she said, "I imagine her physical symptoms are frustrating. She was always so strong."

He finally looked at her. "Strong? I don't think I'd have used that word, even back then. Proud and opinionated, yes. But none of us were strong. Not like you."

He squared his shoulders and faced the door. This time, he didn't scan his card, but he looked into a scanner mounted on the wall. The lock clicked, and he walked through, holding the door for her.

The inside didn't look like any hospital room Mary had ever been in. It looked like an apartment, and not one Mary could afford. She passed a small kitchen on one side and a powder room on the other before the wide entry hall opened to a spacious living room with a six-person dining table at one end.

Alex followed the sounds of voices—one soothing, one sobbing —into a bedroom that was larger than Mary's living room. The sheets on the bed were rumpled, and all the lights were on. A tiny figure hunched in an armchair; she buried her face in her hands as her shoulders shook. An Asian woman in black scrubs sat in the other chair, her hand on Mrs. Villa's back, murmuring softly. The nurse looked up, a relieved expression on her face, when she saw Alex.

"Look who's here, Mrs. Villa," she said. "It's your son."

Although deep grooves surrounded her mouth and eyes, Mrs. Villa was still beautiful. Her long blond hair was now white and stuck up on one side of her head. She wore a light pink satin robe belted over matching pajamas. When she looked up, tears streamed down her face.

"Alessandro, tell these people I want to go home." Despite the waver in her voice, the imperious tone reminded Mary of the orders she used to bark at Alex when they were teenagers.

He dropped to his knees in front of her. "Mama, you know there's no home to go back to. We lost it years ago."

Lost it? What was he talking about?

"I mean your place. You always took such good care of me. Not like these people." She looked down her nose at the nurse, who snatched her hand off her back.

"Mama." His tone was stern. "Umi and the rest of the staff here take excellent care of you. Better than I can do. You know that. We tried, and you didn't like living with me. You were lonely. This is the best place for you." He gathered her into his arms, letting her sob against his chest. To Umi, he murmured, "Did you give her the meds?"

The nurse nodded. "They should kick in any minute now."

"Good." He rubbed a circle on his mother's back. "What's all this about, Mama?"

"They won't let me out," she wailed. "Remember how I used to walk in the garden at night while I was waiting for your father to come home? There's a park outside, and all I wanted to do was smell the moonflower and feel the cool air on my skin."

Alex seemed to deflate. "You can't do that at my place either, Mama. I can't protect you outside the hotel."

"They don't want to hurt an old woman like me," she argued. "It was eighteen years ago. Everyone's forgotten. Besides, we paid them all back."

What was she talking about? Mary stilled to catch every word.

"It wasn't enough for some, Mama. You know that. And what would I do if something happened? What if you fell?"

"Wouldn't be the first time," she muttered, making Mary smile. The feisty woman was back.

Gently, Alex pulled back and looked his mother in the eye. "I'll leave instructions that you can go outside tomorrow. There's a small rooftop garden. Maybe the prickly pear will be in bloom. You'll be safe in the daylight."

Safe from what? Or whom? Mary didn't ask.

Still, Mrs. Villa's gaze caught on her. "Who's that?"

As if he'd forgotten she was there, Alex looked back over his shoulder. "You remember Mary Forza, Mama."

"Hi there, Mrs. Villa," Mary said.

"Hm," she sniffed. "I didn't recognize her. She's gotten so old."

Mary couldn't help it. She patted the shallow creases around her eyes. Did she really look old? She supposed after a full day of work and a night at the club, she might.

"Mama," Alex chided her. "She's gorgeous. Anyone can see that. And she's the same age as me."

Warmth filled her belly. *Gorgeous.* Was that how he saw her, even with dark circles under her eyes and her foundation sweated off?

"She should take better care of her skin," Mrs. Villa said, like Mary wasn't standing right there.

"I think it's time you went to bed," Alex said. He rose to his feet and held out his hands. His mother grasped them and pulled herself out of the chair.

"I'm not a child, you know," she grumbled.

"I know. But you're tired. You'll feel better in the morning." He tucked her hand into the crook of his elbow and guided her to the bed like he'd have walked her into one of the Villas' fancy parties Mary was never invited to twenty years ago. When he tucked her into bed and kissed her forehead, Mary's heart melted. Who'd have thought Alex Villa, Las Vegas titan, could be so kind and gentle?

He murmured a few words to her, then a few words to Umi. Finally, he guided Mary out of his mother's apartment, his expression growing darker as they neared the elevators.

When Alex waved his card at the security pad, she asked, "Is that to keep the residents in or other people out?"

"Both." He didn't meet her gaze. "Some residents have memory issues. Some, like my mother, have trouble controlling their impulses."

When the elevator door slid open, he held it as Mary walked through. Alex again scanned his card, and the elevator doors closed.

"You said it was dangerous for her to go out at night," she said. "What did you mean?"

His broad shoulders slumped as he shoved his hands into his pockets. "My father had enemies. Most he made himself. Others envied what he had."

Mary had only the vaguest idea of what Alex's father did. "He owned a casino. Like you."

"Not like me," Alex growled, his jaw like iron. "He dealt with the Family."

"Whose family?" The door slid open, and she stepped into the lobby. "Oh! You mean the mafia?"

Too loud, the word echoed off the marble floors and wood paneling. The receptionist looked up with wide eyes.

"I mean...organized crime?" Mary whispered.

"He owned the Paradise on paper, but it was the Family—yes, the mafia—who actually owned it. He paid them for security, for casino workers, for produce in the restaurant, and even for toilet paper. And when he ran short of cash, it wasn't good." He cracked the knuckles on his left hand before he scanned his card one final time, and they stepped back into the mostly empty parking garage.

"Shit!" he said. "I forgot about my car."

"It's okay." She held out her hand for the keys. "I'll drive you home."

"Not happening. I'll drive you home. Then I can take the limo back."

"No can do. The lot's covered in security cameras. Michael would blow a gasket if I gave you the gate code."

"Then we'll return the limo together, and I'll drive you home," he said. Stubborn man.

"I could get a rideshare home," she argued.

He only raised his eyebrows.

"Fine." She clicked the lock on the limo but circled to the passenger side. "Though if I don't watch it, I'll get used to riding in a limo instead of driving it."

He opened the driver's side door. "Would that be so terrible?"

She snorted. "You're the riding-in-limos type, Alex. Not me." Though that was dangerously close to bringing up senior prom. So once he settled into the driver's seat, she said, "Why are you afraid of your dad's maf—Family contacts coming after your mother? She doesn't still do business with them, does she?"

He crumpled into the leather seat. "No. And my father didn't, either. Not at the end. There was an incident, and after that, my mother and I begged him to sever those ties. And he did. He bought the Paradise from the Family. But the problem was how he did it."

She let him drive for a few blocks in silence, but when the Forza Elite Motors sign came into view, she asked, "What did he do?"

"He had a reputation as a savvy businessperson. People came to him for financial advice. And that's how he got into trouble. You see, he was not a good man." Alex slowed and stopped at a flashing red traffic light, carefully looked both ways, then proceeded through the intersection.

"I'm sure he was good in his way. He raised you."

Alex only tightened his lips. "He ran a pyramid scheme. He paid out to the initial investors to give people an inflated sense of what their investments could do. But the later investors got nothing. All their money went to buying the Family out of the Paradise."

"What?" How could he have hidden that from her? "When did this happen?"

"He started it when I was in high school. I didn't know about it. Not until later. Mama thought he'd gone legit. We didn't find out what he was doing until the federal investigators came to arrest him one night."

In high school? But they'd been friends then. Surely, he'd have told her if something that big had happened in his life. "When, Alex?"

He slowed to make the turn into the entrance and stopped at the metal gate. He flexed his fingers on the steering wheel and stared through the windshield. "End of senior year."

"End of...do you mean prom night?"

"I think I need the code now," he said.

"Answer me first. Is that what happened on prom night?"

Pain tightened his pretty eyes. "They came that night and stayed for hours, questioning all of us. They confiscated my phone as evidence and wouldn't let me leave."

"Why didn't you tell me after?" She'd cried buckets of tears into her pillow all weekend, humiliated at how Alex had played her when she'd thought there could be something between them.

He stared at the gate. "I didn't tell anyone. Couldn't because of the investigation. And then Mama had to sell the house and the Paradise to pay back the investors. We lost everything, Mary, down to the clothes on our backs. I was ashamed."

She wanted to give him a hug, but Michael's security camera pointed right at them from behind the keypad. She unbuckled her seatbelt and leaned across Alex to enter the code. He sat, stiff as a board, until she scooted back into her seat.

She directed him where to park the limo, dropped the keys into the box, and walked beside him to where he'd parked his flashy silver Ferrari. He opened the passenger door for her and watched as she slid in. He tugged on the seat belt and handed her the buckle, then waited for her to click it.

He took his seat, started the car, and pulled to the gate. As it slid open, Mary chose her words carefully. "So, while I was away at college, you were..."

Alex's shoulders tensed before he said, "Dealing with the mess my father had left and working days at one hotel and nights at another. Driving a taxi on the weekends. Dad had it easy. He was in jail, awaiting trial." He pulled through the gate and turned onto the street toward her neighborhood.

"But if you lost your house," she asked, "where did you stay?"

"Mama had a cousin who put her up, but there was no room for me. I couch surfed," he said. "Luckily for me, I had a few friends whose parents my father hadn't defrauded. A few nights, I slept in my car."

"You got to keep the BMW?"

"No, I had to sell that, too. Bought a janky old Ford Escort. I was grateful for the car repair basics your dad taught me. That car leaked oil like a mother. Never could plug it."

Something tight and prickly settled in her chest. Alex hadn't told her because he thought she'd judge him. Sure, she was upset when he stood her up, but she'd have understood if he'd only explained what happened. Except...

"My brothers told you to stay away from me, didn't they?"

"I'd have done it anyway, but yes. They didn't want me to distract you from your studies."

"We were friends. It would've been okay if you'd distracted me. I'd have wanted to know."

"How does the song go? 'You can't always get what you want.'" He flashed her a grim smile that made her wonder.

"Did you really want to take me to prom? As more than friends?"

He stopped at a stop sign, then reached for her hand. "Of course I did. I was an entitled ass, but I wasn't cruel enough to ask you as a joke."

"But you let me believe it. All those years."

He released her hand and stepped off the brake. "I was a coward. Letting you hate me for something I didn't do was easier than letting you hate me for who I was."

She blinked hard, willing the tears to stay puddled at her eyelids and not run down her cheeks. Fortunately, they'd reached her house, and she used the cover of unbuckling her seatbelt to dab at her eyes.

Alex got out and held the door for her. Silently, they walked side by side up her front walk and ascended to her front porch. She dug in her purse for her key but paused before she slipped it into the lock.

Looking up into his eyes, shadowed in the dim porch light, she shivered, and not because of the cool desert air. He'd smashed everything she thought she'd understood for the past twenty years, and the newly exposed edges of the truth were as sensitive as a paper cut.

"I forgave you a long time ago. You know that, right?"

"I don't know why. I wouldn't have forgiven me," he said.

She smiled. "You do hold a good grudge."

Alex glanced out at her quiet street, then he pulled her into a hug. Into her ear, he murmured, "Never against you."

He loosened his grip on her like he'd step back, but she clung to him. "I liked our dance tonight. Thanks for that. And for, you know, doing my job."

"It was my pleasure."

Suddenly, Mary was aware of how the stiff fabric of their shirts rubbed together. Of their mingled breath. Of the fact that nothing but a few inches of air separated her from his plush lips. She trembled.

His eyes went soft, and he lifted a hand to cradle her jaw. "I'm going to kiss you now. The way I wish I could've kissed you on prom night." But he paused for a second, then another, as he gazed into her eyes.

Realizing that, despite his words, he was waiting for her to make the next move, she stretched her neck, savoring the friction as she rubbed up his chest and landed her lips on his.

It was a closed-mouth kiss, but their lips softened against each other the same way they'd melted their barriers tonight. She understood him at last. All the guilt, pain, and humiliation that drove him to remake that shitty motel into La Villa and thumb his nose at the big players at the heart of the strip. That made him swagger into Forza Elite Motors and pick a fight with her brothers. That kept him silent for four years while she was in college, clueless about his situation and thinking herself the one who'd been hurt. When he'd been hurting all along.

Alex pulled away, leaning his forehead against hers, his breathing unsteady as hers.

A light flickered on at Mrs. Wong's house next door. "You'd better go. I've got nosy neighbors."

"I'll call you tomorrow?"

"Yeah. Maybe...maybe we can go out sometime? Without the birthday party and strippers." She laid a lingering kiss on his lips before reluctantly stepping back.

"A do-over, twenty years late? I'm here for it."

She squeezed his hand. "So am I."

Chapter Fourteen

"I'm concerned," Alex said as they disconnected another call with Rochelle and Rohaan on the first of July.

Mary's heart rate kicked up, and she knit her fingers together on his polished conference table to hide their tremble. Had she forgotten something? Did she seem off her game? She'd practically run here from Twyla and Teagan's dress fitting, but Alex didn't know that. She was holding it together and doing an excellent job on the Richardson wedding with less than a month to go...right?

"Concerned?" she squeaked. He wasn't going to bring up razzle-dazzle again, was he?

"About you. Are you getting enough sleep?"

She forced a chuckle and waved her hand. "Who needs sleep?"

He didn't smile. "Most humans do. Are you getting help at the shop?"

"Rafe and Michael are working just as hard as I am." Harder even, given her split attention lately. She'd expanded into wedding planning to lessen the load on her brothers, but all she'd done so far was hire Evie to free up her own time to work on weddings.

"I'm not asking about their work. A trained monkey could polish a car and vacuum out sequins."

Heat rose in her chest. "That's not all—"

"Sorry." He took a breath. "I just meant that you're the one who does all the customer service and bookkeeping and taxes. I don't know when you have time to work at the shop at all with your new responsibilities for this wedding."

"I have time. I'd never abandon my brothers or our family business." Or tell him how much other work she'd taken on.

"I know. And that's what I'm saying. I have a team of accountants here. I could temporarily assign one of them to your business. Or I could lend you one of my front desk clerks. One of them lives right around the corner from your shop. She'd be thrilled to cut her commute."

"That's sweet of you. But I've already hired a part-timer for the front desk." She was not about to tell Alex who it was. He'd march right over to the shop and try to fire her. Again. "And now that we've made all the decisions on Rochelle's wedding, we're in a bit of a lull until we get closer to the big day."

His concerned expression turned calculating. "A lull, huh?"

"Don't tell me you need help with another wedding. I plan to enjoy a little bit of peace and quiet. And sleep." Tears prickled behind her eyes at the mere thought of eight straight hours of sleep.

"What if I have an idea that fits right in with your plans for peace, quiet, and sleep?"

"You're not firing me, are you?"

"Firing you? Absolutely not. I'm kidnapping you. Have a weekend bag packed and ready to go at noon on Friday."

Her pulse kicked up at the idea of being kidnapped by Alex Villa. But she had responsibilities. "Weekends, especially July 4th, are the busiest times at the shop. We've got two weddings and three bachelorette parties."

"Your new assistant can't handle it?"

"I wouldn't ask her to." Not with the way she and Michael circled each other like a pair of lions protecting their turf.

"Then we'll go during the week. Go home and pack your bag. I'll pick you up at three."

"Three *today?* I couldn't possibly."

"You said you had a lull, and weekdays were your least busy time." He leaned back in his chair, a portrait of smug victory.

"It's unfair to use my own words against me, you know," she grumbled.

"Did you miss it when I said I was kidnapping you? There's nothing fair about this. I'll use every underhanded weapon in my arsenal to get you the rest you need." His brown eyes sparkled with wicked intent.

Mary inhaled sharply, then let out a shuddering breath. She could imagine doing a lot of things with Alex. None of them involved rest.

"What should I pack?"

"Would you prefer mountains or beach?"

"I don't know. I've never been to the beach."

His mouth dropped open. "What? Never?"

"We weren't much of a vacationing family. It's hard when you run a small business."

"That changes today. Pack a swimsuit."

Alex's three o'clock deadline didn't leave her much time, but Mary stopped at the shop anyway.

"Hi, Evie," she said as she walked in. Her new assistant had her back to the door as she pounded a nail into the wall with a little more force than necessary. "Is everything all right?"

Evie's smile was strained. "All good. Just rearranging this display." She hefted a huge framed photo of a happy bridal couple toasting each other in the back of a limousine.

Mary scurried to help lift one side. "Why didn't you ask one of the boys to help you?"

"Doing it myself is easier than asking your grumpy brother to help."

Mary knew exactly which brother was the grumpy one. He said

even fewer words than usual to their newest employee. She stepped back to admire the picture. "Nice work. It really adds weight and atmosphere to the display. But next time, wait for me. Or ask Rafe to help."

"He's not here. Said he had something to take care of."

That was weird. Dependable Rafe never took personal time or even sick days. But speaking of slacking Forzas...

"Will you be okay if I take a few days off? I'll be back by Saturday morning, and our weekend person is scheduled to cover us Friday night."

"Sure. Going somewhere fun?"

"I think so. You've got my number, right, in case anything comes up?"

"Of course." She pointed at the laminated yellow sheet Mary had stuck to the desk. "But I'll be fine. After working at La Villa, this gig is a piece of cake. And speaking of cake, I know I said I needed a break from the bridezillas, but I'd be happy to help with your planning business too. If you need anything."

"Thank you." Mary hadn't yet figured out why Alex had fired Evie. She displayed a strong work ethic. Although she could be prickly at times, especially around Michael, she was professional and courteous even with the most challenging customers. "I'll let you know if anything comes up."

She stepped through the door to the shop, where Prince's "I Wanna Be Your Lover" blasted through the speaker. When she turned down the volume, Michael stilled his polishing rag. He looked up, and when he saw it was her, relief broke across his face.

"What's wrong?" she asked, stepping closer. "Do you need me?"

"No." He resumed polishing Nick Cage. She knew for a fact they didn't need the stretch SUV until Friday night. "Just glad it wasn't Evie coming in to change something else. Did you see she fucked with your display?"

"She improved it, Michael. Not all change is bad, you know."

He circled his rag faster.

"Will it be a problem if I don't come in for a few days?" she asked.

"Nah. It's not too busy this week. Low season for tourists. You working on wedding stuff?"

"Not exactly. I'm taking a short trip. If it's okay with you and Rafe."

He stopped and looked up. "A trip? You never go away. Not even to your college reunion. Or that retreat with your women business owners' group."

"I know. But I could use a little rest. It's been a lot lately, you know?" Her voice wavered, and she cleared her throat.

"I'm glad you're having a little you time. We'll be fine. Rafe and I have got it."

"And Evie. Don't forget Evie."

He scuffed his steel-toed boot on the floor and grumbled, "Can't forget Evie."

She looked back to check the door was shut and stepped closer. "What's your deal with her, anyway?"

"Deal? There's no deal. If having her here means you'll take time off, I'm all for it."

"Okay, then, if you're sure you'll be okay."

"Positive." He folded his rag to buff the fender.

"I'll be back by Saturday."

He didn't bother to respond, which meant he was done with the conversation. She circled the car and bent to kiss his scruffy cheek. "Bye. Be good."

He grunted, and although she knew they'd all be fine without her, guilt dragged behind her like the train on Princess Diana's wedding gown.

Chapter Fifteen

Alex smiled when Mary walked straight through the living room to gape at the picture window that overlooked the beach. The beach house was rented, just like the private jet that brought them here, but a little money went a long way toward impressing Mary.

"It's so...big. Like the desert, but water," she said.

Gently taking her bag from her shoulder, he murmured, "You can go out there, you know."

"I will. After I unpack. And see about groceries. Unless you want to eat out?" She glanced around the living room. "That might be better. I don't want to make a mess that we'll need to clean up before we leave."

"Mary." Grasping her shoulders, he turned her to face him. "Don't worry about making a mess. Someone will come to clean the place after we leave. I've taken the liberty of hiring a private chef for tonight's dinner, but if you prefer to go to a restaurant, that's fine, too. This week is all about relaxing." He kneaded the stiff muscles where her neck joined her shoulders.

Her eyes closed, she rocked her head from side to side. "Relaxing."

"Try it. You might like it."

Her eyes flicked open. "I suspect you don't have a lot of experience with the concept, either."

He laughed. "Maybe not, but I'm committed to trying it for you."

She stared into his eyes for a moment as if waiting to see if he'd take it back. The smile died on his lips. She'd been so young when she lost her mother. Life hadn't been easy for the family before then, but ever since they'd met, that day she stood up for him in fifth grade, she'd been a surrogate mother to her brothers, even her older brother Michael. And she'd kept caring for them for all these years. He guessed she didn't know how to turn it off.

He glanced at his watch, then with mock seriousness handed back her bag. "No unpacking. Just put on your swimsuit. If you're not back out here in five minutes, I'm coming after you."

A smile teased at her lips. "And what will you do when you come after me?"

"I guess you'll find out," he said with his most menacing glare.

"Ooh. Might be worth it to see." With a saucy swing of her hips, she turned away and walked to the hallway with the bedrooms.

"Fuck." He adjusted himself in his pants. He absolutely couldn't go after her, or he'd have to take a cold shower before they went to the beach.

Fortunately, she didn't test him, and he got his erection situation under control by thinking about how cold the water was going to be. Five minutes later, she met him by the French doors onto the deck. She wore a gauzy black cover-up over a black one-piece with a broad sun hat on her head. Alex had put on a white rash guard shirt over his gray trunks.

Mary surveyed him. "You should talk about relaxing. Your beachwear looks just like your business clothes."

"Make another smart remark, Miss Forza, and I'm dumping you into the ocean."

"You'll have to catch me first!" She flung open the doors and, her flip-flops smacking, ran across the deck and scurried down the stairs.

Alex took his time, grabbing the picnic basket from the fridge and locking the door before he followed at a more measured pace. He picked up a pair of folding beach chairs at the bottom of the stairs.

Mary had frozen a few feet from where the sand began. Late on a Tuesday afternoon, most of the families had packed up and gone home, but a teenage boy tossed a ball for his dog and a few couples walked hand in hand along the shore.

"What's wrong?" Alex asked when he stood beside her.

She raised her voice. "It's so loud. I didn't expect that."

Alex listened to the crashing waves and the swooping seagulls' cries. "You'll get used to it. Come on. I'll set these up, then you can dip your toes in."

"Just my toes? I'm not going to miss my chance to swim in the Pacific Ocean."

He eyed the handful of paddle boarders in their wet suits. "All right, then."

He walked to a clear spot of sand and set up the chairs. Nearby were the remnants of a sandcastle that some child must have taken great joy in building, then destroying. He dropped his phone and watch into the picnic basket and covered it with a beach blanket.

Mary stripped off her cover-up, and Alex took a moment to admire her. She'd filled out since their high-school days. The last time he'd seen her in a swimsuit was at a pool party at his parents' house. She'd surprised him by coming. Although they were friends, she didn't like the other kids he hung out with, the sons and daughters of his father's business associates. Entitled, just like him. Hell, he never understood why she liked him. He was certain it wasn't because of his money or his sarcastic teenage wit. He'd feared it was because she pitied him. Poor little rich kid whose dad never noticed him, who had everything a guy needed except unconditional love.

"You're not allowed to stare at my cellulite, okay? I know you've probably never seen it on any of those skinny women you date, but I assure you, it's perfectly normal." Mary pulled an elastic band from her wrist and coiled her hair at her nape.

"It's beautiful," he said, "just like the rest of you."

Flinging her hat onto the chair, she snorted. "That bullshit might work on some bimbo, but I'm wily to your wicked ways, Mr. Villa."

He clucked his tongue. "You excel at many things, Mary. Taking compliments is not one of them."

She gazed at him for a long second. Then, kicking off her flip-flops, she took off toward the waves.

Her running form had never been great, as he recalled from gym class, and she churned over the uneven sand like a battleship. He took a second to admire the half cheek revealed by her swimsuit on one side. It'd be the perfect size for his palm, if he dared touch her. He slipped off his flip-flops and followed.

Mary got as far into the water as her knees before she squealed and turned back, leaping awkwardly against the pull of the waves. Alex was there to catch her and pull her, shivering, into his arms. "Cold?"

"I didn't know water could get that cold." She shuddered against his chest, and he winced at the situation developing in his trunks. He waded around her until the water hit the backs of his ankles, letting the frigid water chill him all the way to his core.

"It'll feel better if we stay where the sand is warm. Let's walk."

When he took her hand, she winced. "What's wrong?" he asked.

"Just my finger," she said. "It twinges sometimes."

"All these years later?" He cradled her right hand in his. Her pinky finger stuck out, away from her ring finger. "If I'd known it'd still trouble you twenty-five years later, I'd have let that kid hit me."

She smiled wryly. "But I wouldn't. You looked so adorable in your pressed uniform shirt and shorts. I didn't want you to get blood on them. I saw your mom when she dropped you off at school. I figured she'd make a fuss."

He'd been a skinny fifth-grader who'd used a snotty attitude to mask his fear of the bullies who'd surrounded him at recess. Mary had fearlessly pushed into the threatening circle. She'd hit her growth spurt earlier and was bigger than most of them. He still remembered the cloyingly sweet bubblegum breath of the kid who'd grabbed him by the shirt front. He'd already resigned himself to going home with his clothes torn and blood on his face. It might get him a few minutes of attention from his dad. And at that point, he was desperate even for his dad to yell at him. But Mary shouted at the kid and then popped him on the chin. When he howled and released Alex, Alex had grabbed Mary's hand and run back to the building.

He stroked her finger. "You should've let the school nurse send you to the hospital. They'd have at least splinted it."

"Back then, I was more afraid of hospitals than I was of pain. Ma spent so much time there at the end. I saw the bills that came in after. Besides, it's not that bad anymore."

He lifted her hand to his lips and kissed her pinky fingertip. "I'm glad we're friends again. I missed you when we weren't."

When she blinked her big, brown eyes at him, he was in danger of kissing more than her hand. And as much as he wanted to do it, this trip wasn't about picking up where they'd left off on her porch last week. It was about relaxation for Mary.

Taking care with her crooked finger, he took her hand and set off slowly across the damp sand. He kept to the ocean side where the icy waves lapped at his heels.

They walked for a minute in silence, Mary's hand warm in his. She tilted her face to the hazy sky, then looked down to the shells left behind by the receding waves.

At last, she sighed. "It's wonderful. Thank you for bringing me."

"It's my pleasure." Truly, it was, to see her cheeks pinked by the ocean breeze and to feel her soft hand in his.

"Aren't you worried about leaving your business?"

"I'll check in with my team a couple of times a day. And with my mother. I don't want you to worry about the Richardson wedding while we're here. I've got Joey monitoring it this week."

She tipped her head and squinted at him. "Why are you personally involved in this wedding? You don't do that for every event at your hotel, do you?"

He could've made up a bullshit reason. He could have told her half the truth. But the words poured out of him. "The Paradise is for sale. And I want it. As you know, Rochelle's father, Ray, is the president of the gaming board. If things go poorly, he can turn the board against me to reject the purchase."

She stared at him for a minute, processing what he'd said and probably what he hadn't. "Good. I mean, not good that your big deal is at stake. But I was afraid you didn't trust me."

"Not trust you? Mary, I'd trust you with my life."

"But you didn't trust me the night of prom," she said.

He sighed. "I was a proud, foolish kid. I didn't want anyone to know about our struggles. But I didn't know the extent of them. That there'd be no way to hide when people found out my dad had stolen their life's savings."

She pulled him to a stop and bent to pick up a sun-bleached sand dollar. "Is that why the Paradise deal is so important? Other hotels have come up for sale, most of them in better condition than the Paradise. You could be instantly profitable with one of them."

"It might not be the most rational decision I've ever made."

"A low bar," she murmured.

He squeezed her hand. "Are you seriously insulting me while I'm baring my soul to you?"

"Your soul?" Her eyebrows lifted.

"Okay, fine. I sold that a long time ago. I'm only revealing my personal business. But that's what it is. Personal. I lost the Paradise once, and every day it mocked me from the center of the Strip as I drove by it in my clunker. When I barely had two dollars to rub together, the Rissos made money off my father's shame and my desperation. Now I have a chance to take it back. I'll tear down that old piece of shit and build something shiny and new in its place. And I'll scrawl my name across it in twenty-foot-high letters. I'll show everyone who spat on the Villa name that I've risen from the ashes my father made of it."

"You could call it the Phoenix."

"Ah, but then people might forget whose building it is. It'll be La Villa Prime."

She snorted. "That sounds like one of the toy robots my brothers used to play with."

"Maybe it's childish of me."

"Maybe it is. But that doesn't make it wrong." Solemnly, she handed him the sand dollar. "You have big dreams. Don't let anyone take them away."

Her eyes were so kind he couldn't bear to look into them. He flung his arms around her and buried his face in her warm shoulder. The edge of the sea creature's skeleton dug into his palm, and he loosened his grip on the delicate shell so as not to crack it. "Mary, I—"

But he stopped himself. He couldn't tell her about the bigger dream he had, that one day he'd be worthy of her. After he'd bought the Paradise and turned her into a world-class resort. After he'd made his first billion. After he'd somehow redeemed himself for the pain he'd caused her so many years ago.

Slowly, her hands came up to rub circles on his back. "Well, I guess you needed to unburden yourself to someone. You know, the church offers that service for free every Saturday. Or a high roller like you could afford a therapist."

He hugged her tighter. "This is better than therapy. And much better than confession with judgy Father Benedict." Though the thought of Father Benedict's hairy knuckles as he set the communion wafer in Alex's mouth was the only thing that saved him from getting stiff against Mary. He tried not to think about the thin layer of spandex that separated his fingertips from her skin.

Finally, when he had his face under control, he pulled back. Mary's hands lingered on his chest.

"Feel better?" she asked.

"God." He took her hand again and led her back toward their beach chairs. "I'm such a jackass for making this about me when it's supposed to be your relaxation time."

"I'm much more relaxed now that I understand why you care so much about the Richardson wedding. I'll stop taking it as a lack of confidence in my abilities."

He pulled her to him and wrapped his arm around her waist. "I'd be lying if I said I wasn't also using it as an excuse to get closer to you."

Her hand landed on his hip. "And I'd be lying if I said I had any interest in resisting you."

"I don't think this day could get any better."

"Oh, I can think of a couple ways."

Chapter Sixteen

"Give me a minute, and I'll do the dishes," Mary said as Alex lifted her empty dessert plate. "I'm too full to move right this second."

"I'll do the dishes," he said, carrying both their plates into the kitchen. "You're relaxing, remember?"

"Hmm." She leaned back in the padded dining room chair as the candles flickered. "Do you even know how to wash dishes?"

He set the plates on the counter and shot her an arch look over his shoulder. "I think I know how to load a dishwasher."

"Good for you. I could get used to this, you know." After their walk on the beach, they'd watched the waves until her stomach growled. When they'd returned to the beach house, she'd taken a quick shower, and by the time she finished, the chef had been putting the final touches on a dinner of local sea bass with garlic mashed potatoes. The green salad had at least eight more ingredients than the salads she usually made herself for dinner on weeknights.

"You should get used to it. It's about time someone took care of you."

It was a dig against her brothers, but she was too comfortable to argue. She tongued a raspberry seed from between her teeth and recalled the tangy taste of the berry tart they'd had for dessert. It went perfectly with the California chenin blanc. She drained her glass, then stood and carried it into the kitchen.

"You're not trying to help, are you?" Alex had to know how fantastic his ass looked in his gray sweatpants as he bent to slot the plates into the bottom rack of the dishwasher.

"Wouldn't dream of it." She reached out a hand to touch his taut glutes, then snatched it back. They'd kissed last week, and he'd given her a heartfelt hug on the beach today, but that didn't mean they were in an ass-touching kind of relationship. "Is there more wine?"

He straightened. "Right here." He lifted the bottle from the counter and poured the last drops into her glass. "Go sit down. I'll join you in a minute."

"Okay. I think I'll figure out how to turn on the fireplace."

"Are you cold?"

Not with the smolder heating his eyes. "It's more for the ambiance."

"Ambiance it up. I'll be right there."

As she walked out, he started humming something, and she paused to listen. Was that "Just The Way You Are" by Bruno Mars? She frowned. It could have been an out-of-tune version of Justin Timberlake's "Cry Me a River."

The fireplace wasn't difficult to figure out. With a click of the remote control, gas-powered flames leaped in a bed of glass rocks. She nestled into the comfortable corner of the giant sectional. Someone could host quite the party here. It seemed a waste for only the two of them to enjoy the huge house by the beach.

Alex entered with two short glasses of something brown in one hand and two tall glasses of water in the other. She plucked the waters out of his hand and set them on the coffee table, then scrambled to find coasters. He handed her one of the short glasses, then touched his glass to hers. "To you."

"To a lovely afternoon at the beach," she said and sipped the drink. Ugh. The pungent aroma burrowed into her sinuses.

"You don't care for scotch?" he asked.

She wrinkled her nose. "I'm more of a wine girl."

He took the scotch from her. "Can I get you more wine, then?"

"No, thanks. I'm afraid I'll fall asleep." And sleep was the last thing from her mind with his gray sweatpants tempting her to find the outline of him, with the scent of vanilla that beckoned to her even under the medicinal smell of scotch, with his dark eyes tunneling into hers like x-rays. He'd made her feel like a queen today. Was it only friendship, or did he want more, too?

"Would that be so terrible?" he asked. "You're here to rest."

She set her hand lightly on his knee. It was warm and solid, just like the rest of him. It was time to be bold. "That's not all I want to do."

He set his scotch on the table. "Tell me what else you want to do."

"Last week...on my porch...we kissed."

"We did." He rubbed his hands on his thighs.

"But nothing since. And now you've whisked me away to this... paradise. With *five bedrooms*. I'm not sure what to think."

"The choice is yours, Mary. We're friends now, and the last thing I want is to fuck it up again. Nothing is worth that. Not that kiss." He swallowed. "Not this getaway, not even the Richardson wedding."

"Are you friends with the other women you...date?"

"I'm sorry. I shouldn't have said we were on a date at the club."

"I don't want to be your girl of the month, Alex. One of those women you date in public for a couple weeks. If I ran into you on the street, I'm not strong enough to trade innuendos and walk away like it doesn't mean anything. When you ghosted me after prom, it broke my heart. If you do it again, I don't think..." She stopped short of telling him her patched-up heart wouldn't survive a second break.

He leaned forward. "You mean so much to me, Mary. This is different. Tell me what you want, and I'll...I'll see if I can give it to you."

"I want friendship. *And.*"

He tilted his head. "You don't mean friends with benefits?"

"No." She shuddered. Even worse than being his arm candy would be being his *U up* text. "I mean more than friends. Friends...and."

"You think I'm capable of friends-and?" His gaze went sharp, crackling the way the silent gas flames didn't.

"You opened up to me today on the beach." She'd been shocked and so, so proud when he'd told her how he felt about the Paradise. She'd felt connected to him when he hugged her. He'd never been so unrestrained, not even when they were kids. She knew he wasn't like that with that Violette woman at the club. "I think you could be what I need. If you're willing to try."

The years dropped away from his face, and he was the teenage boy who'd paused the video game they were playing in his parents' fancy media room to ask her to prom. "For you, I'll try."

Her heart filled with warmth and overflowed. Leaning forward, she kissed him. At first, it was the same kiss they'd shared on her porch last week, tentative, closed-mouth, a test of what could be. Then his lips parted, and so did hers. The bitterness of the scotch had dissipated on his tongue, replaced by a smoky-sweet taste like the mesquite bonfires they used to build in the desert.

His tongue flicked against hers for the first time. Ever since he'd asked her to prom—hell, at least a year before that—she'd imagined what it would be like. Reality surpassed her imagination. His jaw was hard, but his lips were soft, moving gently against hers. His cologne filled her nostrils as his taste danced on her tongue.

And his hands! Big but cautious, they stroked the side of her neck and her waist, hinting at all the places he could use his mouth on her. Warmth settled in her core.

When she opened her mouth wider to lick inside, he groaned like a starving man who'd been presented with a feast but was bound in manacles. Why should either of them be restrained? What they wanted was here for the taking.

She broke the kiss so she could swing her leg over his and straddle him. From her new perch on his lap, she bent and kissed him again, and this time she added a roll of her hips that put his erection right where she needed it, against the crotch of her yoga pants. He loosed a relieved moan and gripped her waist.

She tunneled her hands into his thick hair and rubbed her core against him again, gasping at the pleasure that sparked inside her. He kissed down her neck and as far as the neckline of her shirt would allow.

"Lose the shirt?" he asked.

She found the hem of his shirt and pulled it up over his head, revealing his broad chest. She stroked her fingers across the subtle hills of his abdominals.

"I meant your shirt," he growled.

She traced a finger through the thick hair on his pecs, then circled his nipple, making him hiss. She didn't spend time in the gym like he obviously did, but if she wanted this to go farther, she'd need to expose more skin. Slowly, she rolled up her T-shirt and dropped it on the couch.

His hungry eyes leaped from her lacy bra to the deep valley between her breasts to the swell of her stomach, disappearing into the high waist of her yoga pants.

His gaze flicked up to her face. He set his palms on the cups of her bra and made circles, waking up her nipples. Then he slid his hands around the back to the clasp. "May I?"

She braced her hands on his shoulders. "Go for it."

There was a pinch, then the pressure around her ribs released, and her breasts hung free. They weren't as perky as those skinny girls'—

"Oh, Mary." He dropped her bra on top of her shirt and stared. Then, cradling her breasts with his hands, he buried his face in her cleavage. "I may never leave."

A laugh bubbled out of her as her nervousness evaporated. His scruff burned her skin briefly as he turned his head to lick his way to her nipple. The combination of pain and pleasure made her head spin.

He took a long pull on her breast as he gazed wickedly into her eyes. He watched her as he pinched her other nipple, then petted it, then pinched it again. The sensation rocketed into her core, and her hips bucked against his. She moaned.

He pulled off her nipple and rubbed his stubble against it as he spoke. "Was that a satisfied moan or a frustrated moan?"

"I, um, a little of both?"

"Use your words, Mary."

"For most Catholics, words and sex don't go together."

"We're not most Catholics, and we're going to talk while we do this. How else am I going to know exactly what you want?"

"I, um." *You won't, exactly like every other partner I've had?* "Okay. I like the pinching, but your beard is a little intense right there."

"Perfect." He lifted his chin from her nipple and replaced it with his tongue. At the same time, he pinched her other nipple. Hard.

She gasped. "Yes!"

He chuckled. "Excellent feedback."

"What about...you?" It was difficult to think while he alternated licks and pinches on her breasts. "What do you like?"

"I really like these." He kissed the side of her breast. "Please tell me you didn't have them in high school."

"Of course I had them in high school. But they weren't as..."

"Abundant? No, I think I couldn't have spent as much time playing Grand Theft Auto with you if they were. I want to come on them later. Will that be okay with you?"

"Oh my god, Alex. Do you have to talk like that?"

"Like what? If I offended you, just say it."

"You're so...matter-of-fact about sex."

"Nothing is matter-of-fact about sex. Certainly not sex with you. We'll enjoy it more if we tell each other what feels good and what doesn't. Isn't that worth a little embarrassment?" He took her nipple between his teeth and bit gently.

"Harder," she said.

He obeyed, and pleasure coiled in her center. Then he licked her nipple to soothe the pain away. "See?"

She shuddered with pleasure.

"I like this position a lot," he said, "and I want you to ride me later. But for now, I'd like to suggest a different position."

"Okay," she said quickly. She'd never liked being on top. It put her body on display and made her boobs bounce.

With a scoop and a lift, he flipped them so Mary sat on the couch and he kneeled on the rug. When he turned to push the coffee table farther away, she admired the bunch and strain of the muscles in his shoulders and back. He turned back to her and set his hands on the waistband of her stretchy pants. "May I take these off?"

She nodded, and with a flick of his wrists, they were puddled on the floor. Her underwear, too. Carefully, he pushed her knees apart and gazed between her legs with the same reverence as he'd admired her breasts.

"So wet for me already," he said.

"Do you have a condom?" His sweatpants didn't appear to have pockets. They barely had room for his erection, which strained at the waistband. She couldn't wait to get a peek at it.

"We won't need one for a while," he said, tugging her until her hips teetered on the edge of the sofa. He rubbed his cheek against her inner thigh. "Is my stubble too much here, too?"

She shivered. "No."

"Good. Now, I'm going to eat out this pretty pussy. Tell me if I do something you don't like."

He didn't give her time to think or object before his tongue descended on her, tracing all her secret places. His hot breath skated across her skin as he used his fingers to spread her and explore.

At first, she was too self-conscious to enjoy it. She'd had a few serious boyfriends, and none of them were into performing oral sex. Though they enjoyed receiving it. She'd assumed she didn't taste good, or she did the wrong kind of grooming. But Alex seemed to be enjoying himself, feasting at her wet center.

When he trailed up to her clit and tapped it with his tongue, she forgot to be embarrassed. She moaned, loud and long.

"That's it, baby," he said between licks. "Tell me what you like."

"That," she said. "I like that."

"How about this?" He worked a finger inside her while he tongued her clit.

"Yes. Yes." Her voice rose into a squeak.

She stopped caring about the wet sounds her pussy made as he moved his fingers in and out of her. Her consciousness narrowed down to the sensation coiling inside her. "I—I'm so close."

He didn't change a thing he was doing, just kept going as her body tightened. Finally, when she thought she couldn't stand another second, her release shuddered through her. He stilled his hand when she squeezed around his fingers. He softened his licks on her clit and, when she stopped shaking, planted a gentle kiss on it.

When she opened her eyes, he pulled his hand from between her legs and gave his fingers an obscene lick. "That's my new favorite flavor."

She clapped her hands over her burning face. "Oh my god." Was it wrong to be turned on by something so dirty?

"No fair hiding." He plucked a hand off her face. "I want to memorize what you look like right after you come."

"You do?" Her face was hot and a little sweaty. Her eyeliner was probably puddled around her eyes. And he'd already remarked on the dark shadows under them.

"You're gorgeous." He gazed at her, a satisfied smile on his lips. "Now, let's put you to bed."

"Wait. What about you?" She nodded at the bulge in his sweatpants.

"I can wait until tomorrow. You're tired."

She knew it. She did look terrible. She felt her lips droop. "If you don't want to..."

He surged up to kiss her lips. "Of course I want to. But you need rest."

"You told me to tell you what I want. And I want your cock."

His eyes blazed. "Since you asked so nicely, you can have it."

Chapter Seventeen

"I'll be right back," Alex said. Lust hazed every thought, and he was afraid if he changed anything, he'd miss out on this amazing gift Mary offered him.

"Where are you going?" A worried crease formed between Mary's eyebrows. The firelight made her bare skin glow.

Ah, fuck. She didn't trust him. Not completely. That was fair after what he'd done in high school.

"Condom. I have some in my bag."

"You do?" She raised a teasing eyebrow. "Bold of you."

"Relentless optimism. It's what made my business successful."

"But we aren't having sex on this couch. I've got too much Catholic guilt to do it where people might sit after we leave. Pragmatism. That's my mantra."

"Then we'll find a bedroom, my sexy pragmatist." He held out his hand, and when she took it, he tugged her to stand. His fingertips tingled to trace her naked curves, to tangle in her hair as he kissed her. His balls tightened. "Condom."

He led her into the bedroom where he'd dumped his bag earlier. She'd tossed her bag into a different room, and neither one of them had picked the largest bedroom, the one with the ensuite bathroom with the enormous round tub and the shower that would comfortably fit four people. That made it the perfect neutral ground for a night of play. He grabbed the box of condoms, which he'd conveniently stuck in an outer pocket, and led her into the biggest bedroom.

He flicked on a switch, and wall sconces cast a soft glow on the white comforter and dark wood furniture. A pair of wide brown leather chairs sat in one corner next to a small table and a lamp.

Releasing his hand, she walked to the bed and lifted an armful of throw pillows. She placed them on top of the dresser, then returned to tug back the covers. If it were up to Alex, he'd have tossed her on top, pillows and comforter be damned. But Mary was in charge here, and she knew it. She settled into the middle of the mattress, propping herself up against the upholstered headboard like a queen.

She made an elegant gesture with her hand. "Go on. Strip."

All the blood had raced to his other head, so he had no smart remark on the tip of his tongue. He set the condoms on the bedside table and shoved down his sweatpants. He stepped out of them.

Mary licked her lips and focused on the bulge in his boxer briefs.

Hooking his thumbs into the waistband, he stripped them off and stood before her, naked. His rigid dick pointed him the way to the bed. Since it was the only head thinking clearly, he followed its instructions and climbed up beside Mary. Her olive skin glowed in the muted light.

He leaned over to kiss her plush, pink lips. She reached into his hair, her fingers scratching at his scalp in a way that sent shivers down his spine. How was it that everything she did turned up the dial on his attraction? Once he finally sank into her, he'd have to fight his own body not to finish in a matter of seconds.

He cradled her jaw and tilted her face to deepen the kiss. She tasted like berries and the sweet chenin blanc they'd had with their dessert. She kissed like she wasn't thinking of anything else, not her business, not her brothers, not even their history. Only him. He couldn't get enough. He kissed down her jaw, along her neck where the lamplight gilded it, and up the slope of her breast.

She arched her back and let out a soft moan. Seeing the red patch of beard burn he'd left on her breast, he dropped gentle kisses over it, then licked a circle around her nipple. It was also slightly swollen from his rough attentions earlier. He looked up to check in with her.

Her fingers wrapped around his cock, and she squeezed, making his vision go gray. "Stop teasing me, Alex."

He allowed himself one thrust into her hand. "It's called foreplay, darling."

"A week of foreplay is enough, don't you think?" She gentled her grip and pumped him once.

He doubted anything would ever be enough with Mary, but he couldn't say that. He had to wrest back control or she might see exactly how she affected him.

"Fine, you want my cock? I'll give it to you. Lie down and spread your legs."

He waited until she did what he'd instructed. Her dark hair fanned out across the white pillow, and she bit her lip, turning it darker pink. He took his time opening the box of condoms and slipping one out. He ripped it open, tossed the wrapper on the table, and set it at his tip. Then he watched Mary as he rolled it on. Her eyes didn't leave his dick, and she licked her lips.

Moving to kneel between her legs, he slid his hands up the insides of her thighs until his thumbs met at her center. She was wet and ready, blooming open for him. God, what a gift.

Grasping her hips, he lifted her over his thighs to tilt her pelvis up. His knees wouldn't last long in this position, but neither would his orgasm. And if he did it right, hers would be so intense she wouldn't care.

He notched himself at her entrance, then slowly pushed in. Her lips parted as she watched the flex of his hips.

When he was all the way inside, he paused. "How does that feel?"

"Ah-amazing." Her knees squeezed his sides.

He licked his thumb, then set it on her clit, pressing gently. "And now?"

She arched her back. "Uh—uh huh."

He'd never known Mary to be nonverbal, but it seemed good in this situation. Keeping his thumb in place, he backed up his hips and slid forward. Her tight squeeze took away his words as well. He grunted in pleasure.

She reached forward and grabbed his ass, digging her fingertips into his glutes and spurring him to move faster. He obeyed, rocking shallowly, hoping he was getting close to her G-spot as her breathing grew rapid. Her face glowed pink, and she gasped in rhythm with his thrusts. It was like they were made for each other, created to give each other pleasure. Her channel tightened around him, and it was all he could do to keep his eyes open, watching for the signs of her climax. Because she was coming first, no matter how long he had to hold out. He'd mentally recite his company's mission statement and each of the Nevada Gaming Commission's regulations if he had to.

But with a slight vibration of his thumb, Mary cried out and tightened her grip on his butt. He'd have bruises tomorrow, but he didn't care. He stilled, waiting until her muscles slackened around him.

"Can I come on your skin?" he asked through his clenched jaw.

"Okay." Her smile was loose and relaxed.

He pulled out, ripped off the condom, and groaned as he let go, pulsing wave after wave of his pleasure across her belly and onto the undersides of her glorious breasts. God, if he'd known it would be like this, he never could have held out this long. A week of foreplay? Try twenty years. After that long, he should have known the payoff would be phenomenal. It had been worth the wait to share pleasure like this.

She slipped her hand onto his and tugged him off her clit, then knit their fingers together. She surveyed the stripes he'd painted across her skin. "Oh my god."

He squeezed her hand. "Oh my god."

She flicked her gaze up to his. "Really?"

He knew what she was asking. He had a reputation, and people expected him to be blasé about sex. He'd done it with dozens of women. But it had never meant anything. Not until tonight, with Mary.

"Really. You've bewitched me, Mary Forza."

She narrowed her eyes. "I'm not sure that's a good thing."

He dismounted from her thighs and rearranged her legs more comfortably. Then, bending forward, he kissed her lips. "As far as I'm concerned, it's a very good thing. Hold on, I'll get a towel."

He strode to the bathroom to snag a fluffy towel. He kissed each part of her after wiping it clean. Left breast. Right breast. The curve of her belly. The warmth between her legs. And finally, her smiling lips.

When he returned from tossing the towel into the hamper and washing his hands, she was curled on her side, breathing deeply. He hesitated for a moment. He could leave her here in peace and return to the bedroom where he'd put his bag. They could each get a decent night's sleep alone, like they were both used to doing.

Or he could give in to the temptation of touching her skin all night.

He slipped into the bed behind her and tugged the sheet up over them.

So what if he never cuddled anyone after sex? He'd told her this was different. There was a first time for everything.

Chapter Eighteen

Mary woke, her muscles loose and languid. She pointed her toes under the soft sheets, then reached up to touch the headboard for a stretch.

"Morning, beautiful," Alex rumbled.

He lay with his arms folded under his head, smiling smugly at the ceiling. He was gorgeous, even with his hair rumpled and a crease across his cheek from the pillow.

From the curl that stubbornly poked into her peripheral vision, she suspected she looked anything but beautiful. She hadn't thought to bundle her hair into a scarf or even a ponytail on top of her head.

"I'm not the expert here, but doesn't the sweet-talking usually happen before the sex?"

He rolled toward her. "Who says we're not about to have sex?"

Morning sex? She hadn't done that in a while. How was her breath? She lifted the sheet up over her mouth.

"Okay." He chuckled. "Maybe not yet. How are you feeling?"

"Mmm. Well rested is the term people use, I think?"

Faster than she'd have thought possible, his arm was around her, and he nuzzled her neck. "Or is it well fucked?"

She laid her hands on the back of his head and held him there, enjoying the sensation of his lips on her skin. "Definitely both."

"What do you say to a walk on the beach before breakfast?" His voice came from below her shoulder.

"I think if you keep going, we're not going to make it to the beach before lunchtime."

"Ah, but you see, I've got it all planned out." He sat up. "Walk, breakfast, shower sex, nap—"

"Wait. Did you just list shower sex?"

Playfully, he raised an eyebrow. "Did you just interrupt my itinerary?"

She squeezed her thighs together. "Sorry."

"While you're napping, I'll work for an hour or so. Then we'll drive to the boardwalk for lunch, perhaps some shopping if you're into it. We'll come back here, where I'll ravish you again, probably in that chair over there"—he tipped his chin at a leather armchair she hadn't noticed last night—"and by then it'll be time for drinks on the deck before the chef comes to make us dinner."

She propped herself up on an elbow. "You have our whole day planned, down to the sex position we'll use this afternoon?"

"What can I say? I like to think ahead."

"You mean you like to be in control of everything."

"You didn't complain last night."

No, she'd been too busy orgasming. But it was different in the daylight. Heat surged up from her chest to her face, and she scrambled to sit up. "Just because I liked the way you fucked me doesn't mean I want you to control every part of my day. What about spontaneity? What about what I want to do? Need to do?"

He blinked like she'd slapped him. She wasn't sure if it was because she'd used a crude word or because she hadn't been willing to cede control over the part of her life she spent out of bed. She didn't care, either. She was an adult, perfectly capable of making her own decisions. Her own plans.

She scooted to the other side of the bed. "I'm going to call my brothers."

"What, to come get you?" he snapped. "They don't need to do that. I'll—"

"Stop." She paused at the edge of the bed, her back to him. Took a deep breath. "All I want to do is check in on the shop. After I talk to them and to my new assistant, I'm all yours. Why don't you check in at work, too? Then we can plan out the day. Together. Or just do what we feel like. As I understand it, there's this concept called 'go with the flow' that people sometimes use on vacation."

When she peeked back at him, his dark eyebrows had drawn together, but he didn't look angry anymore. "I could use a minute to check on Mama."

"Good. I'm going to squeeze in a shower, too. Let's meet in the kitchen in an hour. We can agree on what to do next."

"Okay."

She tried not to worry about how the light hit her naked body as she circled the bed and lightly kissed him. "See you in an hour."

He grasped her hand. "We're okay?"

She remembered this from high school. He didn't have siblings, so he didn't know how to argue with someone he cared about. How to give themselves space and come back together.

She squeezed his hand. "We're great."

Mary refused the glass of sparkling wine the steward offered her. She needed to stay sharp to deal with today's disaster. While he was fetching her a bottle of water, she muttered, "I'm sorry we had to cut our vacation short."

"It's fine. It's only a day." The groove between Alex's eyebrows belied his words. "Did you have a good time?"

She grasped his hand across the wide armrest between their seats in the private jet. "The best."

Their two days on the beach had been glorious. Alex had many ideas about how they'd spend their time, but they'd talked it over and decided together. They'd walked on the beach, eaten dinner on the deck with the sea breeze kissing her face, and even driven into town to watch a romantic comedy that neither of her brothers would be caught dead buying tickets for. Alex had handed over his card with a smile and held her hand in the theater.

And the sex? Pure magic. Especially the time he'd bent her over the arm of that leather chair. She wished she had room for one like it in her house. Though she'd have a difficult time explaining to her family why no one could ever sit in it.

The only low point—aside from that one weird morning-after —had been when Evie had called today at noon to tell her about a crisis with Teagan and Twyla's wedding. The caterer they'd chosen had failed to renew their liquor license on time, and now it was tangled in red tape. With the wedding only two weeks away, she couldn't leave it to luck and the local alcohol permit authority. She'd need to find a separate liquor caterer, fast.

Evie had offered to handle it, but Mary wouldn't be able to relax with the crisis looming over her. So she'd asked Alex if they could go back today so she could line up some caterers to visit tomorrow before the shop opened.

"If you tell me about this emergency at the shop," he said, "maybe I can help."

"It's, um, not really a shop emergency. It's my other business."

"The Richardson wedding?" He sat up straighter. "What happened?"

"Rochelle's wedding is fine." She rubbed his suddenly tense shoulder. "It's my other wedding."

"Your other wedding?"

She didn't love the way his jaw had gone rigid. "I have two, actually. Cierra Dallencourt's wedding in August—I think you know her—and one more." She knew for a fact he knew Cierra since they'd dated a couple years ago. And Alex had recommended Forza Elite Motors when Cierra's sister had gotten married. She wanted a classic Rolls-Royce just like Princess Kate. Mary had set her up with a white 1961 Rolls-Royce Phantom V that her dad had lovingly restored back in the day. The bride had been over the moon, and Mary and Cierra had remained friendly ever since. When she'd mentioned her wedding planning side hustle last spring, Cierra had hired her on the spot.

"Cierra's wedding is you? Was the aerialist your idea?"

"She said she wanted something that'd stand out, and I know someone."

"Of course you do. And it'll keep everyone entertained. No one will forget her wedding, which is one-hundred percent what Cierra would want. I wish you'd let me add something similar to the Richardson wedding. Rochelle's going to hate being upstaged by Cierra Dallencourt."

Mary tilted her head. "Will she? Or is that you who doesn't want to be upstaged by your ex?"

"Cierra?" He shrugged. "I couldn't care less about her or her wedding. So what's the emergency?"

She narrowed her eyes, not sure she bought Alex's sudden carelessness. "The emergency isn't with Cierra's wedding. It's another one. Which is in a couple weeks."

"A couple weeks? When?" His stare was flinty like he already knew.

"The weekend before Rochelle's. But it's fine. I've got them both handled."

"Two weddings in the span of a week? No wonder you're so stressed out. We should've gone to the spa like I suggested."

A smile tugged at the corners of her mouth. "I was plenty relaxed on my vacation. Besides, a masseuse might've asked about the"—she lowered her voice—"beard burn on my boobs."

He rubbed his smooth chin. "Maybe I should check it out."

"It's fine now." She squeezed his hand. "Besides, it's only an hour to Vegas."

He leaned closer. "There's a couch in the back. We can ask the steward to go up with the pilot."

The mile-high club would be another first. Would it be worth all the guilt as she said goodbye to the pilot and the steward at the end of the flight if they knew she'd been naked on their plane?

A ping from her phone saved her from the decision. She scanned the screen. "Oh no."

"What's wrong?"

"Now there *is* an issue at the shop. One of our customers got in a fender bender with Christie Brinkley."

"Wait. Actually with Christie Brinkley?"

"No. It's a vintage red Ferrari. Like she drove in *National Lampoon's Vacation.*"

"Is everyone all right?"

She read the latest message. "Fine. But Michael and E—my assistant had to go pick it up."

"Good." He sipped his sparkling wine. "You name all your cars?"

"Every one. It's more fun that way. Our dad started it with the Clinton, his first town car."

Smiling, he shook his head. "Fun and business don't really go together in my world."

"I can't imagine not laughing at least once a day at work."

"You're more naturally vivacious than I am." He wound one of her curls around his finger.

"You don't have to be *vivacious* to laugh at work. You just need to take yourself less seriously."

"I don't think that would fly in my line of work. I have to maintain a certain...presence."

"Customers enjoy working with people they like. We've had customers come back year after year for prom, weddings, parties, even funerals."

"And I've found that people don't mess with people they fear."

She shook her head. No wonder Evie seemed so much happier working at Forza Elite Motors. Except for when she had to interact with Michael, who also had a *certain presence.* A grumpy one. "Someday you should try it. Let loose. See if it works."

He leaned in to kiss the spot below her earlobe that sent tingles straight between her legs. "I let loose with you this week. That's enough for me."

She shivered. "It was pretty good for me too."

"Pretty good?" He licked a line down her neck.

"Okay, pretty fabulous."

"Better." He pulled back. "I'll send Joey to the shop tomorrow morning to help you. He'll work out whatever issue you've got with this other wedding. In fact, you should offload the whole thing to him so you can focus on the Richardson wedding."

"No, I couldn't possibly ask—"

"Don't worry, I'll pay him overtime. Consider him a gift."

The Trojan horse was a gift, too. If she let Joey into the shop, he'd see Evie working for her, and Joey would report back to Alex. Alex would assume Evie was working on the Richardson wedding. Was that the true purpose of the gift? To look into how she ran her business? The back of her neck prickled. He'd all but admitted he was ruthless about his hotel empire.

"No, thank you." She folded her hands in her lap. "I have all the help I need."

He shrugged like he didn't care, but his steely jaw told the truth. "Fine. I can help you in other ways."

"What other ways?" she asked.

"I understand orgasms reduce cortisol levels. I'll just have to reduce your stress levels through the power of organic chemistry."

She shivered. "Stress reduction sounds good."

"So do lots and lots of orgasms."

He was right, as usual.

Chapter Nineteen

W hen she asked him to drop her a block away from the shop, Alex refused. He pulled his flashy Ferrari right in front and clasped her hand.

"When will I see you again?" he asked.

Her brothers read all those comics where the superhero's heat vision melted metal. Alex's gaze seemed to work only on her panties.

"T-tonight?" The reason they were sitting in front of the business had melted away, too. Why couldn't she go home with him right now?

He leaned across the console and kissed her, soft and lingering. "Should I pick you up here?" he murmured against her lips.

"Here?" Where was she, anyway? She glanced over her shoulder and saw the script *Forza Elite Motors* painted on the door. Shit. Her brothers were in there. She hoped they hadn't seen her kiss Alex.

She pushed away from him. "No. I'll meet you at your office. Give you an excuse to stop working on a Friday night."

"Perfect. I'll leave a keycard at the front desk."

"A...keycard?" The idea of a hotel hookup made her skin prickle.

"I live in the penthouse. You can come straight up."

A nervous titter escaped her. "Of course you live in the penthouse." She'd forgotten for a moment this wasn't her friend from high school who knew all the video game cheat codes. He was a stranger who owned an entire hotel and was about to buy another.

But the beach had been fantastic. She'd get to know the new Alessandro Villa. Who lived in a penthouse.

He stroked the inside of her wrist. "Or I could meet you at your place."

Shivers raced up her arm and down her spine. While she liked the control he exerted in the bedroom, it was too much anywhere else. She'd have more power if they went to her place. "Yeah. I'll make dinner."

"I don't want to make you cook. I'll bring takeout."

"Okay. Then I'll make breakfast?" What would it be like to wake up next to Alex in her bed?

"Sounds perfect." He leaned in for another kiss.

She backed away. "Let's, um...keep it on the down-low in front of my brothers, okay? For now?"

He glared at the building over her shoulder. "You think they'll object?"

"Let's just say I wouldn't want anything to happen to your new nose. I'll see you tonight." She pushed out the door and breezed into the shop like she'd just stepped out of her Corvette and not a car that belonged on the set of the *Fast & Furious* movies.

Three stares met her. One incredulous and two infuriated.

"What. The. Fuck?" Michael was the first to roar.

So much for the down-low. "Look, Alex thought I needed some rest. So, he took me to the beach. And we...reconnected."

"Re? Connected?" Evie's eyebrows disappeared under her bangs. "I've never known Alessandro Villa to date the same woman twice."

"He isn't dating her twice," Michael growled. "Because the first time, he stood her up. She cried for weeks."

Mary's face went hot. "He had a good reason."

Rafe shook his head. "I don't know what he told you, but there's never a good reason to break a promise. Michael's right. He was around all summer before you went to college. He didn't try to talk to you once, did he?"

"Because you broke his nose and told him to stay away!" Mary could get loud, too. And right now, she didn't care that they'd dragged her assistant into their family fight.

Rafe stepped closer and squeezed her arm. "If he really cared, he wouldn't have let us scare him away."

She winced. Her brother had a point. They'd gotten so close back then. She'd told him her secrets, including the selfish one about not wanting to rent cars for the rest of her life. He should have called her.

"That was a long time ago." She lifted her chin. "He's changed. Matured."

"I don't know about that," Rafe said darkly. "He came in here and threw those photos in my face."

"He said he got the nude deleted. You haven't seen it online anywhere, have you?"

"God dammit, it wasn't a nude!" Rafe's eyes flashed. "No. They gave it to me with the others so I could use it in my...my portfolio." He ducked his head.

"Your portfolio?" Mary waited until he met her gaze. "You're going to do more modeling?"

He grimaced. "I don't know. Maybe? It was easy money. We could do a lot with the extra income."

"Enough about Rafe's side gig. I want to get back to Alex," Michael growled. "You know what he does with the women he dates. A few weeks, then on to the next one. I don't want that for you."

"*We* don't want that for you," Rafe said, his gaze open in a way Alex's never was, not even when he told her about his dreams for the Paradise.

It was hard to square Alex's past with how he'd been with her at the beach. How caring he'd been. Sure, he'd tried to boss her around, but he'd done it because he wanted to take care of her. He'd washed the freaking dishes and roughed up his manicure. That had to mean something.

"Thank you," she said. "I'll be careful. I promise."

Michael scowled. "We've got your back. And this time, I get to land the punch to his nose, got it, Rafe?"

"I call his kidneys," Rafe said.

"No! No," Mary said. "No fighting. I'm a grown-up, and I can look out for myself. Besides, he's got lawyers now. It won't be some no-consequences schoolyard scuffle."

At the same time, Michael and Rafe crossed their meaty arms over their coveralls. They looked almost like twins if she ignored the grooves of worry on her older brother's face.

"Go back to the shop," she said. "We've got a busy weekend."

They shot her matching mulish glares before clomping in their steel-toed boots through the door to the garage.

"Now," Mary said, "we've got a liquor license problem to solve, Evie."

"I scheduled a couple of phone calls for you tomorrow morning with vendors I've used before. You should be able to work it out pretty easily," Evie said. "I could've done it for you."

"No, you wanted to take a break from weddings. I'll take care of it. Thank you for setting the appointments."

"No problem." Evie bit her lip. "You'll be careful, though? With Alex. Your brothers are right about his dating history. I wouldn't want you to get hurt."

Was it naïve to trust him? She couldn't forget the honesty in his gaze when he'd told her why he never showed on prom night. He might wear custom suits and live in a penthouse now, but inside, he was still the same boy she'd known and loved.

He was worth a second chance.

Chapter Twenty

After his team of executives left his office, Alex ambled to the window overlooking the Strip. As always, his gaze arrowed to the Paradise, just visible on the other side of the Bellagio. In the daylight, she looked sun-bleached and worn as the sand dollar Mary had given him last week on the beach.

Still, the Paradise held her own magic for him, just like Mary. Reminders of past failures. Hope for the future. With both the Paradise and Mary, he'd taken steps to build something bright and new over the disasters of his youth. When he wiped the Paradise from the Strip and replaced it with something modern and gleaming, perhaps he'd finally be worthy of Mary.

When he turned his back to the window, his gaze snagged on the project Yasmin had created for him after she'd seen the sand dollar on his desk. She called it a shadow box. The shallow glass-fronted box held the sand dollar Mary had given him on the beach. It was glued in the box to lean against a printed copy of the selfie Mary had taken of them. Against the backdrop of the ocean, Mary's wild tresses blew against his face and tangled in his stubble. His tongue poked out as he tried to eject one of her curls from his mouth. Laughing at him, she was captivating. She'd sent him other pictures where he looked less ridiculous, but this was the best one of her, the California sunshine sparkling in her eyes like cut topaz.

He resisted the temptation to call her. It was Friday afternoon, and she was working. Instead, he pressed the button on his phone. "Yasmin, get me Lev."

"On it."

Less than a minute later, his phone rang, and he picked it up. "Lev, what's the word?"

"I hear Ray might be softening. Your good behavior is working, boss."

"Any other opposition on the gaming board?"

"Ray's cronies will vote the way he does. I've got most of the rest on your side. Only a couple on the fence. I think the Paradise is in the bag."

Alex found his hand wandering to his crotch to ward off the bad luck. Instead, he muttered, "Tocchiamo ferro."

"What's that, boss?"

He yanked open his top desk drawer and pulled out the old iron amulet his nonna used to wear around her neck. He rubbed the twisted horn shape with his fingertips. "Knock on wood."

"You Italians and your superstitions."

"Watch out, or I'll send you a dozen yellow sunflowers."

"Fuck off. Only my babushka believes in that bullshit."

"Liar." Alex set the talisman back in the drawer and slid it shut. "The vote is August first, right after his daughter's wedding. Anything I can do before then to grease the skids?"

"Stay on your best behavior, and be sure Rochelle is the happiest bride in the world."

Remembering Rochelle was in Mary's capable hands made him smile. "Consider it done." Then another thought broke through his happy haze. "How's Dante Campo doing with the clerical work?"

"Ah. I forgot to tell you. It happened while you were on your trip. He quit."

"Quit? What did you do to him?"

"Nothing at all, boss. He got another job. Something more exciting, he said."

Alex wasn't sure how to feel about that. It was good that Dante was working, but he'd never known the kid to keep a job for more than six weeks. He'd ask Joey about it the next time he saw him.

"Here's hoping he keeps this one."

"I'm just glad he's out of my office," Lev said. "Kid always had bandages on his hands, which meant it took him forever to type up anything. Then he spilled a soda in my filing cabinet. I had to send the whole cabinet out to a document conservation service."

Alex winced. "Sorry about that."

"It's okay. I added it to your bill."

Alex snorted and disconnected the call, but he didn't set down the handset. Instead, he punched in his mother's number. He'd visited her last Saturday morning after they'd returned from San Diego, and he'd go back tomorrow, but he had an urge to speak with her now, and he always went with his gut. Thinking about his grandmother must have pulled her to the front of his mind.

"What a surprise!" she said instead of hello. "The casino must have burned down."

"Mama." He chuckled. "I was only thinking of you."

"Thinking of your poor old mother while you're at work? Is Mary there?"

He'd told her about his fledgling relationship with Mary last weekend. When he was a kid, his mother looked down her nose at the blue-collar Forzas with their faded school uniforms and driveway full of torn-up cars. Now that their business had grown into a respectable one under Mary's leadership, she seemed to have changed her mind. She'd only sniffed and told him he could date whomever he wanted.

"No, Mary's not here. But we're going out tonight. Her brother and his fiancée are in town."

"Not one of the greasy mechanic brothers. The other one?"

"The one who lives in Ohio. The CEO."

"Ah." Approval colored her tone. "You could do worse than Mary Forza. She went to college, you know."

"I know. She's smart."

"You're smart, too, my boy. I wish..."

He wished a lot of things too. But they couldn't change the past.

"You've never dated a settling-down type before," she said.

"Sure, I have. Cierra is getting married later this summer."

"No, I mean someone *you* could settle down with. Like Mary."

"Settle down? I'm not ready for that," he scoffed. Besides, she was too good to settle for someone like him.

"You're thirty-six. If you wait too long, you'll miss your chance to have a family."

"Who says I want a family?"

"Don't you?"

Dammit, she was right. And Mary was the type to want a family, too. He imagined her with a pair of dark-haired kids. Or maybe three, like she'd grown up with. She'd make all of them feel like they were the center of her world. Not a nuisance like his dad had done with him. His heart twinged in his chest. "Families make you weak," he grumbled.

"They can also make you strong. Your father tried to take the right path after the Family threatened you."

"He didn't try long."

"No. But that was because he was weak to begin with. You're a better man than he ever was."

"That's a low bar."

"Don't speak ill of the dead." Her bangles clanked, a sure sign she'd crossed herself.

He was done wasting time on his father. "You're doing all right, Mama?"

"I'm feeling better this week. They let me walk in the garden every day before it gets too hot."

"Good. I'll see you tomorrow."

"Bring back Mary sometime? When I'm made up and not making a scene?"

He chuckled. "Okay. Behave yourself, and we'll see."

He disconnected the call. Then he nudged the shadow box with the photo of Mary next to the photo of his mother. They looked good together, the three of them.

The phone on his desk buzzed. He hit the button to speak to Yasmin. "Yes?"

"A Mrs. Campo is here to see you." Yasmin's tone was frosty. "She doesn't have an appointment."

"S-send her in." Alex had time to crack only the knuckles on his left hand before his door flew open, and Mrs. Campo marched inside. Her hair was gray now, but it was still scraped back into a bun, exposing her blazing brown eyes. The fine lines around her eyes and mouth had deepened. But other than that, she looked the same as the last time he saw her, when she'd come to his parents' house eighteen years ago.

"Mrs. Campo," he said, indicating the seating area at the front of his office, "to what do I owe the pleasure?"

"I'll stand, thank you." She planted her black flats on the carpet and propped her fists on her hips. She wore a black short-sleeved blouse over black slacks. At least she'd ditched the black veil she'd worn when she'd cursed his entire family.

He resisted the urge to cross himself. He hadn't been to Mass for eighteen years. God wouldn't protect him now.

"I suppose I should thank you for taking care of my family since my husband died," she said.

Alex sucked in a breath. She knew? She couldn't. He'd hidden everything so well. She must be talking about Joey. Shaking it off, he flashed her a smile. "I hired your son because he's a good worker."

She smiled proudly. "Joey is a good worker. But that's not all you've done. I'm no fool. I know my husband didn't have a pension." She twisted her lips. "Your father didn't care who he hurt. He only cared about himself. And your mother, she only cared about the money and her status. You're different. You're still a controlling bastard, but you've got a heart in there under that fancy suit."

"Thank you?"

"Don't thank me. I have a request."

Alex held his breath. Proud Mrs. Campo wanted something from him, the boy she'd cursed all those years ago to a life of the same type of pain she'd experienced when her husband died? Not that he believed in any of that. He fisted his hand to keep it off his crotch.

"It's for Dante. I know how you've helped him over the years. And now he and his friends have started a business. An entertainment business."

Alex blinked. He was pretty sure he hadn't seen Dante at the strip show the other night. "What kind of entertainment?"

"They're fire dancers. He's always had a passion for fire." She pursed her lips. "They went to a school for it, and now they're pretty good."

Was that why he'd had bandaged hands at Lev's office? But Alex still had red in his ledger for this woman and her family. He'd never be able to make up for her husband's death. "How can I help?"

"That school was expensive, and now they need work. You could hire them as entertainment for one of La Villa's events." She pulled her phone from her pants pocket, tapped the screen, and held it out to him.

He took it from her. A thumping bass erupted from the phone's crappy speaker. On the dark screen, fire whirled, lighting up bare torsos. The circles it made were hypnotic, and he couldn't tear his eyes from the screen. This would be a thousand times better than Cierra's dull aerialist. It would make the Richardson wedding truly unforgettable.

"They've got insurance?" he asked.

"It was included with the training program."

"Then, yes, I have an event where we can use them."

Chapter Twenty-One

Sunny hugged Mary's arm as they walked into the club. "I love seeing you so happy."

"Happy? More like tipsy." Considering how exhausted she was, it hadn't taken much wine with dinner to give her brain a buzz, and everything had a rosy tint to it, from the crowded tables in the public part of the bar to the screens with the lyrics on them. Even the trio of drunk college girls screeching a Miley Cyrus song sounded good.

"Maybe a little of both. I can see why you're happy." She waggled her eyebrows at Alex, who stood silently behind them, taking in the karaoke club with his eyebrows smashed together.

"Oh, you mean the sex?" Whoa, that came out louder than she'd planned. Her brother, Gabe, winced. She dropped her voice to whisper in Sunny's ear. "Yeah, it's pretty great." Since they'd come back from San Diego, he'd spent the night at her place more often than not. It was another reason she was so tired. But totally worth it.

Alex's hand on her back guided her to the front of the hostess's line. She leaned back against his shoulder and let his vanilla scent embrace her.

But when Sunny pointed to a table near the stage, he leaned around her. "Wouldn't you prefer a private room?"

"For four of us?" Sunny asked. "What's the fun in that?"

"What's the fun in any of this?" Alex muttered.

"I heard that," Mary whispered.

His arm went around her waist. "I didn't mean—"

"I know. It's not your scene. Thanks for being a good sport."

He tugged her closer. "You can thank me later."

She turned in his arms and kissed him. "Believe me, I will."

"Come on, lovebirds." Sunny tapped her shoulder. "Let's sit down so we can get our names on the list."

"Goody." Alex arched his eyebrow.

Mary traced it with her fingertip. "It'll be fun."

"Fun." His full lips pinched together.

The hostess led them to the table. Sunny didn't even wait for the waiter to get their drink order before she asked, "Okay, what do you two want to sing?"

"What do you..." But when she turned to Alex, he wasn't there. He'd stopped a few feet away to talk to a man also dressed in a suit, no tie. "Sorry." She turned to her brother and his fiancée. "He knows everyone."

"Hmm." Sunny's flat lips conveyed her disapproval. "Honey, what do you want to sing? 'Shallow' again?" She leaned toward Mary. "That's our song, you know."

"I love your voice on 'Senorita,'" he said. "Maybe that first?"

They were so cute. Her brother Gabe had seemed so stiff and serious when she'd first met him over a year ago when he'd come looking for his birth family after accidentally taking one of those DNA tests. And here he was, cozied up with professional performer Sunny, about to get up on stage and sing a duet with her.

She wished she and Alex had a song.

"How is Alex's singing voice?" Sunny asked.

She was a little embarrassed that she didn't know. She'd known him for over twenty-five years, and she couldn't remember hearing him sing. He'd hummed while he loaded the dishwasher last weekend. "Okay, I guess?"

"We'll put you down for something that isn't too challenging. How about 'I Got You, Babe'? I think you can do Cher's part, and a semi-trained donkey could stand in for Sonny."

"I don't sing." Alex slipped into the chair next to Mary. "You three can partner up."

"Everybody sings karaoke," Sunny said, narrowing her blue eyes at him.

"I wouldn't argue with her," Gabe said. "She might be tiny, but she's tenacious."

One corner of Alex's mouth tipped up, and a dangerous glint came into his eyes. "I. Don't. Sing."

Mary rubbed his tense shoulder. "Sunny might be a professional singer, but she won't judge your voice. Mine, either, I hope." She chuckled nervously.

"I'll buy the drinks." He signaled the waiter. "And I'll cheer the loudest after you sing."

Sunny opened her mouth to argue, but Gabe put his arm around her shoulder and whispered something in her ear. "Fine," she huffed. "I'll sign the rest of us up. Order me something strong and sweet." She stood and went to the kiosk.

After they ordered their drinks, Alex waved at another patron sitting in one of the booths in the back. "Would you mind if I said hello to a business acquaintance?"

"No, go for it," she said.

Excusing himself, he walked away.

"What's his deal?" Gabe asked, leaning forward and resting his elbows on the table.

"What do you mean? He's just being a guy. Michael would act the same way, I'm sure."

"Michael." Gabe chuckled. "Our brother has a crankshaft up his ass."

"Alex knows a ton of people here," she said. "He has a certain presence to maintain in front of his business contacts. He's working on a big deal."

Gabe's dark eyebrows shot up. "Shouldn't he also consider what makes you happy?"

"He does." She crossed her arms. "He makes me happy."

"If you're sure."

"It's still new. It's not like I'm marrying the guy."

"Okay, okay." Her brother held his palms out. "You don't have to get all defensive."

"Defensive?" But she heard the way her voice rose. She shouldn't have to defend him. Why couldn't he just be a good sport?

"Come on, honey!" Sunny shouted from the kiosk. "We're up."

Her brother, who was a good sport, rose. "You'll be okay?" He glanced toward where Alex still spoke with his business acquaintance.

"I'll be fine. Have fun."

As he walked away, the waiter returned with their drinks, and Mary took a long pull on her Negroni. She grinned as she listened to her brother and his fiancée sing their sexy duet and clapped and whistled when they finished. Alex hadn't yet returned. The ice melted in his whiskey.

Mary finished her drink and ordered another. She didn't even care that Alex wasn't back by the time she and Sunny got up to sing "Dancing Queen."

Much.

Chapter Twenty-Two

When Alex disconnected their now twice-a-week call with Rochelle and Rohaan the following Tuesday, he caught Mary rubbing her temples. The dark shadows were back, and now they were joined by redness around her eyes.

"Another headache?" She'd gotten one Friday night after karaoke, and then she'd been too busy with the weddings, work, and her family over the weekend to see him. Tonight, she was taking her brother and his fiancée to the airport. She had a list as long as her arm of last-minute tasks for her other wedding this Saturday. She was running herself ragged.

"Just a little one," she said, closing her binder and shoving it into her satchel.

"I have a present for you." He walked to his desk and slid open the drawer to pull out the flat package. Yasmin had wrapped it in white paper with a jaunty pink bow.

Mary had followed him to his desk and stared at the shadow box. "You saved the sand dollar? And you printed out our photo?"

"I did. I wanted to remember our trip."

Her gaze darted between it and the photo of his mother. The line between her eyebrows melted. "That's so sweet."

He cleared his throat. "Yasmin put it together. Here." He held out the package. "For you."

Tilting her head, she took it from him and slipped her thumb under the seam of the wrapping paper. Gently, she peeled it off.

She gasped. "You bought me a tablet computer?"

"You can use it to store your notes electronically and sync it with your desktop computer. Or replace that dinosaur altogether. Then you won't have to lug around your bulky binder."

"This...this is too much."

"Consider it an investment," he said. *And a peace offering,* he didn't say. He'd acted like a dick at karaoke. But the place had been packed with his business contacts, including some he needed for the Paradise deal. He couldn't make a fool of himself in front of people he needed to impress.

"I..." She hugged it to her chest. "Thank you."

"You're welcome. And I have another gift for you." He pulled a black card from his pocket and handed it to her.

"A hotel gift card?" She scrunched up her nose.

"It's for you to use at the spa. Unlimited treatments. Maybe you could go tomorrow? You said Wednesdays are usually slow at the shop." The gift was at least fifty percent selfish. A day of relaxation might get them back to where they were after San Diego. When they'd become "friends and."

"Oh. Um. You're right. I could go in the morning. A massage would be nice."

"Stay all day. The spa bistro serves lunch. The ancient grains salad is amazing. And after..."

"After?" Both corners of her mouth quirked up.

"After your day of pampering, I can relax you the way I did in San Diego."

"Mmm. I like the sound of that."

So did he.

The next day, Alex was so distracted by visions of a relaxed, glowing Mary that at noon, he took a break from work to ride the elevator down to the spa level.

The wide-eyed receptionist in her black scrubs stammered, "M-M-Mr. Villa. We weren't expecting you until Friday."

"It's fine, Chantal. I'm meeting Miss Forza in the bistro." He turned toward the men's changing rooms, which led out to the restaurant and indoor pool area.

"Oh! Um, Mr. Villa?"

"Yes?" He turned back impatiently.

"She—she's not here. She left."

"Left?"

"She had the desert sage oil massage and started the parafango wrap, but then she said she couldn't stay. We scrubbed it off, and she...left."

She left before lunch? The spa didn't open until nine. A full day of pampering had turned into an hour or two. "Dammit, Mary," he muttered. The woman could take care of everyone except herself. Would it have been so difficult to enjoy herself for a change? Would it have killed her to let him take care of her?

His breath caught in his chest. Unless something had happened to her. Or to her brothers.

"Are you okay, Mr. Villa? Would you like me to find someone to give you a hand massage?"

He cracked his knuckles. "No, thank you, Chantal. I'll wait for my regular appointment on Friday."

He strode to the elevator and waited until he was back in his office with his resources all around him before he called Mary.

"Hi!" she chirped. "Thanks so much for the spa day. It was lovely."

He let out the breath trapped in his chest. She sounded fine.

"I think you're unclear on the concept of a spa day," he snapped. "A spa *day* involves spending the full day relaxing. If you didn't like the treatments, you could have gone to the sauna. Or the pool."

"I know. And I had a lovely massage. But while I was lying there wrapped in plastic, I couldn't stop thinking about work, and it wasn't relaxing, and I was wasting your employee's time, so I left."

"You weren't wasting my employee's time. They're paid to work."

"I know, I know. And I'm sorry. Though, really, I'm not sure what I'm sorry about. I didn't ask for a spa day. You offered it. And I spent as much time there as I wanted to." Fire crackled in her voice.

Deliberately, he rolled his shoulders. "I'm sorry. I shouldn't have tried to make you feel bad about it. I was—" He cleared his throat. "Concerned."

"Concerned about the Richardson wedding?"

"No, darling. I'm concerned about you. That you had an emergency of some type. That the masseuse pinched a nerve in your beautiful neck. That fucking Michael let a car fall on him."

She laughed, a long, merry tinkle, like wind chimes that danced across his skin. "I had so many lists working in my brain I had to write them down or I'd lose it. I'm sure you know how work can grab you and not let you go."

He understood that well. Work sustained him and challenged him at the same time. It allowed him to achieve success and security for himself and for the people he loved. His gaze fell on the photo of his mother. Then on the photo of Mary next to it.

Fuck.

Did he love Mary, too?

Was that why her photo sat next to the only other person he loved?

His knees wobbled, and he collapsed into his chair. He couldn't, could he?

They'd been friends for so long, and now the sex had produced a flood of confusing endorphins. It was all chemistry.

They hadn't had sex in almost a week. Yet something in him thrilled whenever he heard her voice.

Fuck.

"Alex? Are you still there?"

"Yes, yes, I'm here. I'm glad you're all right." He was holding his phone, so he couldn't do it properly, but he pressed his fist into the surface of his desk until he felt a comforting pop.

"The massage was lovely. Maybe you can come over after work, and I can thank you properly?"

"I like the sound of that. Though you should come to my place instead." He needed the fortification of his own turf. If he went to Mary's cozy little house, he might be lulled into saying something foolish.

"Ooh," she teased. "I finally get to visit your fortress of solitude."

"It's not like that," he muttered.

"Isn't it?"

"Remember, I invited you before. I'll leave a card at the front desk. Again."

"I'll see you at eight," she said.

"Come for dinner. At seven."

"I'll bring dessert."

He lowered his voice. "That had better mean racy lingerie."

She lowered hers, too. "I don't know about racy. I'll try to wear something I bought at the mall and not the clearance rack at Target."

"Target has a clearance rack? I thought the whole damn place was a bargain bin."

"Elitist. I'll take you with me sometime. We'll hit the skincare aisle. You'll be amazed at the value."

"It's a date. And so is dinner tonight." His turf, his rules. He'd wrest back control of whatever emotion had knocked him off his game.

Chapter Twenty-Three

Mary walked out of his kitchen with a plate of cookies and set it down in front of him. "Dessert," she announced with a smug expression.

"Anginetti? I haven't had these since my nonna died."

"Mine used to make them too. I'm so thankful I got her recipe before she passed."

"And yet you've never been to Italy?" His gaze fell on the Venetian glass vase on his kitchen island. It was so showy on its own he never bothered to fill it with flowers.

"No." She looked away.

"I'll take you. When the Richardson wedding is done." Where had that come from? He never took dates on his trips. He preferred to sample the local offerings. He had plenty of memories of curtains dancing in soft Tuscan breezes as moonlight glimmered on the olive skin of stunning women who laughed at his rudimentary Italian. It was like collecting souvenirs without having to find a place to put them when he returned home.

Why did the thought of taking Mary to Italy, of showing her his favorite places, make waking up alone in a beam of Italian sunlight on rumpled sheets seem lonely and pathetic?

Her incandescent smile fell. "I couldn't leave my work that long. Or my brothers."

"They're grown men. They should be taking care of you." Then, under his breath, he added, "I know I would."

He had to shake this off. None of it—inviting Mary to Italy, being disappointed when she refused, that fluttery feeling in his chest—was like him.

He picked up a cookie and stuffed it into his mouth. Sweet almond burst on his tongue and rocketed him back thirty years to the warmth and security of his nonna's cramped kitchen.

"You like it?" Mary asked. "I know you don't like anise, so I used—"

He gripped her wrist and pulled her down into his lap. He kissed her hard, pushing his tongue and the taste of almond into her mouth.

She sagged against him, tangling her fingers into his hair. He didn't let her go until they were both breathless. That was all this was. Sex hormones were fucking him up. He needed her body. He shifted into a familiar gear.

"The cookies are delicious. But I have something else in mind for the next part of the evening." Smirking, he reached for the tiny shopping bag he'd retrieved from the sideboard while she was in the kitchen. He offered it to her.

"Somehow, I think I'm going to wish I'd skipped dessert when I put this on." She reached into the bag and pulled out the pale pink silk nightie so light he'd had to check it was still nestled into its bed of tissue paper. Her lips parted as the silk flowed over her hands. "I don't think I've ever felt anything this soft before."

He swallowed. "Put it on for me?"

She stared at it for a moment. "Okay. Have another cookie while I go change."

"I think I want something else for dessert. We can have the rest of the anginetti for breakfast."

Goosebumps arose on her skin. Good.

"Come on," he said. "You can change in my bathroom."

Taking her hand, he led her down the hall to his bedroom. As they passed the giant platform bed, she tugged him to a stop. But she wasn't looking at the bed.

She tipped her chin at the pair of oversize cognac leather chairs in the sitting area next to the window and its view of the Strip. "Nice chairs."

"Thanks. Though I've got something I think you'll like even more."

"I've seen what you've got," she said. "And I like it a lot."

Like it heard her praise, his dick stirred proudly in his pants. But he wanted to show off first. He flung open the doors to his bathroom and led her inside.

He only ever used the toilet, the shower, and one sink, but even to his jaded eyes, the bathroom was impressive. White marble gleamed against dark walnut cabinetry. The designer had added a few soft elements, like a basket of bath salts next to the clawfoot tub. Each week, his housekeeper dutifully dusted them off.

"Whoa. This is nicer than the spa downstairs. Is the floor heated?" She wiggled her bare toes on the tile.

"It is. And I wouldn't call it nicer. The same designer created it."

She trailed her hand over the heated towel rack. "Maybe I don't need the lingerie. We could just get naked in here."

"I'd like you to try it on." His throat constricted, and he had to swallow again. "For me."

"All right." She set the slip on the counter and turned her back to him. "Unzip me?"

He stepped up behind her and set his fingers on the zipper of her sundress. As he peeled it down, the sides gaped open, revealing a black bra against tan skin. A matching pair of panties peeked out from the bottom of the zipper. Starting at the back clasp of her bra, he traced a finger down her spine. "It's like unwrapping a gift," he said, awed.

She turned, clutching the dress to her chest. "That can't be the first time you've helped someone with a zipper."

"It's the first time I've unzipped you." His feelings for her were unlike anything he'd felt for any other woman.

A shy smile curled her lips. "Give me a minute. I'll meet you out there."

He dropped a light kiss on her lips. "All right."

For a moment, he wished his bedroom weren't so utilitarian. That there was some softness to it to make her feel at home. She'd miss her tiny, squashy furniture and floral prints. There were exactly two decorative pillows on his bed, both made of a stiff, unyielding black canvas. He tossed them to the floor.

Actually...

He picked them up and stacked them next to the bed. They'd make a good cushion against the bamboo floor when he flipped up the hem of her slip. His knees weren't as young as they used to be.

The door opened, and he turned. Mary leaned against the doorway. One hand smoothed over her hip, and the other fluttered self-consciously somewhere around her midsection. Thin shoulder straps held up the pale silk garment. The lace at the neckline framed her gorgeous tits, and the rest of it flowed smoothly down to the tops of her thighs. "You got the size right."

Hell yeah, he had. "Fortunately, the salesclerk had a similar build. She told me which one to get."

She pushed off the doorway and walked into the room. She glanced at the bed.

"Sit on the edge." He prowled toward her, meeting her at the foot of the bed.

"I don't think so. I want to thank you properly for the tablet and the spa treatments and dinner. And this fabulous nightie." She twirled, and the skirt flared out, giving him a tantalizing flash of skin.

He licked his lips. "I was promised dessert."

"You'll get"—she curled her fingers into the waistband of his pants and tugged him closer—"what I serve you." She unbuckled his belt, loosened the fasteners on his pants, and unzipped them.

Instead of letting them drop to the floor, she followed them down until she kneeled at his feet. "Step out."

Gazing into her beautiful face, tilted up toward him, her mouth so close to his dick, he obeyed. While she tossed his pants aside, he tugged off his socks. His heart thudded in his chest as he unbuttoned his shirt cuffs, then reached for his top button.

She rose and put her hand over his. "I've got it." Carefully, she unbuttoned the top button and placed a kiss at his throat. Then she moved to the next button. After loosening each button, she kissed his skin. His breastbone. His stomach. By the time she reached the lowest button, the one that covered his boxer briefs and his straining erection, he was holding his breath, lightheaded with anticipation.

She pushed his shirt off his shoulders and let it flutter to the floor.

She kneeled again and hooked her fingers into the waistband of his underwear. Slowly, she rolled the garment over him and off. He started breathing again when his dick sprang free.

He hissed when she licked the tip. "Okay?" she asked.

"Fuck, yes. Feels amazing. There are pillows. For your knees."

"I won't be here that long. I just wanted to get you a little..." She closed her lips over his head, swirled her tongue around him, then popped off with a sucking sound. "Wet."

He let loose a string of curse words. Anything to keep from going off right then. She'd be upset if he spoiled her new lingerie.

Like she read the thought on his face, she said, "You keep telling me I need to relax. But I think you need it even more than I do. Go sit in the chair."

"What? I—"

"Sit."

He didn't know what he'd been about to say. Probably something to wrest back control of the situation. Being bossed around and not knowing what would happen next made sweat pop along his hairline.

But this was how he'd get what he wanted, which was to sink

into Mary's glorious pussy, so he sat. The soft leather creaked under his naked ass.

"Condoms?" she asked.

"In the bedside table on the left."

He watched the silk shift across her ass as she walked to the table and slid open the drawer. "Mind if I use your lube, too?"

Oh, fuck. "I don't mind."

She carried the tube and the condom to the side table next to him. She squeezed a dollop of liquid onto her finger and reached between her legs.

He grasped the skirt of her slip and raised it to watch her smooth the lube over her labia, then along her slit. Her breath caught when she touched her swollen clit, but then she moved her hand away to press a finger inside herself. He wanted to do it all for her, slick her up and get her ready for him, but all he could do was watch as she slid her fingers across her skin. When he tore his gaze away, he saw the lines of stress around her eyes had disappeared.

"Now you." She gripped his dick with her slippery hand and pumped him. He loosed another string of curses.

"You kiss your mother with that mouth?" she asked, a saucy glint in her eye.

"Bring your pussy here, and I'll kiss it with my dirty mouth."

"Tempting, but I have other plans for your mouth." She picked up the condom and tried to tear it, but her fingers, slick with lube, slipped and didn't hold. "Whoops. Could've planned that better."

"Teeth?" His mouth went dry at the image.

"Gross. No, you do it." She handed him the condom, and he found a dry corner to tear it open. He rolled it on.

She put her knee next to his leg and climbed onto his lap. "I'm doing all the work here, understand? You just let go."

Let go? Unlikely. But he nodded. He lifted her skirt again to watch as she positioned herself over him and, holding him at the base, slowly sank down. With the lube, he slipped easily inside her.

She paused when her ass landed on his thighs and rolled her hips experimentally.

"Fuck," he whispered. Then he lifted his face to capture her lips in a ravenous kiss.

She rolled her hips again, squeezing his dick, and he saw stars. He pushed up his hips to nestle deeper inside.

"Nope. Remember, I'm in charge here." She lifted, then ground down again.

"Yes," he hissed.

"Thought so. You can touch my breasts," she said as if she were a queen, allowing him to kiss her ring.

He slid his hand up the satin-smooth garment to her breast. He lifted it to his mouth and sucked her nipple through the fabric, the silk so thin he could feel every contour against his tongue. He palmed her other breast, rubbing the silk against her nipple until Mary let out a happy sigh.

She started a slow rhythm, lifting and falling in his lap. She added a little squeeze at the bottom of her descent that made his eyes roll back. It wasn't as much compression as when he fisted himself, but being inside her wet warmth, her breasts pushed into his face, and her scent all around him was enough to shoot him to the edge. He gritted his teeth. He couldn't come in less than two minutes. Not before she'd come.

With one hand, she gripped his shoulder, her short nails digging into his skin. With the other, she lifted his chin until he popped off her breast. She kissed him, a hungry invasion of her tongue, and for a minute, he forgot about holding off, about getting her to orgasm, about anything but the way she curled around him and made him feel like the center of her universe.

She kissed along his jaw to his ear and whispered, "Let go."

Fuck it. He gripped her ass, lifted his hips, and thrust up into her once. Twice. Then, shouting something incoherent, he came. He didn't care that he'd broken all his rules. All that mattered was the release that stiffened his muscles for long seconds until he collapsed, boneless, into the chair.

He gentled his hold on her ass. "Sorry," he mumbled.

"Sorry?" she murmured in his ear, squeezing around his over-sensitized cock. "That was so hot."

"But you didn't come," he said. "You only took care of me."

"It's about time someone took care of you, Alex. And I can take care of myself." She leaned back and slipped her hand between them. She touched where they were still joined, and he shuddered. Then she moved her hand up to her clit and rubbed it.

"Let me." Somehow, he'd convince his muscles to move his arm.

"You lie back. Enjoy the show." She put her other hand on the wet spot over her nipple and tweaked it while she continued to work her other hand. Her eyelids fluttered closed.

He watched her beautiful face, her lips parted as she panted. Then he dropped his gaze to her heaving chest and her fingertips plucking at her nipple. Finally, he gazed at her other hand, working fast, her knuckles occasionally brushing his lower belly. He trailed a finger up to her tailbone and caressed her soft skin. He could watch her like this forever. Touch her. Hell, he'd loved curling around her and holding her while she slept. Why had he been such a foolish, proud kid? If he'd only come clean years ago, how many years of this mind-blowing pleasure could they have shared?

She groaned, then twitched. He held her tighter as her hands stilled and her breathing stuttered to a stop, then began again. She collapsed against his chest, burying her face in his neck.

He ran his hand up her spine and rested it at her nape. Her palms settled against his pecs.

It unlocked something inside him, something light and beautiful like a hummingbird or a butterfly. The best feeling he'd ever experienced. *I want to stay like this with you forever.*

But what he said was, "I'd better get rid of the condom." When she nodded and clambered off him, he caught sight of the Paradise through the window. Could he have his hotel empire and Mary, too? Possibly. Assuming all went well with the Richardson wedding. Which reminded him of what he'd promised Mrs. Campo.

"When I get back, let's talk about the Richardson wedding. I have an idea about entertainment I want to run past you."

Mary's mouth was open like she'd been about to say something, but she closed it and nodded. They were partners and lovers. It was goddamn perfect.

Chapter Twenty-Four

The next morning, three days before Teagan and Twyla's wedding, Mary didn't have time for afterglow. Passing on his offer of a leisurely soak in the clawfoot tub that could've easily fit a family of four, she dashed out of Alex's place as soon as it was light. After showering in her tiny, dimly lit bathroom that stayed so choked with steam it was nearly impossible to get her makeup to stay on her face, she tugged on her Forza Elite Motors golf shirt and a pair of jeans and raced to the shop.

She'd just settled at her cluttered desk in the small office when Evie shuffled in.

"What are you doing here so early?" Mary asked.

"Had some stuff to do before the shop opens." Evie set her bag on the chair on the other side of Mary's desk.

"Have a cookie." Mary nodded at the tin of anginetti on the corner of her desk.

"Italian wedding cookies? Mmm. I love the fringe benefits here." Evie set a cup of coffee on top of one of her overstuffed binders. "You look like you could use this."

"Bless you." Mary grabbed the cup in both hands and inhaled the bitter aroma that promised efficient caffeine delivery.

Evie opened the tin, plucked out a cookie, and bit into it. She hummed appreciatively. Her gaze sharpened as Mary guzzled the coffee. "Rough night?"

"No, it was a good night." Although she was starting to consider Evie a friend, she didn't talk with her about her relationship with Alex. Evie didn't have many positive opinions about the man who'd fired her. "Though I had trouble sleeping."

"That stinks," Evie said. "I don't miss that about wedding planning, all the to-do lists spinning in my head. Hang on, I'll be right back, then you can tell me what's going on." She grabbed another cookie and strode out of the office.

Mary was sure Alex hadn't meant to set her brain spinning. He just hadn't thought before he'd brought up work while she was still having aftershocks from an orgasm she'd given herself. Not that she had a problem taking care of her own pleasure. It was what she'd meant to do all along, ever since she'd heard the hurt in his voice when she'd skipped out on lunch at his spa. It was just that...he could've thanked her for what appeared to be a mind-blowing orgasm before he'd asked her to propose a suggestion to Rochelle that terrified her. A change this big with so little time to prepare seemed dangerous.

Long after Alex's breathing had deepened and slowed, Mary had flipped through ways to present the splashy entertainment idea to Rochelle. Then her mind had jumped to how her personal relationship with Alex had tangled with the professional one. She couldn't treat him like any other vendor, or even a client, and tell him she thought his idea was risky, especially if they tried to execute it with less than two weeks to go before the big day.

Working with her lover had suddenly become uncomfortable. She'd even pretended to be asleep when he'd snuggled up against her in the middle of the night and kissed the back of her neck. Was he about to make love to her or make another ill-timed work comment?

She had enough stress in her work life between what had

become two full-time jobs, not to mention her constant watchfulness over her brothers. She should be able to sink into a romantic
relationship and let go of her work stress, shouldn't she? And she
wasn't getting that with Alex, considering the pressure of making
everything perfect to support his big business deal.

Something had to give.

She glanced at her phone. She'd changed the wallpaper, not to
one of the selfies like the one framed in Alex's office but to a less
obvious one, a photo she'd snapped of their feet toe to toe in the
sand. He'd kissed her after she'd taken it, and she could almost smell
the salty ocean air, feel her hair whipping her cheeks, taste his lips.

San Diego seemed long ago. Appropriate, since the relaxation
and lack of responsibility she'd experienced were nothing but a
dream. But the feelings that warmed her chest when she was around
Alex were real.

She loved him. She'd tried to show him last night by taking care
of him. But then he'd brought up work. Clearly, he didn't feel the
same way. Would he ever get there? Mary had always been quick to
fall. And to be honest, she'd never stopped loving him, not even
after he'd stood her up at prom.

Loving someone as driven as Alex was a challenge. He knew
what he wanted. Power. And redemption. To rise above the city of
Las Vegas like a neon sign that said, *Look at me. I'm in charge.* He'd
made sure his previous romantic relationships had been unimportant, easily pushed to the side. Otherwise, they might distract him
from his goal. But Mary could help him achieve what he wanted.
She was doing it with Rochelle and Rohaan's wedding. After
supporting her family for most of her life, she was a professional at
ensuring everyone got what they needed.

But she needed things out of a relationship, too. Namely, not to
have him ask her a question about work when she was about to tell
him she loved him.

For their romantic relationship to work, the professional one
had to go.

Rochelle's wedding was the last project she'd work on for him. Sure, she'd consider La Villa as a venue for future weddings, but she'd insist on working with Joey and not directly with his boss.

She only had to get through this wedding.

Evie returned to her office with an armful of the boys' coveralls.

"What are you doing with those?" Mary asked.

"I noticed a few ripped seams and holes. I thought I'd fix them."

"Fix them?" Mary wrinkled her nose. Her brothers usually wore them until they fell apart, then they ordered new ones.

"It's not hard. All you need are basic sewing skills. Did no one ever teach you? Any of you?"

"I think my nonna sewed, but I was always more interested in learning to cook. And the boys were much more into in her old Chevelle."

"Sewing is a good skill to have. Handy at weddings. I'll teach you sometime. After Rochelle's wedding." Evie pulled a small pouch from her bag and threaded a needle with blue thread. She knotted the end. "Now, tell me what's on your mind."

"Alex wants to make Rochelle and Rohaan's wedding memorable. With fire dancers."

"Like, with actual fire? Where'd he get that idea?"

"I think he doesn't want to be outdone by Cierra's wedding. She's his ex, you know."

"One of many," Evie muttered.

Mary's cheeks burned. "I hired an aerialist to entertain the guests during Cierra's cocktail hour. But I've been planning that for months. I'm concerned about adding this at the last minute."

"They have a fire dancing show at the Blue Hawaiian," Evie said. "I can make some calls."

"Actually, Alex knows someone, and he's already booked them. He says he trusts them, which is saying something. I still have to talk to Rochelle and Rohaan. They might shut down the whole idea."

"That's probably too much to hope for." Evie stabbed her needle into the thick blue fabric.

"Probably. Who wouldn't want half-naked people flinging fire around their guests?"

Evie snorted. "Send me their information. I'll check them out."

"Are you sure? I know you said you didn't want to work on weddings anymore."

Evie looked up from her sewing. "Working with you is a lot different from working with Alex. I could never do anything right for him. He had to put his fingerprints on everything." She raised her eyebrows. "Kind of like what he's doing with the fire dancers."

"This wedding is a big deal for him," Mary said. Alex had promised her he wouldn't interfere with her work. He'd only made a suggestion, right? He hadn't broken another promise.

"That's why he hired you. He shouldn't need to be involved on a daily basis." One corner of Evie's mouth curled up. "Though if he stepped back, he couldn't spend as much time with you."

Mary lifted her coffee to her lips to hide her smile.

"You're a better boss than he ever was. I wouldn't mind helping you out with the wedding work. Is everything ready for Teagan and Twyla this weekend?"

"Everything is smooth sailing at the botanical gardens. The staff there know what they're doing."

"What's their rain policy?" Evie asked.

"Rain?" Mary snorted. "You realize we live in the desert?"

Evie speared her with a glare. "A good wedding planner considers all eventualities. Besides, on my drive here, the radio said something about a storm this weekend."

"A storm? Maybe it'll be one of those quick downpours."

"Or maybe it won't happen at all. Still, you need a plan."

"Right. Okay." Mary could learn a lot about managing risk from her new assistant. "I'll ask them what happens in the extremely remote possibility of rain."

"The last time I planned a ceremony there, they had a tent. They promised everyone would stay dry."

Mary wrinkled her nose, imagining a rotten old scrap of canvas rolled up in a spidery storage shed. "A tent?"

"I checked it out, and it's not as bad as it sounds. They air it out at least twice a year. It's white and plenty big enough for Teagan and Twyla's twenty-five guests. I'll call the garden today to make sure they've cleaned it recently."

"Thank you." Mary sagged back into her chair.

"What about Cierra's wedding? Need any help there?" Evie asked.

"We met with the band yesterday. They're pretty good, and we agreed on the set list."

"What about her fiancé? When she brought him in last week, he seemed like a real piece of work. That business with Rafe..." Evie shook her head.

"I know, right? He just came in to say hi to Cierra, and Sawyer puffed up like a tomcat. How could anyone think innocent Rafe would touch an engaged woman? But that seems to be Sawyer's M.O. He got up in the lead singer's face because he thought he was flirting with Cierra."

"Was he?"

"I don't think so. I pegged him as friendly and eager to please his clients, but Sawyer told him to step off."

"Did he?"

"Yeah. After that, the guitarist did the talking. And he made sure to flash his wedding ring." The last thing they needed was a groom with a hair trigger. Cierra had dated half of Las Vegas and, for some reason, invited most of her exes. Fortunately, most of them, including Alex, had sent their regrets.

Evie tied off her stitch and cut the thread. "Sounds like you've got everything under control. Let me know if you need help."

"I will. Promise." Teagan and Twyla's wedding was small enough for Mary to handle. And for Rochelle and Rohaan's, she could call on the resources of La Villa. She had it all handled.

She hoped.

"Any questions about the shop?" she asked.

"No." Evie stabbed her needle into Michael's coveralls. "Although I failed your brother's test yesterday."

"Test? There's no test in renting cars. Even exotic ones."

Evie grunted. "Someone called in yesterday looking for a red 1982 Corvette to use in a movie. Don't worry, I made them promise it wouldn't be harmed. It's just for the actors to get in and out of in close-up shots. They'll use a different one for the stunts. Anyway, I saw we didn't have one in the inventory system, but we have an '84. So, I told them yes and sent them the paperwork."

Mary winced. "The '84 looks nothing like the '82. It's a completely different body style. Boxier. Less sexy."

"I know that now. After Michael lectured me. He made me go out into the lot and compare them. Then he gave me a pop quiz on the different generations of Corvettes. And tossed in a couple Mustangs just to trip me up."

"Sorry about that. He can be a little...passionate. Did you swap out the '84 for the '78? It can pass for an '82."

"Yes, that's what Michael told me. Who knew cars could be so complicated?"

"Wait until he quizzes you on the difference between a catalytic converter and a muffler."

"Can't wait," Evie said grimly.

"Okay, so today's schedule." Mary woke up her ancient desktop computer's screen. "You should be able to handle the cars. Rentals are pretty light today. I've got to spend some time on the weddings. I'll call Rochelle, and then..." She pulled Alex's gift from her satchel.

Evie's eyes widened. "Oh my god. Are you actually joining the twenty-first century?"

"I guess?" Mary glanced longingly at her stack of binders. "Somehow, I've got to get all that"—she tapped the biggest one, Rochelle's—"into this." She waved the tablet in its box.

"Gimme." Evie snatched the box from her. "By the end of the day, every detail will be loaded into here. Don't worry, you'll love it."

"Will I?" Mary asked ruefully. "Because I really love my binders."

"We'll keep them as a backup, I promise. But that tablet will make you look like the real deal. And be easier on your back."

Alex had said the same thing. She'd suspected at the time it was a power play to insert himself into her business. But maybe he was only looking out for her. Because he cared.

There was also that photo of her on his desk. Maybe he did love her. In his own way.

"If you say so."

Chapter Twenty-Five

A s he hit the button to call the one person who could make him feel better about all this, Alex peered out the window of the hospital waiting room. Rain beat against it. Torrential rain! In Las Vegas! It was like a giant had picked up the snow globe that was his carefully controlled world and shaken it until the casino and his mother had come unfixed from the base to float around with the flakes of fake snow.

Fortunately for him, Mary stayed glued in place. When he'd gotten the call last night from his mother's nursing facility, she'd offered to come to the hospital with him, but he knew she had a big day today with the wedding. Not the Richardson wedding but the other one. The lesbian couple with the funny names that had vacated his brain due to all the stress hormones swimming around in it. He'd kissed her forehead and left her sleeping in his bed. He liked the thought of her being there, one bit of color in the black-and-white world he called home.

"Hi, Alex." Mary's voice sounded high and strained. "How's your mom?"

"She's out of surgery and in recovery. They said it was a clean fracture, so they didn't have to replace her hip. I should be able to see her in an hour or so, they say."

"I'm so glad to hear it. How are you holding up?"

"Besides feeling guilty that I ever suggested she walk in the gardens? I'm all right." He raked a hand through his hair and looked down at his feet. For the first time, he noticed he was wearing one brown loafer and one black one. Shit. He hoped he didn't see anyone he knew.

"That's good. Listen, I'm sorry, but I have to go."

"Right. Wedding stuff. How's it going?"

"Um, it's not." She laughed, but it wasn't her regular laugh. It had a note of hysteria in it. "Have you looked outside?"

Lightning flashed. "Oh, no. Was it an outdoor wedding?"

"It was. And the backup tent isn't going to cut it in this. The whole place is flooded. It's just my luck to get a hundred-year storm during my first wedding."

Alex's heart hurt for her, but why hadn't she planned for this? "There's no indoor space available?"

"Already reserved. We knew when we scheduled it there were other weddings, but..." She sighed. "We're moving it to next weekend."

"Next weekend? But you can't." His heart thundered in his chest. "The Richardson—"

"It'll be fine," she said firmly. "I have an assistant who can handle Teagan and Twyla. You'll have me all to yourself at Rochelle's."

He slowly let out his breath. *All to himself* sounded good. Better than good. Fantastic.

"But really, I have to go," she said. "I have a thousand calls to make to get everything moved."

"Good luck." Even he heard the note of accusation in his voice. How could she not have planned better? Two weddings on the same day, even with an assistant, was too much.

"I'll call you later. And I'll come to the hospital as soon as I can."

His heart twinged. He'd never had anyone he could count on to wait at the hospital with him. He glanced back at the doors that led to the recovery room where they monitored his mother. The doors remained shut.

"I love—" But he could tell from the silence on the line she'd already hung up.

Chapter Twenty-Six

When the zipper stalled, Mary looked over the bride's shoulder into the mirror and caught the shimmer in her brown eyes.

Mary had done nothing but triage emergencies all day, and since the makeup stylist had already left, the most pressing one was the flakes of waterproof mascara mixing with the tear trickling down Rochelle's cheek. Oh, and the fact that her wedding gown didn't fit.

Mary dropped the zipper pull, snatched a tissue from the dresser, and blotted under Rochelle's eyes. "Don't worry. We've got this."

"How?" The bride's voice was dangerously watery, like a Lake Mead's worth of tears threatened just behind the dam.

Exactly. How, genius? "Well, we've got two options. One is a shaper garment." She pulled the black piece of spandex from her tote bag. It was hers, but she'd be happy to look lumpy under her own dress if it meant Rochelle looked fabulous.

"But"—Rochelle rubbed a hand over her midsection—"what about the baby?"

Mary looked over her shoulder. So far, they were alone in Rochelle's bedroom in her suite at La Villa. Her bridesmaids and her mother had gone out into the living room to cruise the array of snacks that had been delivered. Still, she whispered, "I'm sure the baby will be fine. It's the size of a banana. A small one. A little compression won't hurt."

Rochelle's lower lip stuck out.

"Or," Mary continued, "we can go with option B."

"What's option B?"

"We do minor surgery on your dress." Mary circled behind the bride and examined the inside of her gown. There appeared to be enough fabric folded into the side seams to let out and give Rochelle's baby bump a little more space. And she knew someone who sewed.

"Can we? Do we have time?" Rochelle twisted to look at her over her shoulder.

"Of course we have time. You're the bride. Nothing starts until you're ready." At least Alex wouldn't be hovering today, checking that everything was perfect. She silently thanked the thieves who'd stolen the catalytic converter from his car in the hospital parking lot. Rafe had picked him and his mother up from the hospital earlier in the Tank. And now both Villas were at his mother's new rehab facility. Without wheels. Though the many just-checking-in texts he'd sent her indicated sitting with his mother wasn't a full-time job. "I need to make a quick call. Why don't you go have a snack?"

"A snack? Snacks are what got me into this mess. That and Rohaan's IUD-defying swimmers." Rochelle's chin trembled.

"A snack will keep your blood sugar up. We can't have you fainting as you walk down the aisle. How would that look on the big screens Alex set up for you?"

"You're right, I'll eat some carrots."

Mary helped Rochelle step out of the dress and laid it on the bed. After blotting under her eyes, Rochelle put on the fluffy robe with the La Villa logo on the chest and left the bedroom to join the raucous group of women in the main room. It sounded like they were enjoying the champagne Alex had provided. Too bad the bride couldn't drink any.

With the door shut, she called Evie. "I need you here at La Villa," she said as soon as Evie picked up.

"Can't," Evie said tightly. "Bees."

"Bees?"

"The rain last week sent everything into bloom, and now there are bees everywhere."

"I don't suppose anyone has a can of pesticide?" Mary was only half joking.

"Believe me, I asked. But the botanical garden folks flipped out. Apparently, pollination and the health of the bee population are more important than our guests' comfort." Evie's flat tone showed what she thought of the gardeners' priorities.

"Shit. What can we do?"

"The pest control company I called suggested a natural citronella repellent that won't harm the bees. They're on their way."

"Okay, that sounds perfect," Mary said. "I'll ask Rafe to meet them there since he's closer. I'll get there as soon as I can to take over the wedding. Could you come here? Please? With your sewing kit. We need more room for baby in Rochelle's gown."

"Dammit," Evie said. Footsteps scuffed on gravel. "Didn't she just have her final fitting this week?"

"Baby-growing bodies can be unpredictable, I guess," Mary said. "And the shaper garment was a no-go."

"I'll be there in ten." A car chirped.

"Same." Mary picked up her bag and walked out to give her bride the news.

This bride's tears were one hundred percent Mary's fault. And they weren't even the worst part of the situation. Mary rubbed Teagan's back as she sucked on her inhaler.

"I'm so, *so* sorry," Mary murmured.

Twyla gripped her bride's hand. "She'll be okay now that we've got her medicine."

Teagan set aside her inhaler and took a tentative, shallow breath. Her voice came out raw and scratchy. "Better than Aunt Beth would've been if one of those bees had stung her. God knows if she has an EpiPen on her."

Mary made a mental note. She needed one of those for her wedding kit. "Better now?" she asked.

"Yeah. I just need to stay away from the flowers and that citronella spray. Remind me next time I get married to do it indoors."

"Next time?" Twyla smacked her arm. "Here I am, beside you in sickness, and there you go—"

Teagan stopped her with a kiss. "It was a joke."

"You're not allowed to joke after almost dying on me."

"Hey." Teagan patted Twyla's hand. Twyla's knuckles were white as she gripped Teagan's other hand. "It's all good. We're married."

"We are. Finally." Twyla leaned forward and kissed her bride.

A smile spread over Mary's face. Moments like this were why she'd taken the risk of starting her wedding planning business. The love overflowing the brides' eyes made all the stress, the late nights, and the time away from her own loved ones worth it. Seeing the brides happy together in this private moment was better even than the kiss at the end of the ceremony Mary had so carefully choreographed.

"Now, let's fix your makeup so we can get this party started," she said. Fortunately, Teagan and Twyla had done their own, and it was much less formal than Rochelle's makeup. A little powder, mascara, and a fresh application of lip gloss had them both looking refreshed and ready despite Teagan's red eyes and pale cheeks.

Mary had just re-steamed the back of Teagan's gown and handed her a bottle of water when her phone rang. Alex. She sent it to voice mail and instead tapped out a chipper text.

No time to talk, but everything's great!!!

Three exclamation points were a little much. She backspaced over one of them. It still looked like she was trying too hard. She backspaced again. One exclamation point was good. It expressed excitement and didn't make it seem like she was lying at all. Shit, now she'd spent entirely too much time on a one-sentence text. He'd have been watching the bubbles and be concerned that it had taken her that long to type it. He'd know she was lying. She backspaced one more time. No punctuation sounded breathless and distracted. Two accurate descriptors of her current mood. She hit send.

She'd have added a thumbs-up emoji or three if she had the time.

"Everything okay?" Teagan asked.

"What? Everything's fine." If she repeated the lie enough, it might come true.

Teagan sighed and looked out the window of the small class-room they'd been given as a brides' room. Holding glasses of champagne, their guests meandered through the bee-free garden. "I'm so glad you're here. We couldn't have had this gorgeous day without you."

Mary grinned. All the stress? Totally worth it. "Thank you. When you're back from your honeymoon, I'd love it if you'd write a short testimonial. But now, if you're feeling up to it, you should rejoin your guests. And have something to eat."

Twyla put a hand on her wife's back. "Come on. I want one of those mini empanadas while they're still hot."

The wives left the room, hand in hand, and Mary had only a second to smile with pride before her phone rang again. She reached to silence it—could Alex really not understand that she was work-ing?—when she saw it was Evie. She tapped to answer.

"Bad news."

Mary sucked in a breath. "Again?"

"You remember Devon, Rohaan's nephew?"

"He's the ring bearer. Oh no, did something happen to his suit?" She'd had her doubts about his tiny all-white suit, but Rochelle thought it was adorable. Mary envisioned a greasy stain like the one on the garage floor from the time the transmission pan on Michael's Mustang had rusted through. Maybe it was still salvageable.

"No. But he got into my sewing kit while I was fixing Rochelle's gown."

That didn't sound so bad. "How did the dress alteration go, by the way?"

"Great. Plenty of room for the bride and the bump. But the little thief stole my scissors while I wasn't looking."

Mary imagined his little jacket hacked with jagged holes like a slice of Swiss cheese. But Evie had said his suit was fine. Uh oh. "What did he do?"

"He snipped the rings off their pillow so he could try them on."

"No!" Silently, she started praying a Hail Mary.

"Fortunately, his dad, the best man, discovered it and took the rings away."

"Oh, thank God."

"Hold on. There's more. When the best man went to get his backpack with some toys for Devin out of his rental car, he reached into his pocket for the key, and the rings fell out."

Mary sucked in a breath.

"They rolled into a drain. It's got one of those grates on top, and we can't reach them."

"Holy Mary mother of God!" Both rings gone? Could she find a substitute? She still had her parents' bands. She could run home to get them. But Rochelle and Rohaan would notice that they weren't using their custom engraved rings. They didn't need that kind of stress on their wedding day.

"I think we might be able to rescue them," Evie said. "Do you have some tools to fish them out?"

"Tools?" She looked at her bag. She had needle and thread, safety pins, and a curling iron. Then she remembered the shop.

They had a pry bar they could use on the grate. And if that didn't work, they could use the borescope to look inside the grate and a flexible grabber to retrieve the rings. "Of course! I'll get Michael to bring them to you."

"Michael?" She could picture the curl of Evie's lip.

"Rafe is still here with me on bee duty."

"Okay. Fine. Just make sure he's courteous. We don't need him to stomp in here all surly and make a scene."

As much as she hated to admit that either of her brothers had a flaw, Evie was right. She encouraged Michael to stay in the back of the shop for exactly that reason. "I'll talk to him."

The moment they disconnected, she called her brother. It rang seven times, each second torture. When he finally answered, he said, "Everything okay?"

"Not really. Are you okay?"

"I was under a car."

If she'd asked Google to translate what he'd said into English, the screen would read, *Why the hell are you bothering me? But I'll be nice to you since you're my little sister.*

"Listen, I need a favor. The rings for Rochelle's wedding went down the drain in the parking lot. I need you to take a pry bar, the boroscope, and one of those grabby things to the parking lot at La Villa to get them out. And be subtle, please. I don't want anyone, especially the bride and groom, to find out."

"Can't you ask your boyfriend for help? He's got an entire maintenance crew."

Mary sucked in a breath. What would Alex say if he found out what had happened? Between the dress and the rings, he'd think her incompetent. She might not want to be his wedding planner for any future weddings, but a word from him would ruin her reputation in the city. It might even break the fragile trust they'd rebuilt. He wasn't like her brothers, who'd forgiven her again and again, who understood what it was like to be fallible.

"I'd rather he didn't find out. Can you help? Please?"

"Okay. I'll be there in ten."

"And don't drive anything ostentatious, okay?"

He snorted. "Ostentatious? Me?"

"No, seriously. I—"

But he'd already disconnected.

It would be fine. Especially since, with his car missing a catalytic converter, Alex was stuck at the rehab facility with his mother and couldn't see the wedding teetering on the brink of disaster. Between Evie, Michael, and Mary, they'd turn it around. She squared her shoulders and strode out into the warm evening to ensure that this wedding continued with no more catastrophes.

Chapter Twenty-Seven

Alex's first tip that something was wrong was the giant pickup truck in his reserved space. It was the kind where you needed a step to get into the cab even if you had long legs like his. The bed extended at least three feet beyond the painted white lines.

"What the fuck?" he grumbled, turning the wheel of Rafe's black Land Rover away from his usual spot. He'd bullied Rafe into leaving it with him after he'd dropped him and his mother at the rehab facility. Now, he was taking advantage of his exhausted mother's nap to check on the Richardson wedding. His nerves buzzed, and a million wedding disaster scenarios fought each other in his brain. Each one resulted in Ray Richardson publicly berating him and promising he'd use every tool he had to ensure Alex never got his hands on the Paradise.

He carefully pulled the SUV into a space at the end of the row. "Show up late one Saturday and everything goes to hell," he muttered.

Though since it was probably one of the Richardson wedding guests who'd stolen his spot, he'd overlook it this once. This wedding, if it was successful, put everything he wanted in his grasp. And that was the reason he'd left his mother in the care of the nursing staff to check on the results of Mary's careful planning. It wasn't that he didn't trust her, not exactly, but that the stakes were too high for anything to go wrong.

He stepped down from the Land Rover. As he turned toward the hotel, a small crowd of people in the middle of the next row of cars caught his eye. A maintenance person wearing coveralls—though they were blue instead of La Villa's standard-issue black—crouched on the pavement. Standing next to him was a Black man in a tuxedo and...was that Evie McAlister, his former employee? He strode toward them for a better look.

Before he reached them, the man in coveralls leaped up, his hand in a fist. "Got them!" he roared triumphantly.

Alex froze. That voice...that enormous build...it was Mary's brother Michael. What the fuck was he doing here?

Michael dropped something into Evie's hand, and she polished it with a cloth, then handed it to the man in the tux. He hugged Evie, then opened his arms to hug Michael but at the last minute, thought better of it and clapped him on the shoulder. Smart man, if he wanted to keep blood off his tux. The well-dressed man strode toward the main entrance to the hotel.

Evie looked up at Michael with an elated smile, but soon it faltered, and she glanced away. She stiffened when her gaze fell on Alex. She punched Michael's arm and muttered something.

Alex forced a careless swagger into his stride. "Miss McAlister. As I recall, you no longer work at La Villa. May I ask what you're doing here?"

Someone who wasn't paying attention might have missed it, but he noticed Michael edging slightly in front of Evie.

"It's not your business what she's doing here," Michael growled. "We're not inside La Villa."

"As a business owner, certainly you understand that my property extends to the parking lot, which you were clearly tampering with." Alex nodded at the crowbar next to the displaced grate at Michael's feet. "I ask again, what are you doing here, Miss McAlister? Or do I need to call security?"

"I'm all the security—"

Evie silenced Michael with a hand on his arm. "One of the guests lost an item in the drain here. Mary asked us to help."

"I see. And where is Mary?"

"She's...um...I'm sure she's close by. I'll call her."

Alex's blood turned to resin in his veins, stiffening his body. "No, I'll call her." He lifted his phone to his ear.

Evie nudged Michael. "We'll just..."

"Stay," Alex barked as Mary's phone rang. She'd ignored his call earlier. Would she pick up now?

"Hi, Alex. Everything's going great. How's your mom?"

Everything didn't sound great. More like she'd taken someone's Adderall and washed it down with Red Bull.

"She's fine. How are you?"

"Great. Just great. Everything's perfect," she chirped, her voice too high.

"Then why are your brother and Evie here?"

"Here? Oh! You're...here."

"Yes, and I'd like to speak with you. Can you come to the parking lot?"

"I...um...I'm really busy. With the bride."

"You mean Rochelle?"

He heard her suck in a breath and sigh it out. "No. I had to put out a fire at my other wedding. Evie and I swapped."

"You mean to tell me that Miss McAlister is managing the most important wedding of my life? After I *fired her?*"

Evie winced at his raised tone.

"Yes," Mary said, "she is. I needed her skills. She's come through for us today. Everything is on track."

"It is not on track if she's here and Miss Richardson's wedding coordinator isn't. I need you here. Now."

Suddenly, Michael was in his face. "Don't order my sister around like that."

Alex glared up at the bigger man. "She is working for me, Michael. I can issue her orders as I would any other employee."

His face went red. "Any other—"

"Hand the phone to Michael, please," Mary said, her voice low.

He did and narrowed his eyes as Michael said a few "okays," then handed the phone to Evie. Alex stood with his hands on his hips, sweating in his suit. The top of his head was going to blow off any minute. Mary had let him down and was running the Richardson affair like someone's backyard tent wedding. Even though she knew how important it was to him. It only proved he was wrong to think he could rely on anyone besides himself.

Evie disconnected the call and handed the phone back to him. "She's on her way. Come on, Michael." She turned toward the hotel.

"Where do you think you're going?" Alex said, jogging to get between her and his building.

"Until Mary gets here, you need a wedding coordinator. The entertainment is scheduled to start in twelve minutes. Unless you want to delay?"

Fuck his life. She knew he hated anything to run late. He had to wrest back control. "Not him. I can't have a grease monkey walking into my lobby."

Evie stuck her nose in the air. "We're going in through the service entrance. This way, Michael." She strode off, her heels clicking on the pavement.

Twelve minutes? He had to get going if he wanted to check that Ray Richardson hadn't noticed his daughter's wedding going to shit. And talk him down if he had.

At the back of the ballroom they were using for the ceremony, the stage was set up for the fire dancers. Good. And the large video screens he'd added to the setup yesterday stood in front of the red-curtained windows. They extended along both walls to the other end of the room, where the ceremony would take place. No one would miss a moment of this showcase for the La Villa brand.

Black-suited servers passed hors d'oeuvres. That was Mary's uninspired idea. His addition to the cocktail hour stood out: the walking bar. One of the most attractive athletes in La Villa's gladiator show had agreed to move through the crowd inside a rolling metal rack shaped like a chariot. Guests could admire his muscles as they plucked a glass of champagne from the rack. In his short tunic and leather spaulders, he seemed popular with the female guests.

Alex breathed out a relieved sigh. After the shit week he'd had, something was finally going to plan. Even if Mary herself wasn't here.

He scanned the room until he found Ray Richardson talking to Rohaan's father, Omar. Alex made his way to his favorite bartender's setup.

"Evening, Mr. Villa," Elton said, already reaching under the bar.

"Make it two, please, Elton. And whatever the father of the groom is drinking."

Elton carefully poured out two glasses of Macallan. As he filled another glass with club soda, Alex asked, "How's the event so far?"

"Folks seem to be having a good time. And I'm looking forward to the"—he lowered his voice as he returned the bottle of scotch to its hiding place—"surprise entertainment. Though I'm glad my bar is way over here." The bartender chuckled.

"It's perfectly safe," Alex said.

"If you say so, boss. I just want to keep fire far away from all these high-proof spirits. Cheers."

Alex gathered the three glasses and made his way to Ray and Omar.

"Evening, gentlemen. Congratulations." He handed the club soda to the father of the groom and the scotch to the father of the bride. "Are we enjoying ourselves so far?"

"It's certainly...entertaining." Ray nodded at Luca, the gladiator.

"Speaking of entertainment, what's happening on that stage back there?" Omar asked.

"Ah-ah-ah," Alex teased. "We've got a surprise lined up. No one will forget Rochelle and Rohaan's wedding." Cierra's aerialist would be a pale shadow of tonight's spectacle.

"For what I'm paying, I hope not." Ray chuckled. He sipped his scotch. "You have something special here, Alex. A surprisingly pleasant balance of elegance and over-the-top panache. I think you could bring a fresh perspective to the heart of the Strip."

His heart pounded. "Thank you. If I'm approved to purchase the Paradise, you won't regret it. La Villa Prime will be even more spectacular."

The lights dimmed. When he looked toward the stage and spotted Mary standing behind it, his heartbeat slowed, and warmth spread through his body. She was here. Everything would be all right.

"Gentlemen, would you like to come with me to get a better view of the entertainment?" he asked.

Omar eyed the crowd pressing closer to the stage. "I think I'll enjoy it from back here."

"So will I," Ray said. "Where can I get another glass of this? Somehow, I don't think it's the scotch I paid for."

"It's my gift to you. Go see Elton." Alex waved toward the bald bartender. "He'll take care of you."

With a nod, he made his way toward Mary. He'd just reached the roped-off safety zone around the stage when the entertainers emerged. Wearing slim-fitting leather trunks, Dante Campo and two other muscular men stepped onto the stage. They carried staffs and chains, and Dante set a pair of buckets at the front of the stage. The guests gasped and stepped back when fire erupted from each container with a whoosh.

One man lit the ends of his staff and twirled it, the flames leaping in a hypnotic circle. The crowd oohed, and Alex relaxed. This wedding was going to be magnificent. Unforgettable. Not only that, but he was helping the Campos. Donna Campo's curse didn't stand a chance. Everything he wanted was in his grasp.

Dante lit his prop, a small ball that dangled from a chain. He swung it slowly, then faster. When the third man lit another staff, the spectacle was complete. Heat billowed from the stage and prickled Alex's skin. The whirling fire whooshed over the sound of the crowd's gasps. The guests cheered when the three men synchronized their movements and three wheels of fire spun in parallel.

Alex glanced over at Mary to share a look of triumph. But she wasn't there. Instead, Rochelle stood against the wall in her dazzling white gown, gazing at the performance, her lips open in awe.

This. This was perfect. Rochelle would never forget her wedding. No one would. Especially not her father. The Paradise was his.

But where had Mary gone? She should be here, at his side, so he could whisper to her about the great work they'd done together to pull off the wedding of the year in less than two months. So she could whisper back that his idea for the fire dancers was brilliant and not the potential disaster she'd called it when he'd first suggested it. Maybe she'd brush her fingers against his, acknowledging the less public side of their partnership and reassuring him that everything in both his professional and personal life was coming together in a way he'd never dreamed possible.

He glanced back at the stage, and that was when it happened.

Something flew off Dante's chain into the audience. No, not into the audience. A flame ignited on the spaulder covering Luca's right shoulder. He shrieked, a higher-pitched sound than Alex could've imagined coming from such a large body. He ripped off the blazing leather and flung it off, making his champagne glasses rattle ominously. The spaulder hit the wall, and less than a second later, fire licked up the red window curtain.

Half of the guests kept their gazes locked on the stage. They must not have seen the fiery projectile. The other half backed away from the flaming curtain.

Alex pushed toward the fire. "Luca, are you okay?" he asked the gladiator.

"Yeah, sorry, I didn't mean to—"

"Help me put it out." Alex grabbed two glasses of champagne from Luca's chariot and tossed the wine at the curtain. Although the velvet had ignited quickly, he knew it had been treated with a fire retardant. No casino owner worth his gaming license would allow any flammable furnishings in his establishment.

But panic was almost as damaging as fire, and he couldn't allow it to take hold. He and Luca splashed the flames with glass after puny glass of champagne. They managed to keep it from spreading further, but fire blazed through the velvet. So much for that fire retardant.

Foam exploded from his right and coated what remained of the conflagration. Mary was a Valkyrie with her legs spread, bracing against the extinguisher's kick, her curls wild, an inferno glowing in her eyes.

He had never craved her more than in that moment.

She dropped the extinguisher, shook out her hand, and turned to the closest guests. "Are you all right?" she asked. That was Mary, always looking out for everyone.

"You good, Luca?" Alex asked.

The gladiator's hand trembled as he picked up a glass of champagne and poured it down his throat. He wiped his mouth with the back of his hand. "I think so."

Alex turned back to the guests. "Everything's fine. Here, have more champagne." He passed glasses from the rack to the guests. The smell of burning chemicals prickled in his nose.

"Oh my god!" Rochelle rushed up in a swirl of white satin. "Is everyone okay?"

"Everything's fine," Alex repeated. "You can all go back to watching…" But the show had stopped, and now every eye turned his way. "It's all good," he announced, louder, hoping that saying it would make it true.

"Rochelle, do you need to sit down?" Mary asked.

It was only then he noticed the bride shivering. Like he had an extra sense for his bride's health, Rohaan rushed up to her. "Baby, are you all right?"

"I—I think so. Do you think we need to cancel the wedding?"

"Cancel the wedding?" Alex's pulse whooshed in his ears, louder than the muttering guests. "Over a little fire? No need. Look, it's already out."

"Alex." Mary set a hand on his arm. "Give her a minute to process."

"Process?" Fear licked up Alex's spine, faster than the blaze had moved on the curtain. "There are five hundred people here. To see a wedding." What would Ray Richardson think if he'd spent six figures on a wedding that didn't happen?

"Baby." Rohaan rubbed Rochelle's bare arms. "We're okay. All our friends and family are okay. Even the gladiator and the fire dancers are okay. And I'd really like to marry you tonight. Take all the time you need."

Alex winced. The longer they delayed the wedding, the more upset the father of the bride was likely to be. Richardson was no prude, but how angry would he be if it was Alex's fault his grand-child was born out of wedlock?

"If I may," he said. "I think we should all take a deep breath. Let's try it. Breathe in blue. One...two...three...four. Hold it. One... two...three...four. Then let it out pink. One...two...three...four... five...six. Now repeat." He led them through the exercise again, and even Luca joined in. By the fourth time, Rochelle's face had returned to her natural color, and her hands were steady.

"Better?" Alex asked.

"It's okay if you need more time," Mary said.

Alex scowled at her. It was anything but okay.

"I'm good," Rochelle said. "Though if one more thing goes wrong, I'm going to take it as a sign."

"Nothing else will happen," Alex promised. "Your wedding will be as glorious as we planned. Now, should we go set up?" He tipped his head toward the other end of the room where the wedding dais waited.

"Okay." Rochelle gathered up her skirts and headed toward the main doors.

"Joey," Mary muttered into her earpiece. "Please have the ushers seat the guests."

Alex took another calming breath. The flaming gladiator would be a funny story the Richardson family could tell at their next gathering.

"Rohaan, please gather your groomsmen at the front." Mary waved at the dais.

The ushers were already organizing the guests into their seats. Good. Though it would take a few minutes. Five hundred people didn't do anything quickly.

"Don't forget the video monitors," he said.

He caught her eye-roll before she said, "Joey, the screens."

Along both sides of the room, the video screens lit with a prepared slideshow of Rochelle and Rohaan, from baby photos to their engagement portraits. All except one. The screen closest to the fire-blackened curtain remained dark.

He tapped Mary's shoulder. "That one's not working."

"I'll check on it." Then, into her earpiece, "Evie, you've got eyes on the bride?" She walked to the video screen, tapped the power button, then circled to the back of it.

"Oh," she said. She moved behind the massive screen.

A second later, the room went black. Someone shrieked.

It was black like only an interior room can be, the darkness so thick it pressed on his eyeballs. It was dungeon-dark. Desert-dark, but without the starlight. Doomsday-dark.

A few camera flashlights flicked on. Giggles and murmurs filled the guests' initial startled silence.

Alex tapped on his camera's flashlight, strode to the nearest window, and tugged the heavy curtain open. Outside, La Villa's tower was a void against the streetlights and the neon of the nearby businesses. Shit. His building, and only his building, was dark on a Saturday night. He could almost feel the money draining from his bank account.

"What happened?" Ray Richardson's voice rose above the others.

Mary's face lit from underneath, just like when they used to joke around at Halloween when they were kids. Her voice wobbled. "It looks like we have a slight electrical problem."

Slight? His entire fucking building was out of power. He could only imagine the chaos in the casino below them. In fact, he didn't have to imagine it. Text messages erupted across his lock screen, and the device vibrated with a call. Two. Three.

"Everyone, if you could, please turn on your flashlights," Mary said. "Stay seated if you can. Ushers, please help guide people to their seats. We'll start in a few minutes."

"Start?" Alex cracked his first knuckle. "How are we going to—"

"We'll get through this," Mary said. "Don't worry."

Too late. Alex's lungs felt a size too small, and his heart battered against his ribs. He'd lost control of the situation. He was as powerless as he'd been that night the investigators pounded on their door.

As his phone screen lit with a cascade of texts, it buzzed again with a call from his casino manager. "I've got to take this. Are you sure—"

"Go." She nodded at his phone. "Take care of that."

In the dim light of the guests' phones, he made his way out of the ballroom to the relative quiet of the hallway.

He was fucked, and not in the good way that he and Mary had been doing.

In fact, sleeping with Mary and letting himself be distracted by hormones and fucking *feelings* was what had made him take his eye off the prize to begin with. He'd made a mistake in trusting Mary with this critical event.

He'd always known he could trust only himself.

Chapter Twenty-Eight

S he knew what had happened. The rogue flames from the damned fire dancers Alex had insisted on, not to mention his ridiculous gladiator's vegan leather armor, had burned the wall behind the curtain and shorted the wiring. And when she'd plugged the faulty screen into a nearby outlet, she'd overloaded the circuit. She hadn't thought the screens were necessary in the first place since they weren't at a flipping sporting event and likely wouldn't need to do an instant replay of the I-dos.

Though she'd known from the beginning what a control freak Alex was. She should've known not to believe him when he'd promised not to interfere in her planning.

She still wasn't sure why the overloaded circuit had taken down power to the entire hotel, but she knew one thing: she was the wedding planner, so it was her responsibility.

And from the squinty-eyed look Alex had given her before he'd turned away to take his call, he agreed.

Not that she blamed him. Losing power in the building had to be stressful. How many hotel guests, diners, and gamblers were complaining, blowing up Alex's phone? Was anyone injured because of her mistake in plugging in the silly video screen?

She clenched her fists, digging her nails into her palms. She couldn't worry about that now. She had to get the wedding back on track.

Thank goodness her walkie-talkie system was battery powered. "Joey, do you have the judge and the groomsmen ready?"

Joey's voice chirped in her ear. "Rohaan, the judge, and the guys are ready. I've even got the ringbearer up here. Want me to send him to you?"

"No, without the lights, better keep him there with his dad. You've got eyes on both rings?"

"They're here, thanks to Evie's needlework."

Mary sent up a silent thanks to St. Anthony for helping her brother find the lost rings. She'd give one of her spa days to Evie to thank her for saving the day. Twice.

"Evie, are Rochelle and the bridesmaids ready?" she asked.

There was a brief silence. "I think we need you, Mary."

Her heart skipped a beat. "Are you in the bride's room?"

"No, we're outside by the pool."

"Oh, God. Not *in* the pool?" Could Rochelle have accidentally fallen in? Mary hurried out of the ballroom.

"No. Just come. Quickly, please. I'm no good at this."

She broke into a run as soon as she reached the hall that led to the exit nearest the pool. When she pushed open the exterior door, she easily spotted Rochelle's white dress. It caught the light from the neighboring casino and seemed to glow as the bride paced across the pool deck.

"Hi, Rochelle." Mary approached her cautiously. "How are we doing?"

"Not good. Not good." The whites of her eyes were wild in the dim light. "This is a sign. I thought the baby was a sign we should get married, but now the universe is telling me it's a mistake."

Evie melted into the shadows. She really wasn't good at this.

But Mary had to try. "The universe?" She stepped closer. "So we had a tiny fire. And a blackout. You should see the ballroom with everyone's phones lit up. It's so romantic."

"And my dress. And I know about the rings falling into the

drain. Devon told me about it. I'm afraid if I step down that aisle, Rohaan's going to get struck down with appendicitis. Or Daddy will have a heart attack."

Mary held out her palm. Rochelle looked at it for a moment, then laid her trembling hand on top. Mary clasped it.

"You don't have to get married tonight," she said.

Evie gasped in the darkness.

"You don't," Mary said, her voice stronger. "But there's a reason you decided to marry Rohaan. Even before you knew about the baby. Do you remember why?"

"I love him," she muttered. "But that doesn't mean I have to marry him."

"No, it doesn't. Why do you love him?"

Rochelle paused. "I'm the best version of myself when I'm with him."

Mary's heart fluttered. She felt like that with Alex, too. She wondered briefly if she made him a better person. Then she forced her attention back on the bride. "Sounds like a good reason to stay with him."

"Of course I want to stay with Rohaan," Rochelle snapped. "But marriage? It's a big commitment. What if all these disasters are telling me it's not right for us?"

"In the big scheme of things, none of the things that have gone wrong are all that important. Everyone's safe. You're glowing. And Rohaan wants nothing more than to be your husband. Do you want me to get him?"

"No. No," Rochelle muttered, pacing away. "He'll just hug me and kiss me and make me feel better. I'll think more clearly on my own."

"Will you? I always do my best thinking with someone else. My brothers. My employees. And Alex."

"Alex?" Rochelle snorted. "He has a nice hotel, and he's bent over backward to accommodate this wedding because of Daddy, but you're the one doing all the work. Meanwhile, he's getting all the credit."

"You think so?" The flutters died in her heart, and her stomach felt heavy. She remembered the curl of Alex's lip when he turned away from her in the ballroom. If he didn't appreciate her help, why was she even doing it? Her tripled fee and the spa treatments weren't worth the time away from her brothers. The near-disaster at the reception for Teagan and Twyla, who'd believed in her when few others did.

"Rohaan would never take credit for my work. He always shines the spotlight on me."

"He sounds like a winner." Mary's voice trembled. But this wasn't about her problems. She cleared her throat. "You sure you don't want to prove how much you love him by walking down that aisle despite everything that's tried to get in your way?"

"Maybe you're right. Maybe it's a test."

"Like God tested Job," Mary said.

"God was an asshole to Job."

Mary was glad for the darkness that hid her shocked expression. She and her brothers had a healthy respect for God, who'd done a lot of taketh-ing away in their lives.

Rochelle continued, "And the universe has been an asshole to us tonight. But I'm going to show everyone, including the fucking universe, how strong we are together." Rochelle pointed her middle finger at the sky. "Screw you, universe. I love Rohaan, and we're going to live happily ever after, starting tonight."

Mary sighed her relief. She tapped her earpiece. "Joey, start the processional. We're on our way."

It would take two massages to release the knot of tension in Mary's shoulders. And it would be a long time before she could have a glass of wine to relax her jangled nerves. She hadn't even spared a thought for the wedding banquet. Was the kitchen able to keep everything warm without power?

One disaster at a time.

And from the sound of it, they were approaching another one.

Ray Richardson's raised voice echoed down the hall. "What kind of second-rate, cheap-ass establishment doesn't have a backup generator?"

"We've got a fucking generator. It just hasn't come on yet. My maintenance chief is working on it."

Mary winced at Alex's volume. "Rochelle, just a second. I'm going to make a call."

"Okay," Rochelle said. "I'm going to see if I can calm Daddy down." She marched toward the arguing men.

Mary plucked her phone out of her pocket and dialed her brother. "Michael, are you still here?" she asked as soon as he picked up. "There's an issue with the generator at La Villa, and—"

"Evie already called me. I just met up with one of the maintenance guys, and he's taking me to it."

"Good. Thank you."

"No problem. Need me to call Rafe to raid the church supply closet for candles?"

Mary imagined five hundred candles lighting up the wedding. Romantic, but open flame hadn't been a friend to them tonight. "Better skip it. The phone flashlights are doing the job."

"Okay. Looks like I'm here. I'll have this bad boy purring like a kitten in no time."

"Thank—" But her brother had already disconnected.

Alex and Ray Richardson were still arguing, a little more quietly now that Rochelle clasped Ray's arm.

Mary spoke into her earpiece. "Ready, Joey?"

"Bridesmaids are lined up. Just waiting on the bride," he said.

"Okay, we're on our way to you."

Pasting a falsely confident smile on her face, Mary stepped between Alex and the Richardsons. "Ray, Rochelle, we're ready for you. It's time to get married."

Rochelle's grin was fearless. "I'm ready to show the universe who's the boss. And it's Rohaan and me. Come on, Daddy."

"But—" Ray protested.

"Not now, Daddy. I want to get married. You can fight with Mr. Villa later."

Her father's frown melted as he looked down into his daughter's face, lit up by her phone's flashlight. "You're so beautiful. Even in the dark."

"Thank you, Daddy. Now, walk me down the aisle."

He crooked his arm toward her, and his daughter threaded her hand through it. Together, they walked toward the ballroom door, their flashlights lighting the way.

As Rochelle proceeded toward her groom and her future, a tiny flame lit inside Mary, making her chest expand like a hot-air balloon. She sighed. She'd never have a father to walk her down the aisle, but maybe she'd find her groom someday. If things kept going well, the man beside her might want the job.

She shot him a tentative smile. But he was too busy scowling at the father and daughter to see. She took his hand. "We did it," she said softly.

He flicked off her hand like he'd been stung, and when he turned to face her, his eyebrows smashed together. "What, fucked everything up?"

"It wasn't that bad. Accidents happen."

"Accidents don't happen in my hotel. Today has been humiliating to Ray Richardson. He'll never forgive me."

"Accidents are a part of life. It's how you deal with them that's important. And a beautiful wedding is happening right through there." She waved at the ballroom door, where Evie stood, staring at them instead of watching the ceremony. A few curious people in the back rows of chairs leaned back, watching them too. She turned her back to them and tried to shield their conversation from the nosy guests. "You've had a trying day with your mother and all. When's the last time you ate? We can probably find something in the kitchen. I've got a granola bar in my bag."

"You can't solve a problem like this with food!" he shouted. "Everything that happened today was one hundred percent preventable. If you're in control of your work. And your personal life."

"What are you saying, Alex?" She kept her voice low and even. "Everyone did their best. That's all we can ask of anyone, including ourselves."

"That sounds like some nursery-school bullshit. I live in the real world, where results are what's important. And a dark casino on a Saturday night and a disaster of a wedding aren't results I can be proud of. I'll never get the Paradise now." His face twisted with pain. She'd never seen him lose control like that before, not even when they were kids.

"Wait. *That's* why you're upset? Because you won't get to buy that stupid casino? Not because Rochelle and Rohaan might've missed their chance at happiness, or because someone might've been injured in the dark?"

"Stupid casino?" He finally lowered his voice. "I explained to you what it means to me."

She put her hand on his arm. "You don't need the Paradise to prove you're a better man than your father. Anyone who knows you already believes it."

"Not Ray Richardson. Not the gaming board. Not anyone who matters."

The flame in her chest flickered and died. The balloon shriveled up, leaving her heart enshrouded in ice. "No one who matters?"

"Without the support of the gaming board, I might as well call it quits. They'll take pieces of my business away from me until I've got nothing left."

"Nothing?" She squeezed his arm. "You'd have friends. People who love you."

"Yeah, right," he scoffed. "People only care about what I can do for them. I learned that when we lost everything. Even you dropped me." Finally, he met her gaze. "This is a business relationship. Don't worry, you'll get your fee despite how shitty everything turned out."

She gasped and snatched her hand away. A business relationship? Sure, she'd done everything in her power to make this wedding a success. But she'd taken it on for personal reasons, despite knowing it was too much with the rest of her responsibilities. She'd lost sleep. She'd endangered the shop. She'd even taken her eye off her brothers. And when one thing after another had gone wrong, she'd called in favors from Evie and her brothers. All to help Alex.

Was he grateful? No! He said it himself: she didn't matter. Cold realization swept through her like the dawn breeze in the desert, scouring out all her pride, all her happiness, all her hope. She'd let herself become one of his disposable women. He'd pampered her and flattered her as part of their *business relationship*. How long was he going to lead her on after? Weeks? Days?

She was worth more than that.

He'd crushed her heart half her life ago, and she'd forgiven him. All these years later, she'd made the mistake of entrusting the sad, patched-up thing to him again, and he'd dropped it on the hard marble-tiled floor, smashing it into a million pieces.

Alex didn't care about her. He'd only been using her to get what he wanted.

No, he wasn't. Not anymore.

"I quit. You can keep your damned fee." When she hitched her heavy tote bag onto her shoulder, her weak finger twinged, but she ignored it. "And we're through. You can lose my number. Again. Goodbye, Alex."

Mary turned on her heel and marched out of La Villa, her flashlight guiding her into the starry night.

Chapter Twenty-Nine

Alex stared at Mary's back as she marched out.

He'd hurt her. He had to, even though as he'd watched the light go out in her eyes, his gut felt worse than when Michael and Rafe pummeled it all those years ago.

If he hadn't pushed her away, she'd have stubbornly kept shoving her quarters into the slot until her bucket was empty. He'd never pay out. Especially not now that the Paradise was lost.

When had it all gone wrong? When had he lost control? It happened long before he'd agreed to hire Dante and his gang of human liability risks. It was the moment he'd allowed his personal life to seep into his business.

When he'd hired Mary for all the wrong reasons.

He hadn't hired her because she was the best. Vegas was thick with wedding planners, all with more experience, and he could've brought in any one of them. He'd insisted on Mary Forza because of the hope buried deep inside him. Hope that she could forgive him. That he could be worthy of her love. That if he let her in, they could be stronger together.

It was utter bullshit.

If he'd been thinking with his head instead of with his pathetic heart, he'd have seen that Mary had too many other priorities to give this wedding the attention it required. He'd witnessed her exhaustion when she'd almost fallen asleep in that meeting with the bride and groom. He should've replaced her then. If he'd done that, maybe he could've separated his professional life from his personal one and pulled off a successful wedding.

That pitiful little spark of hope inside him whispered, *Maybe then Mary could've loved you.*

No. He should've stayed away from Mary Forza altogether. He'd built his business from nothing, relying only on himself. He'd never allowed himself to have feelings for anyone. Not until Mary.

Emotional entanglements were for chumps.

He was a chump.

Despite what Mary said, vulnerability was a rabid dog, and it had bitten him in the ass. He'd lost everything, and to save Mary from being tainted by his failure, he'd shoved her away again.

It had been surprisingly easy. She must not have cared that much.

He didn't know if that made him feel better or worse.

Realizing he was staring at a closed door, he shook his head.

None of it mattered now. His wedding planner had quit, and he had to keep up the farce of it all until the bitter end. Although his business was in the shitter, he had some pride left. And it was pride, not any soft feelings for the bridal couple, that forced his feet toward the ballroom.

He'd organize whatever chaos was happening in there. He didn't need help. Especially not from Mary, with her tumultuous curls and those soul-shattering eyes.

Crossing her arms, Evie glared at him as he approached the ballroom.

"Your boss quit. You should leave too," he barked, brushing past her into the dark room.

He pulled up short. Inside the ballroom was...enchantment.

The guests' phone flashlights pointed forward, illuminating the bridal party and the officiant with a soft glow that reminded him of candlelight Mass on Christmas Eve. Even from behind the back row of seats, Alex heard Rohaan's teary "I do" across the electrified hush of the ballroom as clearly as if the microphones and video screens had been powered on.

The witnesses broke the silence with soft murmurs and *awws*. The couple's brilliant smiles dazzled in the dim glow of five hundred white LEDs.

Alex's heartbeat slowed. This was pure magic, and for a second, he wished Mary could see it.

With a sudden whoosh, the air conditioning surged on, and light blinded him. The guests groaned, blinking in the restored electricity.

Shielding her eyes, Rochelle called out, "Turn off the lights. But keep your phones on."

Behind him, someone flicked off the chandeliers and plunged them back into darkness. The guests gave a pleased murmur and pointed their phones again toward the couple.

"Let's wrap this up," Rochelle said. "I'm ready to be married."

Even the dour judge cracked a smile as she read out Rochelle's vows. After saying, "I do," Rochelle didn't wait for the judge's instruction. She threw her arms around Rohaan's neck and pressed a kiss to his lips.

Alex sighed. A wedding was something he was now certain he'd never have for himself. His mother would be heartbroken when he told her to stop hoping for grandchildren to dote on. But it was his fucking life, and if he wanted to live it alone, wallowing in failure, that was his right. Fortunately, he'd socked away enough cash to take care of Donna Campo and Mama, regardless of what happened to La Villa.

Turning on his heel, he led the way to the reception in the ballroom next door. The chandeliers blinded him. None of the magic from the ceremony lingered. It was just a regular wedding reception with dinner, a band, and cake. Even Joey could handle that. He'd set up the seating map and was guiding the guests to their tables.

Too bad Mary's fingerprints were all over the event, from the crispy potatoes she'd said were a better choice than pasta to the heirloom cake topper she'd admired when he brought it to the shop.

After a stop at the bar, he took his drink to a corner where he could practice being a lonely old curmudgeon.

Hours later, Alex wished another blackout would shut down the reception. He was tired of guests walking up to him to thank him for the work Mary had done.

One of the groomsmen had towed a tiny boy in a white suit up to him to ask where Evie had gone. He wanted to thank her for rescuing the wedding rings.

At least fifty guests told him how wonderful the ceremony had been. They called it enchanting and charming. Not at all how he'd have described the building-wide blackout.

Even his hotel manager texted him to thank him for sending Michael Forza down to help the engineers with the generator. Apparently, it was Michael's extensive knowledge of internal combustion engines that identified and repaired the problem.

He'd just picked up his third scotch from Elton when Rochelle towed her father up to him.

"Hello, Alex," she said.

"Congratulations on your wedding." Alex cleared his throat. "I'm sorry it didn't go as planned."

"No one will ever forget it." She shrugged. "I'm just glad to be married. And my father has something to say to you."

Ray sucked his teeth. Then he said, "I'm sorry, Villa. I know it wasn't your fault the power went out."

Alex blinked his eyes wide. It wasn't?

Ray continued, "I appreciate the creativity with which you resolved the problem. The ceremony really was beautiful."

"I—it wasn't me," he admitted. "Mary Forza had the idea for

the candlelit ceremony. And her brother Michael fixed the generator."

Ray twisted his mouth. "As I recall, you and the Forzas haven't always gotten along."

"We had a disagreement back when we were all younger."

"Good to see that you got past it. Seeing your collaboration with the Forzas gives me hope that you and the other owners on the Strip can come together to revitalize the Paradise."

Alex's heart pinged like one of the slot machines downstairs. "The Paradise? You mean—"

"I spoke hastily earlier, and I regret it." Ray Richardson's hand landed heavily on his shoulder. "I admire how you all worked together to ensure Rochelle married the man of her dreams."

"When I got cold feet," Rochelle said, "Mary reminded me of why I wanted to marry Rohaan in the first place."

She did? "And what reason was that?"

"I'm a better person when I'm with him."

Was Alex a better person with Mary? He'd felt amazing when they were together in San Diego. Like his burdens were lighter once he shared them with her. But he hated how out of control he felt tonight. How bile rose in his stomach and his eyes prickled.

Emotions made him weak. He'd known the danger of allowing Mary behind his defenses. He'd resisted letting anyone close for exactly this reason. With Mary, he'd done exactly what he'd laughed at so many others for doing. He'd allowed his feelings to get in the way of his business.

He'd endangered what he wanted most in the world: to tear down the Paradise, that symbol of his shame.

He stood up straight, willing the hard shell to re-form over his vulnerability. Despite what Ray thought, Alex was better off on his own. But he didn't have to share that conviction with him. "At La Villa, we have a whatever-it-takes attitude to ensure our guests' comfort and enjoyment," he said. "That will be our mantra at La Villa Prime, as well. I'll make the property a star on the Strip again. I'll rebuild it into a world-class resort."

"You're committed to the city, and the Strip?" Richardson asked. "Can I count on you to work with us for everyone's success?"

Mary had taught him that. How to combine his strengths with hers to make something better than he alone could have done. Alex's heart felt blackened and blistered like the wall in the other ballroom. "Of course."

"Then you have my vote in favor of the purchase," the older man said.

Alex waited for the satisfying feeling of a missing piece slotting into place. It never came. Instead, the empty pit inside him deepened.

He was hungry, like Mary said. Or stressed. Or too focused on this wedding to enjoy the victory. He half-wished he could tell Mary the news.

But he couldn't. He'd burned that bridge.

Tomorrow morning, he'd tell his mother instead. She'd be proud of him. Then he'd feel whole.

He forced a smile onto his face. "Thank you. You won't regret it."

Regret. That couldn't be what muffled the elation he should be feeling.

Chapter Thirty

Going to Mass always made her feel better, though the sacrament had a lot to overcome today after she'd been humiliated and heartbroken. Still, when the organist played a flawless run, Mary's heart fluttered weakly in her chest like a butterfly with an injured wing. She crossed herself and eased off the kneeler onto the seat.

Someone had taken the spot next to her on the pew. Michael looked pained in a collared shirt that strained across his broad chest and a pair of chinos with a knife-sharp crease over his shin. On his other side was Rafe. His shirt was new. Fashionable. The right size. Was this even her brother? She'd have gotten some holy water to sprinkle on him, but then she noticed his cuffs were rolled up over his hairy forearms. That was her Rafe.

"What are you two doing here?" Mary whispered. "It's not even Christmas."

Rafe leaned around Michael. "Hey, I come when it's not Christmas. I came with you last month at Pentecost."

Mary tightened her lips and raised her eyebrows, waiting.

"We wanted to check on you after last night." Michael ran his palms down his thighs where the fabric stretched tight across them. How long had it been since he'd worn anything but jeans and his coveralls? "Mary. Stop thinking about taking me shopping. Tell us what *you* need."

She blinked up at her brother. "What I need?" She kept her voice low. "I need to focus on the shop. After yesterday's fiasco—*fiascoes*—no one else will hire me for wedding planning."

"No. That's not what we're asking. What can we do to help you? We know you're hurting."

Rafe leaned around again, a wicked gleam in his eye. "Need us to go rough up that dickhead?"

Mary glanced around. The woman in the pew in front had turned to stare at them.

"We're in church!" Mary hissed.

Rafe shrugged. "Jesus flipped tables in front of the temple. I think he'd support a little violence when someone hurts our sister."

"No," she whispered. Then, more loudly, "No." Someone shushed her, but the nosy lady in front had to hear that her brothers weren't going to beat anyone up. Especially when it wasn't Alex's fault things had gone completely to shit yesterday. The wedding was her responsibility, and she'd blown it.

"Okay, then." Michael's big hand landed on her shoulder and awkwardly petted it. "What can we do? Want us to put up a flyer on the bulletin board outside the Fellowship Hall? Or at the gym?"

"A flyer? For what?" Around them, people surged to their feet as the priest and the lector walked up the aisle toward the altar. Mary and her brothers stood.

Michael leaned to whisper in her ear over the organist's crescendo. "For your wedding planning business."

"I'm done—" But the priest was talking. She muttered the response and crossed herself. As the congregation took their seats, Mary whispered to Michael, "I'm done with all that."

"What's she saying?" Rafe poked his head around Michael's bulk.

"Shh," someone behind them said.

Michael whispered to his brother. Rafe scowled. But it was time to remember their sins, and all three Forzas bowed their heads in silence.

The priest didn't give her enough time to recite them all. From not having a fire blanket on standby to not insisting the seamstress put extra give in Rochelle's gown to allowing Twyla and Teagan to plan an outdoor wedding in July, all the way to sleeping with Alex. She should've kept it friendly and professional and not let herself hope—

Mary joined in the penitential rite. She hadn't spared a thought for the risk to the family business. When every minute of her time was precious, every moment she'd spent on Alex was wasted. And all her hopes for the wedding business had been futile. Splitting her attention with her side hustle, what if she'd forgotten to do something important, like pay their taxes? Was Rafe still interested in modeling? Should she have supported his dreams? What about Michael? She had no idea what was going on with him.

At last, it was time to sit quietly for the readings. The words, "Give to your servant a teachable heart," struck her chest like an airbag. Unlike Solomon, she hadn't been given a teachable heart. She'd learned nothing. She'd let Alex break her heart a second time. How foolish was she to let him back in after he'd confessed that he didn't trust her enough to tell her about his father's crimes? She'd jumped in to help him, eyes closed, hoping that if she did, he'd trust her. She swallowed. Love her.

She shouldn't have been surprised when he'd pushed her away after she'd made a mistake. Many mistakes. She'd failed him. Forgiveness came with love, but none of the help she'd given him, none of the things she'd done for him, had made him love her.

Mary stood for the reading from the Gospel, but her mind was too busy to comprehend it. She'd always taken care of her family. Her mother's death had made her a caretaker. She loved taking care of others. Every time she helped someone, her heart glowed in her chest. She remembered all the little things she'd done to make Teagan and Twyla's wedding perfect, or as perfect as it could be, considering the bees and the asthma-inducing citronella. She remembered how Rochelle's eyelids fluttered closed in delight when she'd taken that first bite of cake at the tasting.

But love shouldn't come from what someone did for someone else. She loved her brothers because they were her brothers. Because they supported her no matter what. Because they were willing to beat someone up who'd broken her heart. As much as she appreciated their appearance at Mass this morning, she didn't love them because of anything they'd done.

Didn't she deserve the same?

Why had she thought anything she could do would make Alex love her?

Fuck him if he didn't love her, failures and all.

She crossed herself and silently recited an extra Act of Contrition for thinking a swear in church and tried her best to listen and pray during the rest of the service.

When Mass ended, her brothers hustled her outside into the bright sunshine, hardly allowing her time to wave goodbye to some old friends of her parents and the women's club. Michael had parked his pickup in the shade of a crooked tipu tree, but when they clambered inside, the black truck felt like an oven. Sandwiched between her brothers in the front seat, Mary fanned herself with her copy of the church bulletin while they waited for the air conditioning to turn cold.

"So, what's this all about?" she asked.

"You can't give up on your wedding planning business," Rafe said. "It makes you happy."

"The family business makes me happy. I love working with you two. And the wedding planning was a flop."

"It wasn't," he insisted. "Twyla and Teagan loved their wedding. And so did their guests. That aunt of theirs—"

"Aunt Beth?" Mary asked.

"The one who's allergic to bee stings. She cornered me and gushed about the garden and the food. She asked me if you did birthday parties, too."

"What did you say?" Her business was so new, she didn't know if she did birthday parties.

"I told her she'd better call you on Monday to get on your schedule because it's filling up."

"Rafael Paschal Forza. You did not lie to that woman."

"You know I hate my middle name," he growled. "And I didn't lie. You've got Cierra's wedding coming up in a couple of weeks. And your schedule will fill up. You're an amazing planner."

"Besides," Michael said, "you're fired."

"I quit, actually." Mary looked down into her lap. "He was about to fire me, though. In front of everyone."

"No. You're fired from Forza Elite Motors. Evie said she'll take over your responsibilities at the shop."

"What?" She stared at her brother. "You hate Evie."

"She does good work. I'll just keep to the shop."

Panic clawed up her throat. "But you can't fire me. I'm a Forza!"

"You'll still own a third of the shop. But you can't work there anymore." Michael crossed his arms.

"You can come visit if you want," Rafe said, patting her arm. "But you'll have to clear out your office. Otherwise, you'll be distracted from wedding planning when you come in."

"But Evie doesn't know how to run the shop. She hardly knows the difference between a Mustang and a Corvette."

Michael gave a disgusted snort.

"She'll learn," Rafe said. "You know you'll be happier helping people celebrate their love than shuttling people to the airport or making sure no one pukes in Nick Cage."

The thought of never having to hold back another bachelorette guest's hair filled her with relief. And envisioning happy couples like Twyla and Teagan in their wedding finery filled her with the peace she normally felt after Mass.

Michael exchanged a glance with Rafe. "Besides, Rafe has some news, too."

"News?" She raised her eyebrows.

"Yeah. I...um...I'm going to do more modeling. My agent has me booked on some gigs in LA next month."

"Your...agent?"

"Yeah." His cheeks went red. "But my buddy Axe is going to start working at the shop."

She spun to face Michael. "And you're okay with this?"

He shrugged. "Guess I have to be. You two have gotten too big for the car biz. Rafe's earning more for this LA gig than we make in a month."

Mary spun back to face Rafe. "Holy shit. I guess you'll be okay without me."

"Of course we will," Michael said. "We'll all be okay. Financially. The question is, are you okay after what that asshole Alex did?"

"He's not an asshole. He just...his business is important to him. I fooled myself into thinking he cared about me, too." She'd thought her picture on his desk meant more than it did. His cleaner probably moved it next to his mother's photo.

Rafe put his hand over hers. "You do so much for everyone. It's about time someone took care of you. Let us do that for you. Until you find someone who's not a selfish pig like Alessandro Villa."

Mary hummed like she agreed with him. But after Alex had shredded her heart so thoroughly, she wasn't sure she could patch it up again for anyone else.

Chapter Thirty-One

A ball of wadded paper bounced off his forehead, startling Alex out of his thoughts of warm sand, icy water, and dark curls tickling his cheek.

"There you are," Lev said.

He leaned forward in the leather chair and set his elbows on the conference table. "Sorry, what?"

Lev rapped his knuckles on the table. "You need to get more sleep."

"I'll sleep when this deal is done," Alex grumbled. "Are we ready to close or not?" He glanced through his office window at that eyesore, the Paradise.

"I'm ready on my side," Jack said. "I'll wire the money when Lev says go."

"We're a go to close on Monday," Lev said. "You two will be the proud owners of the most dilapidated casino on the Strip."

"Bring in the demolition crew on Tuesday," Alex said, leaning back in his chair. Lev was right. He could use some sleep. He hadn't slept well for two weeks. Since...her. His room was too quiet, and the bed felt too big, too cold, too empty.

"I can't get the permits that fast," Lev said.

"Call in favors. Make it happen," Alex snapped. "I want to look out my window on Wednesday morning and see a crater where that dump used to be." He waved at the window.

Lev grumbled something Alex couldn't hear, but he started tapping furiously on his laptop.

Jack leaned back, too. But he wasn't looking at the Strip. He was assessing Alex. "There's something going on here. More than your history with the Paradise."

"He broke up with his girl," Lev muttered, still typing. "Been a right svoloch since then."

"Your girl?" Jack raised his bushy white eyebrows. "Since when have you had a girl?"

"What is this, a sorority house?" Alex snarled. "You two about to start painting each other's nails and talking about who's taking who to the big dance?"

Jack ignored him and turned to Lev. "Who's he dating?"

"Mary Forza. The pretty brunette with the fantastic rack and the brothers who want to kill him."

"Your event planner?"

Alex said nothing.

"Not anymore." Lev stood. "She quit." He walked to the far side of the office and lifted his phone to his ear.

"I should never have hired her," Alex grumbled. What hurt the most was that he'd needed her. He didn't want to need anyone else ever again. "It was better when she hated me. When she didn't want anything to do with me."

"This is fascinating," Jack said. "She hated you?"

"I stood her up in high school. Because of the investigation around my father. She didn't speak to me after." Though Mary, with her soft heart, had forgiven him as soon as she'd moved back home. If their situations had been reversed, Alex would never have forgiven her.

"Sounds a bit like your relationship with the gaming board," Jack said. "You pissed them off, but then Ray Richardson took a risk when he trusted you with his daughter's wedding."

"That was more the bride's choice, but, yeah, I guess so."

"And now you're buying the Paradise. You've got a foothold in the center of the Strip."

"True." Pride swelled in his chest. "How are those permits coming along, Lev?"

"It's fucking Friday afternoon, boss," he called from the other side of the room. "It's going to take me a minute."

"Just get it done."

"And Mary," Jack said, making Alex's stomach clench. "She planned the wedding. She helped you win Richardson's support."

"Barely." Alex pulled his prickly emotional shield around himself like a coat. The thing was, it was scratchy and too small now. Like Mary had tossed it into the wash on hot and handed it back to him, a triumphant gleam in her eye. Stubbornly, he kept it up. "The wedding was a disaster. There was a fire, and we lost power."

Jack cocked his head. "And still, Miss Richardson got married? And her father was so pleased he rallied support for your bid?"

"Yeah. Everyone lit up their phones, and it was fucking magical." Except for the fact Mary wasn't there.

"Seems like it turned out all right in the end. Why'd she quit?" Jack asked.

"Because we thought I'd lost the Paradise. Because she was cutting her losses."

"Is that what she said?" Jack asked. "Mary didn't seem like the type to care about that. Didn't you say she forgave you after things went down with your father?"

"But...but she shouldn't want to tie herself to a loser."

Jack caught his gaze and held it. "Alessandro Villa, you're no loser. Whether you've got the Paradise or not. Whether you've got a casino or not. You're a good man. Mary saw that. So why did she quit, really?"

Alex couldn't look at Jack, so he sank his face into his palms and rubbed his itchy eyes. "Because I pushed her away. I thought I'd be better on my own."

"On your own? You've got Lev and me and a whole staff here. You're not on your own. As a CEO, you should know about delegating. I'd be concerned about my investment if you thought you could do it all."

"I know how to delegate." Alex lifted his head to nod at Lev, still sweet-talking his contacts at the permit office. "See?"

"Sometimes others will do things their way, not a way we'd have done it. If I'm not mistaken, you'd have marched into the permit office and knocked some heads to get what you want, right?"

Alex narrowed his eyes. "Probably. Though I'd have wasted time driving there."

"And you might have missed anyone who worked from home today. So, Lev's way might be more efficient."

"True. And I'm letting him do it his way. What's your point?"

"Partnership isn't only for business. One thing I've learned from forty years of marriage is that you can do anything with the right person at your side."

Alex lifted his head from his hands, though his eyes still burned. "That might be true for you, Jack, but even if Mary were the right person for me, she'd never forgive me a third time." He didn't deserve happiness, anyway. Eighteen years ago, Mrs. Campo had speared him with that uncanny, unblinking stare and told him he deserved to live the rest of his life in misery.

She was right.

"You can't know she won't forgive you if you don't ask her," Jack said. "It might be worth it to have a partner like Mary. Love is like the frosting on a wedding cake. It makes something tasty even more delicious."

"Love?" Alex scoffed. "I never said anything about love. Besides, feelings have no place in business."

"I'll have to disagree with you there, boss," Lev said, walking back to the table. "The sweet old lady at the permit office, the one who goes to my church and pinched my cheek after my confirmation, just promised to get our demolition approved on Monday."

Later that afternoon, after Jack and Lev left, the sinking sun blazed off the glass of the shadow box on his desk and speared him in the eye.

Instead of tipping the box over like he should've done and continuing to scan the spreadsheet on his screen, he leaned back in his chair, out of the beam of reflected sunlight, and rubbed where his forehead ached.

He should hide that shadow box away. He had no right to keep the photo anymore. Not after how he'd treated Mary. Every time he left the casino, he half-expected her two meaty brothers to be waiting outside, ready to jump him and give him the beatdown he deserved. He'd welcome it. Maybe then he'd feel something other than numb.

When he took his hand off his face, a person dressed all in black stood in his doorway. He jumped to his feet. "Mrs. Campo. What are you—would you like to come in?"

She lifted her chin and strode into his office, her black flats silent on the thick rug. She wore a short-sleeved black blouse and a longish skirt that flared slightly at her calves. She carried a black handbag large enough to fit a human head, and a gold cross gleamed at her throat.

She reached into the bag, and Alex had a vision of all the noir films he'd watched as a kid, when the woman pulls out a Glock. He held his breath.

"For you," Mrs. Campo said, holding out not a gun but a bottle of brown liquid. "Take it," she urged him.

He took the bottle from her. Even sealed, it gave off a strong alcoholic aroma.

"Nocino. My nonna's recipe," she said.

So, it wasn't poison. Probably. "Thank you." He set it on his desk next to the shadow box. He studied the tiny woman. In the fifteen years he'd been secretly supporting her and her family, she'd never come to see him, and now she'd visited twice over a summer.

"Dante talked to you?" she asked.

"Yes. I appreciate his apology." He smiled, bitter. "Though

someone wise once told me that accidents are a part of life, and it's how you deal with them that's important."

"That was a wise person." She squinted at him. "I hope you took those words to heart."

"I did." He'd lain awake every night since the wedding, thinking of all the ways he could have better dealt with the disaster.

"But have you really?" she asked, stepping closer.

"Yes, of course. I even gave Dante a testimonial to use on his website. Though I think he should raise the limits on his liability insurance."

"No, no." She slashed a hand through the air between them. "I mean you. And your guilt over what your father did."

Alex ground his teeth. "What he did was no accident."

"No. But it wasn't your fault." She raised a hand. "I know, I know. I told you it was. I was angry. Heartbroken. Grieving. But deep down, I knew you were a victim, just like my family and me."

"I...but..." His stomach pitched like he was falling. He'd lost control of this conversation, unable to predict what the woman would say next.

"What you did after, giving everyone back their money, working so hard, supporting my family, taking care of your mother, and building up a business that employs so many—" She waved her hand in a circle to encompass La Villa. "That shows character. It proves you're not like him."

That sounded a lot like what Mary had said. The words he'd been too afraid to accept as truth. *You don't need the Paradise to prove you're a better man than your father. Anyone who knows you already believes it.*

"Thank you. That means a lot, coming from you."

For the first time, she looked down. When she looked up, she pursed her lips. "I shouldn't have cursed you. You were only a boy then. You're a good man now."

Stepping closer, she touched his forehead and muttered something under her breath. Then, stepping back, she said, "It's gone."

"Wait. You lifted the malocchio?" Like a lot of Italian Americans, Alex had grown up under a mysterious cloud of superstitions from the old country. He'd never really believed in them. Well, except sometimes he had an irrepressible urge to touch his left nut or to hold something made of iron. But older people like Mrs. Campo sure as hell believed in them. And he'd never known any of his elders to take back a curse.

She scoffed. "You said back then you didn't believe in that nonsense."

He squared himself up. "And I don't." *Ninety-nine percent.*

"Regardless, it's gone. You can live your life with happiness now."

"Thank you." He still felt off balance, like he was in a funhouse.

"Now, what are you going to do about it?"

"I...I guess I'll keep working. Open up La Villa Prime and hire back the people who worked at the Paradise."

Mrs. Campo growled, "Not about work. About the Forza girl."

His shoulders slumped. Did everyone know about what he'd done to Mary? "We broke up. It's over."

"Is it?"

"I've humiliated her twice now. I don't think I can come back from that."

"Pride is your sin," she said, "not Mary's."

"You think she'd take me back?"

"Isn't that what you want?"

He remembered how Mary had squealed in the surf in San Diego. How they'd made love in all five bedrooms of the beach house. How the firelight flickered across her thighs spread for him. How her warm hand had gripped his as the sea breeze tossed her curls and kissed her skin.

"It doesn't matter what I want. I'll never be worthy of her," he said.

Her brown eyes pinned him. "Don't you think that's something she should decide?"

Let someone else make a decision that affected him? *No, thank you.*

When he was silent, Mrs. Campo tutted. "I think you've been hiding behind that curse. And now it's gone, you don't know what to do."

Alex took a few steps toward the door and was relieved when Mrs. Campo went with him. At the door, he paused. "You know I don't believe in that stuff."

"Don't you?" She narrowed her eyes. "Then why are you so afraid to seize your own happiness?" Turning on her heel, she marched away toward the elevators.

Alex almost spat out his sip of the bitter brown liquid. It burned down his throat and into his stomach. Mrs. Campo's nocino might not be poison, but it was the most disgusting stuff he'd ever tasted.

He plugged up the bottle and stashed it in his freezer. Bad luck to throw away a gift from a wise woman.

Shuffling into his bedroom, Alex switched on the lamp next to his lonely bed, then the gas fireplace. His penthouse seemed so much colder without Mary. Even though everything about her seemed out of place in his ordered world, from her chaotic curls to the smear of her red lipstick on his pillowcase.

That was the thing he couldn't wrap his mind around. He didn't want to change anything about her. Not her scrappy little business, not her cozy house stuffed full of tacky mementos of three generations of Italian Americans, not even her knuckle-dragging brothers.

Mrs. Campo's words swirled in his brain. Was he worthy of Mary's love? And did he have the courage to ask her for it?

To be loved—to let Mary love him—he knew, had always known, he had to change himself. To open a window and let Mary peek in. To open a door and let her poke around and rearrange things.

And that scared the shit out of him.

But now, all alone in his penthouse, he realized that was what he had to do. Let her bring the plastic La Pieta and her pothos with the tiny Italian flag jammed into the soil. Let her invite her surly brothers to track grease onto his rug and threaten him with a thrashing on the regular. All he wanted was to nestle into a pile of flowery cushions, drink a glass of too-cold Chianti, and soak up Mary's love.

She'd lit up the gloom within him just like she'd lit up that blacked-out ballroom. Now he couldn't face returning to the darkness. Even if it meant he had to compromise. If he had to trust. If he had to jump, not knowing what lay below.

If there was the slightest chance Mary might catch him, he had to leap.

Chapter Thirty-Two

F orza Elite Motors didn't open until noon on Saturdays unless you had an appointment, which Alex definitely did not. He'd already tried Mary's house, but her car wasn't in the driveway, and she didn't answer her doorbell. So, he waited outside the Forzas' business until he saw Evie—of course, it had to be Evie—drive up in her little gray compact and put her key in the lock.

"Hi, Evie," he said, emerging from his Ferrari.

She jumped. "You scared the shit out of me. What are you doing here?"

"I'm looking for Mary. Is she here?"

Her lip curled. "No, just me."

"Do you know where she is?"

She gave him a long, ball-shriveling look. "Yes." She walked inside, letting the door bang shut behind her.

When Alex wrenched it open, the bell jingled merrily. "Where is she, Evie?"

"I think she'd have told you if she wanted you to know."

"Look, I need to find her and tell her—"

The bell tinkled behind him. "Who let this asshole in?" a deep voice rumbled.

Alex turned to keep both Evie and Mary's brother in sight. He knew better than to turn his back to a Forza. Especially Michael.

Evie glared at Michael. "He just walked in. How did you expect me to keep him out?"

Michael glared back. "I'll show him out." He advanced on Alex, looking like an offensive lineman protecting his quarterback.

Alex let his knees go loose, prepared to dart and evade Michael's clutches.

The bell tinkled again. "What's going on?" This time, it was Rafe. His biceps bulged under the short sleeves of his blue T-shirt.

"Just showing this asshole the door," Michael growled.

"Wait," Alex said. "I came in to find Mary."

"She's not here," Michael said, taking a step closer.

"I need to find her."

"Why?" Rafe asked. He'd always been the more reasonable one. Except that time he'd broken Alex's nose.

Alex spoke to him, keeping his back to the wall. "I made a mistake when I let her walk away. I need to apologize."

"She doesn't need you or your fucking job," Michael spat. "She's just fine without you."

"Better than fine." Rafe stuck out his chin. But his eyebrows drew together in a way that belied his words.

Alex hesitated for a moment. Then he sucked it up and laid himself bare. "I'm not fine. I was a fool. I—I need her."

"We just told you she doesn't need you, asshole." Michael clenched his fists.

Alex stood his ground. He deserved a punch, and he'd take it like he'd taken their fists after prom. "Don't you think Mary should decide that?"

"You've hurt her enough." The lines around Michael's eyes deepened like he hadn't meant to say it.

The ache was back in Alex's belly. "I know. And I want to make it right."

Michael opened his mouth, but Rafe spoke first. "How do you plan to make it right? What you did was shitty on multiple levels."

"I'll do whatever she asks. Buy her gifts. Grovel at her feet. Tell her I'm sorry. Walk naked down the Strip while tourists pelt me with frosé if that's what she wants." Hell, he'd let both her brothers pummel him if that was what she wanted.

"Recommend her services?" Evie asked. "As an independent contractor. You get no cut of her fees."

"Of course," he said. "For every wedding until her schedule is full."

"If you're going to grovel, I want video proof," Rafe said with an evil smile. "Payback."

Fuck, he should have known he'd pay for showing the Forzas those photos of Rafe. "I'll ask Mary to confirm my grovel, all right?"

Rafe's mouth turned down. "I guess."

"I don't know, Rafe," Michael said. "I think he'll look better with a fat lip."

"That'll just make her feel sorry for him," Rafe said. "She's more likely to stay mad if he goes in there looking slick." He gestured at Alex's suit.

"You've got a point," Michael said. "Let her decide. And if she decides to stay mad"—Michael smirked—"we'll break your fancy new nose."

"Fair," Alex said. It was what he deserved. "Where is she?"

When Rafe told him, he realized it wasn't only Evie and the Forza brothers who had it in for him. The universe or God or karma wanted a piece of him, too.

Outside the country club at dusk, guests gathered in the green space next to the empty driving range to watch Mary's friend the aerialist.

Red silk wrapped her body as she twirled, suspended from a four-legged rig. The guests gazed up in awe, their sparkling wine forgotten.

Dante and his fire dancers had been more impressive. Though

given they'd cost him over a hundred Gs, including the damage to the wiring and the losses from an hour of downtime in the casino, an aerialist had been the smarter move. Little chance of injury to the guests, at least.

Hitching up the heavy box under his arm, Alex skirted the gawking guests on his way to crash his ex's wedding.

According to his plan, showing up mid-reception would be the least disruptive to Mary. Coming to the ceremony might invoke all those terrible rom-coms where the ex showed up to say his "I object," and the last thing he wanted to do was stop Cierra from marrying what's-his-name. Besides, Mary would be busy supervising the videographer and the photographer, organizing the bridal party, and ensuring Cierra's mother wasn't seated next to her father.

While he'd waited for the appropriate time to crash the wedding, he'd run out for a sorry-I-lied-on-my-RSVP gift and cracked his knuckles while the store wrapped the ugly piece of crystal. Then he'd changed into a different suit and even pulled out a wedding-appropriate floral silk tie to prove his sincerity.

Although he'd intended to show up after dinner, while Cierra and her groom spun blissfully on the dance floor and most of Mary's work was done, patience wasn't his strength. When he walked into the reception room at the country club, the dance floor was empty. A few people milled around with drinks while servers tempted them with trays of hors d'oeuvres. A piano played Fauré in a corner of the room, and the band was still setting up on stage.

Alex wandered around the edges of the room, searching for Mary. No luck. This would be a busy time for her. She'd be ensuring dinner was almost ready, coordinating the bride and groom's entrance, and preparing to coax everyone into their assigned seats.

He hated waiting, but he'd do it for Mary.

Determined to find an out-of-the-way spot to lurk, he set his gift with the others on the skirted table and walked back outside. But before he could find a bench, he was rewarded for his good intentions by a glimpse of Mary emerging from inside, followed by the bride and groom. She wore her black dress, the one with the teasing diaphanous sleeves, the one she thought faded into the background like a roadie on stage. It didn't work. Mary's dark hair and dress stood out against Cierra's puffy white gown, making her all Alex could see.

She fluffed Cierra's skirt, stepped back, and nodded. Then she said something to the couple, turned, and disappeared through the door again.

Without engaging his brain, his feet moved him a few steps closer to the door. That was when the trouble started.

"Hey! What are you doing here?"

Alex ripped his gaze from the spot he'd lost sight of Mary. Yes, that was the groom. Shouting at him.

Innocently, he put a hand on his chest. "Me?" he asked.

The groom strode toward him. "Yeah, you."

"I was invited." God, he wished he'd paid more attention to that invitation. Then he'd remember the groom's name.

"You?" the groom sneered. "I don't think so."

Alex tried to relax his shoulders as he shoved his hands in his pockets. "Cierra invited me."

She stepped up to them, and the overpowering, fruity scent of her Miss Dior perfume almost choked him. "As I recall, you sent your regrets." A smile curled her lips, done up in demure pink. But there was nothing sweet about the dangerous glint in her eye.

Cierra loved drama.

"Congratulations," he murmured, bending down to brush his cheek near hers in what he hoped would be a friendly, tension-defusing air kiss.

But Cierra turned her face at exactly the wrong moment, and his lips met hers. Alex stumbled back. "Sorry, I—"

"What the *fuck*, Villa?" the groom roared. Around them, people Alex hadn't noticed before gasped.

"I didn't mean to—"

"Parking lot. Now." The groom's face was red.

"I'm not going to the parking lot with you," Alex said. "I'm just here to—"

"I know why you're here. You can't have her back!" the groom roared in a soap opera–worthy performance. It seemed he, too, had a flair for the dramatic.

Behind him, someone stopped the aerialist's music.

Alex put up his hands. "I don't want—"

"Fuck what you want." The groom grasped his arm and tugged him along the path toward the parking lot.

Alex had two choices: dig in his heels and resist, which would surely get him punched and might splatter blood on Cierra's gown, a problem Mary would have to deal with; or go with the groom, also with a one-hundred percent chance of getting punched but likely to create fewer problems for Mary.

Shaking off the groom's grip, he walked beside him along the path to the concrete parking lot. That was going to hurt—a lot—when he fell. Why couldn't it be sun-softened asphalt?

Sunset turned the pavement rosy pink. Alex squinted against the golden rays that speared into his eyes. "Look, I'm not here for Cierra. I'm here to see—"

Pow.

Alex doubled over at the unexpected pain radiating from his midsection. Cierra's husband didn't punch as hard as Mary's brothers, but any blow to the solar plexus hurt like hell. Blinded by the sun, he hadn't even braced for impact. He coughed on his shiny dress shoes, willing the bile not to rise into his throat.

"Stand up and fight!" the other man shouted.

Still bent at the waist, Alex held up a hand. "I don't want to fight you. It's your wedding day."

"I'll fight anyone who touches my wife!" He grasped Alex's shoulder and pulled him up.

Pain sizzled in Alex's stomach as he straightened. Resisting would make everything worse. This time, he saw the groom's fist coming for his face, and he braced. Agony lit up his jaw, and his head snapped to the side. He stumbled back, lost his balance, and fell on his ass.

Fortunately, his suit saved him from road rash. Unfortunately, the thin linen split with a ripping sound.

The groom grunted and shook out his hand. His chest heaved.

Sitting on the concrete, Alex touched his jaw, then worked it around. No teeth loose, and nothing appeared broken. "We good now?" he muttered, glancing at the crowd that had gathered. Of course their phones were out, recording his humiliation. His tongue felt thick, and his words slurred.

"Yeah." The groom examined his reddened knuckles. Then, louder, he said, "Stay away from my wife."

"Got it." Alex lowered his voice. "Know where I can get some ice?"

"Kitchen. There's an entrance around to the right."

"Thanks, man." Alex squinted at the guy. "Good luck to you and Cierra."

The groom stepped closer. "You better fucking stay away from her."

He held up both hands. "I promise. I came here for your wedding planner."

The groom laughed. "You came here for the wedding planner?"

"I love her. I came here to tell her that. Say one word about her, and the punching bag punches back."

"Nah, we're cool," the groom said. "I wish you'd told me that before...you know."

He ached too much to argue. Instead, he held out his hand. The groom took it and pulled him up. A breeze cooled his ass. "I'll go find her in the kitchen."

"Actually," the groom said, "I have a better idea. Cierra's gonna love it."

Chapter Thirty-Three

M ary pulled the knife from the cup of hot water and smoothed it over the frosting of the lowest tier of the cake. The bakery had delivered the four-tier monstrosity in perfect shape, but when the catering staff had wheeled it from the walk-in cooler, they'd knocked into a rack of salads, and a sizable chunk of it had broken off and fallen on the floor. Mary had trimmed what was left so it was more or less even, then patched it with some bread and a batch of frosting she'd whipped up herself. It wasn't a perfect match, and her cake decorating skills weren't the best, but she'd ensure they lowered the lights in the dining room before they wheeled it out and didn't serve the part that wasn't actually cake to any of the guests.

Was this failure, on top of all the others, enough to ruin her chances of ever planning another wedding?

With the back of her hand, she wiped the sweat from her brow. Maybe she wasn't cut out for wedding planning after all. If she begged her brothers, they had to take her back at the shop, right? They were family.

Though she didn't want to return to her old job. As much as she loved her brothers and the idea of continuing their father's business, she'd never loved it. Not like she loved planning weddings. The fragrant flowers, the delicious food, the unique venues and wedding traditions. The romantic kiss at the end of the ceremony. Her heart beat a little faster on days she was working on a wedding, and it wasn't only adrenaline from dealing with emergencies, big and small. Weddings brought her joy. Helping a couple celebrate love in front of friends and family made her romantic heart sing.

If this was the last wedding she ever planned, a little part of her would die along with her dreams.

She stepped back and gazed critically at the cake. She'd ensure the patched-up part was closest to the wall. She circled to the other side of it. Nothing looked amiss from the front. She reached up and adjusted the topper, so the couple faced her. It would work. And long after Cierra's wedding was over and Mary got paid, she'd tell Cierra about it, and they'd laugh together.

Until then, she'd pretend everything was perfect.

Everything at the wedding, that is. Because there wasn't a person in Vegas, it seemed, who didn't know precisely how her life had gone off the rails. The other night, her neighbor, Mrs. Wong, had brought her a batch of lotus-seed mooncakes and suggested she get on "the app store" to find a man. At church last weekend, the woman sitting next to her had clucked her tongue and shook her head during the sign of peace. And when she'd picked up her dress from the dry cleaner, the owner had slipped her a chocolate bar along with her receipt.

She'd show them all she was doing great despite her personal and professional humiliation. She'd find someone who hadn't heard she'd screwed up the wedding of the season, offer them a massive discount, and start over.

But first, she needed to find the photographer and ensure she only photographed the cake from the front.

"Hey." She walked to where the kitchen manager stood, supervising the servers as they transferred the salads from their racks, one with a smear of white frosting on the side, to their trays. "Cake is good to go. Please be sure the patched bit faces the wall when you wheel it out, and remind the servers not to serve that part, okay?"

"Got it," he said. "I'm sorry about the accident."

Mary shrugged. "It happens. I should know."

"I heard." The manager's eyes crinkled in sympathy.

Ugh. Maybe Mary needed to move to Salt Lake or Phoenix to escape her reputation. "I'm going to talk to the photographer. I'll be back to check in before the main course."

She paused to take one last look at the cake. It didn't look so bad, did it? Maybe she could borrow a couple of frosted rosettes from one of the upper tiers to help disguise the patch.

"Miss Forza!" One of the servers stood at the kitchen's swinging door, an empty tray under her arm. "You've got to come out."

Mary's heart kicked in her chest. "What happened?" Visions of guests puking from an outbreak of food poisoning, a rowdy drunk uncle shouting his political views from the stage, and the bride and groom tossing their rings at each other all popped into her mind. That third one was actually pretty likely. Cierra had brought the drama to her wedding and seemed determined to poke Sawyer until he did something rash.

"Come see." The server tossed her tray onto a counter, grasped Mary by the wrist, and pulled her out into the dining room. Mary took a deep breath. Whatever had happened, she could handle it.

In the dining room, something seemed...off. Anticipation crackled in the air. People stood on the dance floor when they should have been seated, ready to start the salad course. She'd have to talk to the emcee, who should have handled that.

She scanned the room for the bride and groom. There they were, also on the dance floor, arm in arm. She sighed, relieved. No emergency there. Hopefully, no drama either.

Murmuring erupted around them as the server dragged her toward the stage. Oh, no. Was there a problem with the emcee? Had he walked out? Or experienced a medical emergency? Silently, she recited a Hail Mary as she jogged toward the stage.

"There she is!" Cierra squealed, pointing right at her. "Go, Alex!"

Alex?

A spotlight lit up the stage. But instead of the band's scruffy lead singer, a suited man stood in it, his glossy dark hair haloed in the bright light. Alex.

Mary's stomach dropped. Shit, had he followed her to her next wedding to warn everyone of what a screw-up she was? Had he come as a favor to his ex, Cierra, to rescue her wedding like he'd done for Rochelle's? Her cheeks burned.

"Mary," he said, cupping his hand over his eyes against the glare of the spotlight. "Where are you?" His voice sounded thick, and his words slurred slightly. There was something wrong with his face, too. Even in the color-sapping spotlight, his jaw looked red.

A tall groomsman stood in front of her. She could hide behind him, shake off the server who still manacled her wrist, and then slink back to the kitchen. No, Cierra had spotted her. She had to face the music. Not literally, since it was only Alex, and he'd pointedly told her at karaoke night that he didn't sing.

Pulling her arm away from the server, she straightened her shoulders and stepped to the front of the crowd below the stage. Her stomach churning, she said, "Here I am."

"Mary," he said into the microphone. His eyes crinkled. Was that pity? Or...remorse? She couldn't identify the unfamiliar expression. "Thank you for coming."

She narrowed her eyes, partly in disbelief and partly to examine his strange appearance. His top half was impeccable as always, his light linen suit jacket looking especially crisp, his shirt extra white, and his tie...his tie? She'd only seen him wear a tie at funerals. This one was a bright, cheerful floral.

But his bottom half was even stranger. Instead of linen suit pants to match his jacket, he wore a pair of cheap-looking black slacks, shiny with polyester, like what the caterers wore.

None of it mattered to her pattering heart. His face was familiar and beloved and gorgeous despite the shadows the spotlight made under his eyes.

"You're thanking *me* for coming?" she said. "This is my job. I'm supposed to be here. You're not."

He chuckled, and so did those guests close enough to hear her. "I deserve that." Then his voice turned serious and deep and so, so loud through the speakers. "Mary, I'm sorry for doubting you. For being afraid to trust you. That was my failure, not yours. I should have let you do your job, which you do so well. Isn't this a great wedding, everyone?"

There were a few claps.

"Hey!" Cierra shouted. "This is a great wedding!"

A few more guests obliged her by clapping.

"Tough crowd," Alex said. "Though maybe that's my fault. I'm making it weird. But after publicly humiliating you, I had to make my apology just as public."

"You really didn't," Mary said, glancing around at the guests.

"Didn't I?" His brown eyes sparkled in the spotlight. "Someone wise told me I had to let go and be vulnerable to truly love. Mary, I love you, and this is me being vulnerable to prove it to you."

He nodded to the guitar player, who strummed out a quick rhythm.

Alex raised the microphone to his lips and warbled the first words to "If I Could Turn Back Time."

Mary gasped. Alex was singing? To her?

And...it was terrible. His voice cracked and wobbled. The man standing beside her groaned. Even the guitarist winced.

But Alex? His eyes didn't leave Mary's as he put his breath, his heart, into the song, note after painful note. Voices like Alex's were why they'd invented Auto-Tune. And he'd forgotten everything they'd learned in the children's church choir about breathing. When he ran out of breath, he sucked in, loud, sometimes missing a word or two.

Was he nervous?

Mary stared up at him. The apples of his cheeks were bright pink, and his posture wasn't as straight as usual. Yet he kept singing despite the tremble of his fingers on the microphone stand.

Her heart cracked just a bit.

When the drummer joined in with a riff and drowned out the vocals, Alex sounded a little better.

He paused his singing to say, "Come on, folks. Help me out here."

And even though it was an old song and none of the younger wedding guests would be caught dead listening to an adult contemporary radio station that played Cher, this was Vegas, and everyone knew her songs.

The tall groomsman beside her belted out the words, and so did Cierra's parents, and soon every person on that dance floor, from the bride and groom to their grandparents, was helping Alex express his regret and pleading for Mary's forgiveness.

And by the time Alex and the rest of the guests belted out the last line of the final chorus, the crack in her heart had grown so wide that it split open. But unlike the first time Alex had broken her heart, when she sat alone in her sparkly dress on prom night and her heart shattered like crystal, this time it cracked open like a seed, allowing her love to push out of it, vigorous and vibrant. Her love bloomed, colorful and beautiful as his tie, watered and nourished by the proof of his love.

"Mary?" he said over the buzz of the guests. "I know I can trust you. With my secrets, with my business, and with my heart. I promise I won't shut you out again." His gaze caressed her face. "I love you. Can you love me back?"

Her heart opened like a sunflower. "I do."

"Hey, that's my line!" Cierra called, laughing.

The emcee stepped up to grab the microphone from Alex. "And mine is to remind you all that the first course is served. Everyone, find your tables, and let's celebrate Cierra and Sawyer."

Alex crouched, wincing as he put his palm on the stage and hopped to the dance floor. In a moment, he stood in front of Mary. "Really? You love me?"

She stepped closer to him and put her hands on his chest. His shirt front was damp with sweat, but she didn't care. He'd put himself out there for her. He'd exposed his broken parts to her and everyone else at the reception. Her chest filled with a golden warmth.

"I always have."

His mouth landed softly on hers, his kiss both familiar and new. There was a gentleness to it, an openness that welcomed her in. It told her they'd be starting the next leg of this road trip together, once they agreed on where to go. He'd let her take the wheel when he was tired, and they'd get off the highway when they needed to refuel.

Mary's kiss promised she was more than along for the ride. She'd tell him what she wanted and needed, and she'd remind him to stop and take in the sights along the way.

But as she deepened it to hint at what she wanted from him later, he grunted and pulled back.

"What's wrong?"

"Just a...a gift from the groom." He touched his jaw gingerly and worked it around. "Nothing I didn't deserve for showing up unexpectedly to my ex's wedding."

She skimmed her fingers along his swollen jaw and laid a gentle kiss on it. "I'm glad you came. But from here on out, you get a pass on karaoke."

"Thank God. I never want to do that again."

"It was a sweet gesture. I wouldn't mind if you sang to me in the shower."

"In the shower? I think I've got a much better use for my mouth than singing."

Her skin tingled. "Show me after I'm done here?"

"Maybe I can show you now in the locker room." He nipped her earlobe.

"Sorry, I'm on the clock. Which reminds me. You sent your regrets. I don't have a seat for you."

"I'm not a guest tonight. I'm part of your staff. Give me a job to do."

"A job?" She glanced at his manicured hands that for many years hadn't done anything more strenuous than click a keyboard. "Come on. I'll show you how to cut a wedding cake."

"Good. So I'll know what I'm doing at our wedding."

Her pulse hammered. "Our wedding?"

"You should know by now that once I decide I want something, there's no stopping me."

"But...we haven't talked about it. And you haven't asked me. I want a story to tell our grandchildren."

"Grandchildren?" He swallowed. Then a slow smile broke across his face. "Don't worry. I'll give you a story that'll make our grandkids blush."

Epilogue

3 MONTHS LATER

When Mary stepped outside the Sistine Chapel, the November drizzle barely hit her new red cashmere beret before Alex flipped the umbrella up over her head.

"Thanks," she murmured, tucking her chin into her also-new cashmere coat. It was a luxury, and her old parka would've done the job, but a honeymoon in Rome called for something special. Or so Alex told her when he offered to buy it for her.

But she'd proudly used her own card and the profits from her wedding planning business. Alex had also advised her that as a business owner, she should pay herself first.

The toasty-warm, soft cashmere was worth every penny.

"Put your beanie on." She reached for the handle of the umbrella and ogled her new husband only a little as he pulled his blue knit cap over his dark waves. Despite his dorky hat, he was so handsome she couldn't resist rising on the toes of her walking flats to kiss the pink tip of his nose.

"What was that for?" he asked with a grin.

"I've never seen you in a beanie before. It makes you look like an art student. Or my sexy art professor." She bit her lip.

"Wicked woman. If I have to take you back to the hotel to satisfy your fantasies, it's going to throw off our schedule. If we want to make it to St. Peter's Basilica, we've got to leave now. It'll be faster if we hail a cab." He stepped toward the street, scanning it for a taxi.

"Wait." She stilled him with a hand on his arm, her new wedding ring glinting next to the giant engagement ring she hadn't yet gotten used to. "We're in Rome. I want to slow down and enjoy it."

He stepped back under the umbrella, his face only inches from hers. "You really want to go back to the hotel and do the art professor roleplay?"

She laughed. "Not really. But I do want to sit in a café with my husband and watch Rome go by."

Heedless of the other people on the sidewalk, he gathered her into his arms. "I thought you wanted to see all the sights on your honeymoon in Rome."

"I did. But then I remembered that there's a joy in going with the flow, too. I'm sorry to mess up the itinerary you worked so hard on."

She could see the effort it cost him to relax his shoulders as he let go of his carefully structured plans. "It's fine. We'll make other trips to Italy. We'll see the basilica next time. Right now, I want to do whatever my wife wants to do. And if that's sipping wine at some overpriced sidewalk café in the rain, then that's what we'll do."

"Thank you." This time, she kissed his lips. "And after the café, I want to buy one of those beautiful scarves I see the Italian women wearing."

"Then we'll head toward the Spanish Steps. And I'll buy you the most beautiful scarf you can find."

"Mmm, yes, please. I know exactly how to thank you when we get back to the hotel."

"You can give me a little taste now." He pressed his lips against hers, his tongue teasing her lower lip.

She jerked back. "We just came out of a church!"

"But we're on our honeymoon in Rome. Jesus would understand. The Pope too, I bet."

"Come on." She seized his hand and pulled him along the street she thought led toward Rome. Though if it was the wrong direction, Alex would guide her back to the right path. He had an unwavering sense of direction. Well, except where she'd been concerned. He'd taken a long, meandering journey back to her after high school. But they'd both ended up exactly where they needed to be.

Together.

He held tight to her hand and led her straight out of Vatican City. They had to stop in the souvenir shops, of course. She hadn't yet found the Pope John Paul II bobblehead she wanted to surprise Rafe with. Apparently, everyone else wanted him, too.

And when their leisurely, romantic walk in the rain ended at a boutique near the Piazza di Spagna, there were too many beautiful scarves to choose only one. Alex bought her three. He wrapped the red patterned one around her neck, the silk quickly warming against her skin.

He didn't check his phone once at the outdoor café as they sipped the most delicious wine Mary had ever tasted. He seemed content to look where she pointed—at an adorable dog, or a man who looked like Michael, or even a cute handbag—and almost always agreed with her.

It was dusk when they returned to their hotel to change for dinner. Their room overlooked the Trevi fountain, lit up in greens and golds, and Mary paused in front of the window to admire it.

"It's not quite as showy as the one at the Bellagio at home, is it?"

"Showy?" His arms came around her, and his familiar vanilla scent loosened her joints until she felt as supple as her new scarf. "Today, we saw some of the world's most famous art. And people have been admiring that fountain for hundreds of years. Yet you compare it to a garish hotel in the most lurid city in the world?"

She turned in his arms to put her back to the view. "Don't think I haven't loved every minute we've spent in Italy. But I guess I'm a

Vegas girl at heart. I want a little zhuzh." She traced the sharp line of his jaw. "I guess that's why I like you so much."

"You're saying I'm more of a Bellagio fountain than a Trevi?"

"You're almost too pretty for everyday use. Like my grandmother's china."

"Almost?" His lips tipped up into a smirk.

"Almost. But I like having you every day." She rose to her tiptoes and kissed him.

"And I love you. Every day."

"Even when I'm not appreciative enough of the most famous fountain in the world?"

"Maybe you'll appreciate it more if we associate it with something even more pleasurable." He led her to the wingback chair next to the window and guided her to sit. "You can see the fountain?"

"It's hard to miss. It's big and lit up and...oh."

He'd dropped to his knees and flipped up her skirt. He worked her tights and panties down over her hips and knees, then tossed them aside. "Watch the fountain. I've got something even more beautiful to appreciate."

A thrill raced over her skin as his hot breath gusted across her center.

"Mmm. Already so wet for me." He smoothed his thumb over her, then licked it. He laid his glistening thumb on her clit and vibrated it.

She bowed her back, almost rising out of the chair.

"Ah-ah-ah." His smile was devious as he used one hand to guide her hips back onto the chair. "Remember, you're watching the fountain."

"I'd rather look at you." But she dutifully gazed at the fountain, at the people gathered around it who'd never be as lucky as she was, with her sexy husband about to make her come.

"Good girl," he purred, making her shiver.

In the three months since he'd sung to her at Cierra's wedding, Alex had seemingly made it his job to learn all the things that made her body sing. He plunged two expert fingers inside her and curled them to reach the spot that lit her up inside. At the same time, he vibrated his thumb, sparking pleasure that tingled to every nerve.

"Eyes open."

His words made her realize she'd squeezed her eyes shut to savor the sensations he was giving her. Her eyes flew open, and she kept them on the fountain's main figure, Oceanus, imagining him as Alex, wielding his power over the waves of pleasure that crashed through her. It didn't take her long to reach her peak, and she moaned as her body tensed under his fingers.

He kept his thumb still on her clit as she came down, her body loose.

"Did you find a new appreciation for Rome?" he asked, his lips curling up.

"I already loved Rome. Just like I'll love anywhere we go together."

He surged up to kiss her, long and slow. Then he stood and adjusted himself. "Stay there. I'll get a washcloth to clean you up, then we'll go to dinner."

"But I'm not done yet." She gave him a mock-serious look.

"Oh, I'm sorry." He mirrored her teasing expression. "I thought I just gave you an earth-shattering orgasm."

"Consider it the opening act. Now I'm ready for Wayne Newton." She put a hand on his belt buckle, feeling him stiffen under her palm.

"I can never tell you no," he said, unbuckling his trousers.

"I love that about you, too." When he lowered his pants and boxers, she stroked him from root to tip.

His eyes rolled back. "God, Mary, how'd I ever get so lucky?"

"Luck had nothing to do with it. It was all hard work and persistence. How many other men would have tried again after my brothers broke your nose?"

He kneeled and nudged inside her. "One hundred percent worth it."

And as they surged together like the rush of the water outside their window, she knew he was right. All the hurt that had broken them years ago had made them who they were, and they were stronger for it.

They were irrevocably joined, and nothing could split them apart now.

Not a wedding, and certainly not an old feud.

Thank you for reading! Did you enjoy? Please add your review because nothing helps an author more and encourages readers to take a chance on a book than a review.

And don't miss more from Michelle McCraw coming soon. Until then read ELEPHANT AND CASTLE by City Owl Author, Hannah Ledford. Turn the page for a sneak peek!

You can also sign up for the City Owl Press newsletter to receive notice of all book releases!

Sneak Peek of Elephant and Castle

BY HANNAH LEDFORD

Nora Shrapsan spun in a slow circle on a street just south of the Thames. Not that she knew which direction was north or south or which way was to the river or to Buckingham Palace. Seven years ago, Nora had zipped through the streets of London like a local, hopping on red double-decker buses and hailing midnight cabs, emerging from the labyrinth of underground stations with the ease and confidence of someone who'd lived there for years, though it had only been one summer. Nora had found her way around the city without any problems when she was a teenager with few responsibilities and nowhere in particular to go, so she had foolishly assumed that she could just pick up right where she left off in her relationship with ye olde London Town. She had assumed that she —an expert traveler and experienced tour-book copy editor—could jump on the Tube with ease and get to where she was going.

She was wrong.

When she'd gotten off the Underground and pulled up the address on her phone, the little blue arrow kept spinning in circles, changing its mind about which way she should turn. If Nora didn't figure it out soon, she was going to be late for the first meeting with her new editor, and she was going to have moved all the way across the Atlantic just to get fired, which would really be a shame, honestly. She'd been preparing for months—paperwork and visas, packing and parting words to friends. She had even broken up with her super-hot boyfriend, abandoning the comfort of upstate New York and regularly scheduled above-average sex. The breakup was a thrill for her mother, who always said that she shouldn't bother with Brandon anyway. Too pretty, too shallow. According to her mother, above-average sex wasn't worth the hassle of dating someone who made you watch Monday Night Football, but Nora was quick to point out that this was coming from a woman who wasn't getting laid at all.

"We're very comfortable together," Nora had explained to her mother again and again.

Kathleen Shrapsan, cancer survivor and member of the Binghamton City Council, did not take "comfortable" for an answer. They had the same conversation in perpetuity: "Brandon is very easy to look at," her mother would say. Even she couldn't deny it. "And he's nice to you. Heck, I feel comfortable with him too, but that doesn't mean he has any interest in marrying and impregnating you."

"Mom—"

"And you're too smart for him," her mother complained. Nora stopped arguing that a lot of men didn't care as much about *smart*.

"I want you to get married and have lots of babies and be happy, happy, happy, but I don't want you to do any of that with a man whose favorite book is *Sports Illustrated*. Also, not getting laid is a choice."

As usual, Nora knew her mother was right. Kathleen had been overjoyed when she heard the news about the London job, and she immediately waved off all the guilt Nora felt about abandoning her in-recovery matriarch. That was just a minuscule con in a long list of pros: no more football, no more dinners with finance bros, no more Brandon. With little regard for any of Nora's fears or concerns, her mother was praising the Lord that she wasn't going to just be *comfortable* anymore.

Even though her breakup was so fresh, and Nora kind-of-rudely told him two weeks before leaving the country, she was only partly concerned about the end of her relationship with Brandon and only slightly more concerned about the fact that she couldn't read a map. There was also the matter of the diary. A diary that had turned up while she was searching for her passport. A diary that was still sitting at the bottom of the overstuffed backpack slung over her shoulder, practically throbbing like it was a freaking tell-tale heart.

Nora decided she better just pick a direction and take her chances. She had done this before, after all; she'd trekked all over that city by herself or with her British boyfriend and his friends. She'd walked in the footsteps of The Beatles and Anne Boleyn and Idris Elba, probably. She shouldn't have a problem finding a company office in Southwark. She lifted her chin and marched down the sidewalk.

"Make a U-turn," her phone said. Nora wanted to fling it into oncoming traffic.

The diary had only started taunting her recently, and in fact she didn't even remember it existed until a few weeks ago when she'd opened an old shoe box, praying it wasn't going to be a smelly pair of Keds. Inside, there were old photographs, ticket stubs, a crinkled map, and a loose bunch of old tampons (not used, obviously). There was no passport, but underneath it all she found a diary with a pink, faux-leather cover that she recognized immediately. With her fingers touching the fake leather, Nora couldn't help abandoning the search for items that may have actually had some use to her as she prepared to move to a different country, and she took the little book over to the couch where she could sink into the cushions, crack it open, and remember for a second what it felt like to be nineteen. It was impossible not to memorize the words while studying the pages like an anthropologist who had uncovered a discovery that could unlock the secrets of a lost world.

London, June 5

Hugh keeps saying such romantic things, things that I don't know if I believe, but it's nice to hear them anyway. "I was perfectly content before I met you," he says, "but now I can't imagine what I'll ever do without you." He tells me he's sure I will ruin him. I know in my head that it's cheesy and he probably says stuff like this to every girl he dates, but I can't help feeling like it might be possible that he's falling in love with me too.

London, June 29

   Here's the honest truth. There is nothing like getting kissed by a British man in an elevator at three o'clock in the morning...

London, July 7

   I have never slept with anyone before...well until now. I have roommates, and Hugh has roommates, so it's not like we get a lot of privacy, and even when I would stay over at his place just to cuddle, I still felt a little embarrassed at what Dev might be thinking. One morning I walked out, and Julian was over, and I think we both turned bright red. Dev eavesdropping on my love life is one thing, but Julian...he's so sophisticated and shy. So Hugh got a hotel room, and that's where we went. "I think maybe I'm a bad influence on you," he said. Maybe he's right. He's five years older, and he's a man, and I know very little about men. But I wanted it to happen all along. I wanted him to take me somewhere private. I wanted to kiss him all over, even if I was worried about looking like an idiot and not knowing what I was doing. When I was there with him, I didn't really worry about that at all.

Nora could admit that discovering this significant artifact may have had something to do with her breakup as well. Sure, she'd been preparing to leave the country, but long distance was a thing. She and Brandon could have tried that. She wasn't sure exactly how long she would be in London; they could get back together when she returned. But after reading those pages and remembering how she felt that summer, Nora thought maybe she had known Hugh Jeffries better than Brandon from just three wonderful British summer months. She knew she was probably being stupid and idealizing their whole relationship. For one, she had been so young and had never been abroad before, and she was already inclined to indulge in romantic notions. Then there was the man himself. Hugh was a musician. With an accent. And he wrote songs about her. How could you not be head over heels for someone who wrote songs about you? It really wasn't a fair fight.

If she had stayed, she would have grown up, and the rose-colored glasses would have come off. They would fight, and she would get bored, and he would get lazy and messy and forget her birthday after spending more time in the pub with his friends than making her happy. They had just never gotten to that part. A long time ago, she stopped fantasizing that Hugh Jeffries would show up on her doorstep and sweep her off her feet.

Still, Nora realized as she shuffled down the street—slightly frazzled and increasingly panicked—one part of her brain was looking for her office, but another part was disobediently searching for Hugh, as if she could imagine him into existence just by standing on a street in the city where he lived. You would think that someone who had finally gotten the chance at her dream job—or at least a lot closer to her dream job than sitting in a tiny office copy editing articles about beautiful places she would never get to visit—would have more important things to think about than men they'd been in love with when they were teenagers. She should be worrying about money, or how to actually do well in her new position, or the fact that she would only be freelance and the company could drop her contract and abandon her in the UK at the drop of a hat.

So no more NSFW British ex-boyfriend fantasies. She should probably wall the diary up behind a big stack of bricks and never look at it again. *Oh, wait. That was "The Cask of Amontillado."*

Nora was relieved to find that she had finally picked the right direction when her phone didn't command her to turn around again. With her eyes focused on the screen, she almost walked into a couple of well-dressed Londoners before she discovered the small office space with a big window and little yellow sign with purple lettering that read "99 Flamingo Publishing." Perhaps for the first time since exiting the Tube, Nora exhaled.

It was cozy inside—little desks blocked out at different angles, an office and a conference room in the back, and the sound of constant clacking as each person in the main room banged away on their keyboard. It wasn't exactly what she had imagined when she packed up her life and left America. She'd been picturing a big corporate office with elevators and a first floor Starbucks. This was kind of a rinky-dink operation, a one floor, very cramped, and very brown workplace situation. She knew publishing didn't have the budget it used to, and 99 Flamingo was only a very small imprint of a larger press, but this was still a surprise.

"Nora?" A woman at the front desk stood up and removed her glasses.

Nora did a double take, wondering if she should already be acquainted with this person. Surely the arrival of one American writer was of little significance to this place. "How did you know?"

The woman smiled warmly. "Well, we don't get a lot of people wandering in here, and we're expecting you." She reached out a hand for Nora to shake.

"I found the place," Nora said. It was an obvious statement, but she meant it more as an affirmation for herself than a conversation starter, as if she weren't a travel journalist with a terrible sense of direction.

"Give me a minute, and I'll take you back to Darcy," the woman said. "Also, I'm Jasmine. Did I mention that?"

Nora had forgotten how much she loved being surrounded by British accents, the way it made her feel as if she had stepped into a Jane Austen novel or a George Bernard Shaw play. It made her want to shout "hear, hear!" in raucous agreement whenever anyone said something exciting. She smiled to herself while she waited for Jasmine to introduce her to Darcy—of course her editor would be named Darcy. She wondered if it was a man or a woman. Perhaps it was a Mr. Darcy and her wildest *Pride and Prejudice* fantasies would play out in the little publishing office.

"Come on back, Shrapsan!" a smoky voice called from the back office, and Nora jumped. The other people in the main room kept their heads down with their eyes on their computer screens as she passed by them. *Friendly,* Nora thought sarcastically.

She popped her head around the corner and peeked inside the back office to see a mess of books and papers, maps and notes, ashtrays and takeout containers. Behind the desk was a beautiful woman in her mid-thirties with giant dark eyes and round cheeks. Her black hair was pulled back from her face, and her lips formed a displeased pout.

"Have a seat," Darcy said, and Nora quickly did as she was told. Jasmine slipped back out of the office, leaving Nora alone in a sea of publishing debris with her new boss. Actually, Darcy was just her editor, but Nora couldn't stop thinking the word "boss." She'd thought it so much that it didn't totally seem like a real word anymore until she saw Darcy. She appeared to embody the term, and despite the fact that she looked the opposite of Mr. Darcy in every way, she did exude his same sternness and derision. Nora had been practicing this moment in her mind, planning her first impression, but she didn't even get a chance to say hello before Darcy started going on in her raspy voice.

"Well, here you are then," she said, not looking up from the note she was writing on her desk. "They insisted on having an American do some research and writing for the project, though I find it unnecessary. We can easily write the book on our own city and every other place they throw at us."

"Right," Nora said. "Well, I suppose they just want multiple perspectives for the app."

Darcy scoffed. "Our perspectives are good enough, I think. But we do have a bit of ground to cover in a relatively short amount of time, so I'll want you writing and editing blurbs as quickly as possible. Am I correct that this will be your first time writing this kind of content?"

"Yes," Nora said quietly. She didn't know how to elaborate. She was pretty sure that she would be great at this. She'd been waiting for the chance for so long, but this woman was already making her doubt herself.

She tried to give herself a mini pep talk in her mind. *You can do this.* She could focus on her writing and publish incredible travel guides and forget that she was once again in the same city as the most beautiful man who had ever touched her. A man with stormy eyes and incredible fingers, the first man to ever give her an org —*Nope, get it together, Nora.*

"We'll check out the first place on the list together, go over what kind of details we're looking for," Darcy was saying. "That will be your training. It may be unusual, but I think it's important that you get a feel for the tone of the book." Nora nodded. "This isn't just a run-of-the-mill guide. It has personality and a special appeal for young, chic travelers. There's a restaurant in Kensington they want to include. A couple of new clubs in Piccadilly. A hotel in Marylebone. Those are going to get bigger write-ups in the book, but there will be even more content on the app. God knows I'm too old to go to the clubs, but you can do that with Timothy. Did you meet everyone?"

"No, not yet," Nora stuttered.

"Timothy!" Darcy called, and a pencil-thin, dark-haired man appeared in the doorway almost immediately. He would have looked like a steampunk villain if only he'd been sporting an oddly manicured mustache. "This is Timothy. He does some writing, some IT, and whatever else," Darcy announced, as if that gave Nora all the information she would ever need to know about him.

"Hello, lovely, it's a great pleasure to make your acquaintance," Timothy said, running his hands through his hair. His accent wasn't as charming as she would have expected.

"That's enough," Darcy snapped, and Timothy was gone again. Nora felt terrified but also like she should be laughing her head off at the same time. It was not at all the nurturing mentorship she had been expecting with her new editor in her dream job. "Anyway," Darcy said, "about the museums..." She proceeded to talk about the project as if in bullet points, not pausing even when Nora tried to ask a question. Nora jostled the things in her backpack, searching for a pen as quickly as possible so she could take notes on everything

Darcy was firing at her. Darcy wasn't even looking in her direction while she was talking—she was simultaneously typing an email on the computer. Nora tried to say something, but Darcy cut her off again. "You'll need to get to know some locals, as it helps to get some context about the different neighborhoods from their view. You want to get input from the kind of people that pass by these places every day as well. We're not just writing reviews or telling people about the latest events. We're telling a story. Though, you know, there will also be a lot of brochures to collect and facts to check."

"Ok, what do you think about—" Nora tried, but Darcy cut in again.

"I guess now is as good a time as any. Let's go."

"Go?"

"To the new restaurant. Training. Have you been paying attention?"

She mostly had been paying attention; there was just that one little part in the middle where she really zoned out. Maybe if she burned the diary, she could somehow stop her weird memory/fantasy life from taking over.

Darcy stood. "Come on then, let's get started."

When Nora was starting college, she wasn't quite sure what she wanted to do with her life. She loved studying English, but that wasn't really one of those majors that led to an easy, specific career path. She loved books and stories, but she didn't want to teach, which seemed to be the only thing that anyone expected you to do if you got a BA in Literature. She loved true crime and mysteries, but she didn't have the constitution to be a detective, and even the thought of blood made her queasy. When she found out about the study abroad program in London, it was the closest she had ever come to figuring out what she wanted as a career, because she wanted exactly that, to read Shakespeare and go to plays at the Globe Theatre, and take walking tours around beautiful, historic cities. How did one turn that exact thing into a job that paid you money?

Finally, her chance had come, which was perhaps a testament to the power of perseverance, or even more likely it was proof of the power of begging. The company where she'd been sitting at her cubicle for years had given her a shot in their most low-stakes writing position, and now that the job was hers, she was working hard not to let Darcy's persistent negative attitude depress her. In fact, as they sat in a dim restaurant that was going to get a tiny write-up in the book, Nora was beaming.

"Why are you making that face?" Darcy asked.

"What face?"

"That face like a puppy and a unicorn just had a baby, and it's going to carry you around the Froufrou Forest and grant you three wishes."

"I'm not sure what that means," Nora said.

"Stop smiling so damn much," Darcy barked. "This restaurant isn't even good. It would get one out of five smile emojis in the book."

"My soup isn't bad," Nora said.

"Who orders soup when it's thirty degrees out?"

"Is that hot? I don't know how to convert the temperature to Fahrenheit."

Darcy shook her head, as if embarrassed by Nora's stupidity or perhaps by the stupidity of all of America. "Aren't you dying? My whole body is covered in a layer of sweat. I look like a slimy sea lion."

Nora inspected Darcy for a moment, considering this comparison. "The only thing about you that reminds me of a sea lion," she said, "is your big, dark eyes."

Darcy snorted. "You're forgetting about my whiskers. Anyway, look at this chicken. It looks like my nan made this in 1976, and they've just defrosted it. It's actually wrinkled."

"Is that what you'll write in the review?"

"You're writing the review," Darcy said. "Though I don't really think this place deserves to take up space. This is why you can't trust anything you read on the internet. Now tell me the categories you need to cover in your 150 words."

Nora concentrated. "Year established. Convenience of the location. Atmosphere." Nora didn't mention that she had no idea about the convenience of location for anything, since she didn't know where anything was and would almost certainly get lost on her way anywhere.

"Yes, yes," Darcy said, "but none of that matters when the food is such shite. I'm at least going to try the pie. Excuse me!" Darcy raised a hand to flag down the waiter.

As Darcy bit into a slice of chocolate pie that she absolutely despised, Nora decided to steer the conversation away from the lacking quality of the restaurant. This "training" lunch was the perfect time to get to know Darcy a little better and to see if there was a way to break through to some kind of positive working relationship.

She could almost hear what her mother would say. Kathleen always seemed to understand what was at the heart of people immediately. She would recognize all of Darcy's little insecurities, the way she kept brushing her hair out of her face and gripping the table. She would say it was all a mask, that Darcy was really just scared of something, and she would probably know exactly what that something was, even if Nora hadn't quite put her finger on it. Her mother would know how to handle it too, how to talk to Darcy in a way that put her at ease or put her in her place, whatever was necessary in the moment. Nora just knew how to be nosy.

"So how long have you lived here?" she asked.

"Forever," Darcy said, shutting down any further inquiries. "Have you ever even been here before?"

Nora smiled. "I studied abroad here, and I fell in love with it. I took afternoon strolls through Regent's Park, I browsed record stores near Abbey Road, I went on the Eye at sunset. It's my favorite city in the world."

"The weather's terrible," Darcy said, but Nora could tell that she couldn't complain too much about her hometown. This was where Darcy had grown up, and while she could dislike almost anything, Nora was sure her boss couldn't hate London. "People are idiots too. Brexit? Come on."

Nora laughed. "The people I met here were wonderful."

"Oh gross." Darcy scrunched up her face.

"What?"

"You met a guy here, I can tell."

"What? How can you tell?" Nora looked around the room furtively.

"*The people I met here were wonderful.* Sigh. Wistful look. Memories stirring behind your blue eyes. I can read you like a book, Shrapsan. You batted those long eyelashes all over town, and you fell in love."

Nora stared. She must be so obvious, but she was also relieved. She'd been dying to talk to someone about Hugh, to say everything she'd been thinking for the past seventy-two hours—or maybe the past seven years—out loud, but now that she had the floor, Nora wasn't sure Darcy was the right person to talk to, and she didn't know where to start. It was so much more than a teenage romance to her, but how to explain it so that Darcy wouldn't think she was a dramatic weirdo? Maybe she shouldn't have decided to spill the beans to her boss in the first place. "He was my first love," Nora said. She cleared her throat.

Scenes from the life of nineteen-year-old, losing-her-virginity Nora kept playing in her mind. Make out sessions on Tower Bridge in the rain. White teeth glowing in black lights while they danced at Ministry of Sound. Steam wafting from hotel bathrooms, droplets of wine dotting the side of the bathtub.

"Well, that is serious," Darcy said, and Nora blinked hard, forcing herself back into the present.

"We met at the pub where he worked, and he was in a band. It sounds silly now, doesn't it?" She tried to shrug nonchalantly. "The first time he ever spoke to me, I could tell immediately there was just this *something* about him. He told me I couldn't handle my liquor and I'd be 'Oliver Twist' in no time. I didn't know what that meant, even though I love the musical.

"You Americans always fall for that Cockney bullocks," Darcy said. "A couple of rhymes, 'Oliver Twist' instead of 'pissed,' and you're completely charmed."

Nora laughed. "I totally was. I fell for it immediately. Even when I thought logically this guy is just charismatic and I shouldn't be so smitten, I couldn't help it. I was done for. And he was right that I couldn't hold my liquor."

"Wow, you're gullible." Darcy shook her head. "Seriously. How do you survive in this world?"

Nora was on a roll, and she ignored Darcy's comment. "I liked him, but I didn't take him that seriously. We always had an expiration date. I knew it would just be a summer fling. But then I got to know him... The band was actually amazing. I think it clouded my judgment." Nora looked off into the distance wistfully.

"So he gave you the struggling musician bit, and you ate it right up. You were probably throwing your panties on stage in no time." Darcy laughed at her own joke. "What was the band?"

Nora was still in another world, remembering all the things that Hugh had said to her, how much she'd wanted to believe him. When he'd told her he loved her. That had been real, right? That wasn't just some line to get in her pants. "Oh, it's not like you would have heard of them. They were just—the Pet Rockers," she said finally, and Darcy actually did a spit take. She had cider dribbling down her chin.

"You're fucking with me," Darcy said, suddenly alert and completely invested in the conversation.

"What?"

"You did not date a guy from the Pet Rockers. You're good, Shrapsan. I didn't think you had it in you to make up such a load."

Nora stared at her, eyebrows wrinkled. "What are you talking about? You know about a band called the Pet Rockers?"

Darcy was shaking her head. "I don't know whether to believe you or not. They are a relatively well-known local band, at least if you're into the music scene at all. They do shows all over the city. In fact, I have tickets to a special event they're doing just north of here."

"That's crazy," Nora said. "There's no way it's the same band, right? I mean, literally no one knew who they were when they used to play at the Goose and Cobbler."

Darcy stared at her as if trying to solve a puzzle. "No, that's it. You're not fooling me anymore. What's this bit you're doing? I don't get it," Darcy grumbled.

"What are you talking about?" Nora suddenly felt sick, and she wasn't sure if it was from the soup or some other kind of nausea.

"The show this weekend—*this* fucking weekend—is a special show at the Goose and Cobbler." Darcy tossed down her fork as if the sheer ridiculousness of this situation wouldn't allow her to hold it a second longer. Nora sat in stunned silence, but everything felt too loud. Her head was cloudy, as if she was just waking from a strange dream. Darcy was still saying something, but she couldn't quite make out the words. The diary in the bottom of her bag still seemed to be beating, and Nora couldn't hear anything else.

"You really aren't making this up, are you?" Darcy said, her voice finally breaking through. "I was going to have my roommate go with me, but she doesn't care about it anyway. I would much rather take you and see you reunite with your boyfriend."

Nora's mouth was hanging open. She'd been having the stupid debate in her head, ever since she found the diary, about whether or not to pop into the Goose and Cobbler for old-time's sake. She never thought Hugh would still be there, behind the bar, waiting for her. And she really never thought that his now semi-famous band would be playing a show in the very place where she had first laid eyes on him. She was trying to convince herself that there was no way any of this was possible—there was no actual way that she could set foot in the pub and fall in love with Hugh Jeffries all over again after seven years. But as Darcy sat there snapping her fingers in front of Nora's face to try to break her from her total state of shock,

Nora realized the truth. There was no way in hell she was missing that show.

Don't stop now. Keep reading with your copy of ELEPHANT AND CASTLE.

And sign up for Michelle's newsletter to get all the news, giveaways, excerpts, and more at linktr.ee/michellemccraw.

Don't miss more from Michelle McCraw coming soon and discover all of her books at www.michellemccraw.com

Until then, discover ELEPHANT AND CASTLE by City Owl Author, Hannah Ledford!

If only there was a guidebook on how to land the London boy of your dreams...

Nora Shrapsan is literally writing the book on London, and she's not going to let fantasies about her sexy British ex-boyfriend break her stride. So what if she has been reunited with semi-famous rock star Hugh Jeffries, and their chemistry is still palpable? He's engaged, and Nora needs to focus on...anything besides Hugh's lips.

Julian Rhodes is Hugh's best mate, and his secret feelings for Nora are one thing that won't stay in the past. When a desperate Nora begs him to help her navigate London, Julian has to say yes—strictly to keep her from getting fired, of course. Surely, they can go to murder tours, magic shows, and museums without any feelings getting in the way. No problem.

But the more time Nora and Julian spend together, the less Nora finds herself thinking of Hugh. Maybe her second-chance romance didn't go according to plan, but that doesn't mean Nora could ever fall for her ex's best friend, right?

Please sign up for the City Owl Press newsletter for chances to win special subscriber-only contests and giveaways as well as receiving information on upcoming releases and special excerpts.

All reviews are **welcome** and **appreciated**. Please consider leaving one on your favorite social media and book buying sites.

Escape Your World. Get Lost in Ours! City Owl Press at www.cityowlpress.com.

Acknowledgments

A book is like a child in that it takes a village to bring it to maturity. I'd like to thank my publisher, City Owl Press, Tina Moss, and my editors, Tee Tate and Yelena Casale, for your faith in this story and your dedication to making it the best book it could be. Thanks to my agent, Amy Brewer, who encouraged me when it was just a few scenes and a vague summary, and who has supported me through this wild process that is publishing.

Thanks, also, to my amazing writing friend Carla Luna and the Wide RomCom Discord for your feedback and inspiration. Writing is more fun with comrades.

Finally, I couldn't write a book about an Italian-American family without mentioning mine. They live in Dallas, not Vegas, but I infused this story with so many memories of them: raucous laughter, good food, warm hugs, and Sundays on the kneelers of All Saints Catholic Church. I'm not a big fan of the Church these days, but I will treasure those remembered scents, tastes, and embraces for the rest of my life. I know we're far flung now, but I love seeing the photos, old and new, on social media and making the old recipes when I can get back to Dallas.

About the Author

MICHELLE McCRAW writes swoony, steamy contemporary romance that just might make you laugh. Her stories center on characters passionate about science, engineering, and technology. A native Texan, she now lives in Georgia and enjoys reading, travel, drinking bourbon, and spoiling her extraordinarily ill-behaved but adorable dogs.

Follow Michelle on social media and get her VIP love notes for writing updates (and, not gonna lie, TONS of puppy pics) at linktr. ee/michellemccraw.

facebook.com/MichelleMcCrawAuthor

instagram.com/mmowriter

goodreads.com/michellemccraw

bookbub.com/authors/michelle-mccraw

About the Publisher

City Owl Press is a cutting edge indie publishing company, bringing the world of romance and speculative fiction to discerning readers.

Escape Your World. Get Lost in Ours!

www.cityowlpress.com

facebook.com/CityOwlPress

x.com/cityowlpress

instagram.com/cityowlbooks

pinterest.com/cityowlpress

tiktok.com/@cityowlpress